THE RIDDLE OF MONTE VERITA

THE RIDDLE OF MONTE VERITA

Jean-Paul Török

Translated by John Pugmire

The Riddle of Monte Verita

This book is a work of fiction. The characters, incidents, and dialogue are drawn from the author's imagination and are not to be construed as real. Any resemblance to actual events or persons, living or dead, is entirely coincidental.

First published in French in 2007 by France Univers, 3, Rue d'Estienne-d'Orves,
92110 Clichy-la-Garennes as *L'Enigme du Monte Verita*
Copyright © France Univers 2007

The Riddle of Monte Verita
English translation copyright © by John Pugmire 2012

For information, contact: pugmire1@yahoo.com

FIRST AMERICAN EDITION
Library of Congress Cataloging-in-Publication Data
Török, Jean-Paul
[*L'Enigme du Monte Verita*. English]
The Riddle of Monte Verita / Jean-Paul Török;
Translated from the French by John Pugmire

Author's Note:

Two objectives of unequal weight motivated me to create this work. The first was to write a mystery novel obeying the rules of what is often termed the Golden Age style, and to write it – word by word and line by line – in a manner consistent with French language usage of the time: the nineteen-thirties. The second, far more obscure, was to write a novel whose last sentence was that of John Dickson Carr's 'The Burning Court' which, even more than the book itself, has forever exercised a fascination over me. It caused me to undertake the strange mission of writing a story from back to front, so to speak, while still remaining faithful to the rules and conventions of the classic locked-room novel.

I

It was about six o'clock, maybe six-thirty. The sky-blue convertible weaved its way smoothly and rapidly between the vineyards and the chestnut woods. The Delahaye's motor, seemingly reinvigorated by the evening air, purred almost musically. The wild mountain scenery of Bellinzona – passes cleaving sheer cliffs and deep, menacing valleys between snowy peaks – was behind them. The road now crossed slopes that fell gently away towards unknown parts; everywhere there were meadows, and in the meadows there were vines, and between the vines there were mulberry trees and plantations of corn. In the tiny villages clustered around the church towers, good folk came to the windows to see and those taking the air outside on the porch looked up with interest. It felt as if they were already in Italy, not by virtue of official frontiers or national customs, but because of the nature of the surroundings; and it was the scent of Italy that floated in the warm breeze that stirred the green countryside, so seductive and so full of life.

Solange drove with her customary ease. She was wearing a white sports skirt and sweater; a light jacket fluttered casually on her shoulders and a few strands of her chestnut hair escaped from under her petite cloche hat.

'Ah! Can you smell the sweetness in the air? Did you see all those roses in the gardens and all those golden grapes on the vines? I never knew there were so many vineyards in Switzerland. Isn't it marvellous?'

She took a couple of deep breaths and threw her head back.

'Aren't you tired?' he said admiringly.

'Not at all.'

'Are you sure?'

'Yes, of course.'

They had spent the night in Lucerne. She had taken the wheel that morning and had not relinquished it the whole day. ("I know it's your

7

car, darling, but it's better that I drive. Sometimes your head seems in the clouds.") In fact, it was she that had bought the Delahaye without his knowledge and had presented him with it the day before their departure. ("You wouldn't have wanted to turn up in Locarno in your old Citroen 5CV, would you? What would your colleagues have thought?"). She had driven with such dexterity down the steep roads and through the hairpin bends that Pierre, who was normally tense when others were at the wheel, was able to relax and admire both the scenery and the profile of his young wife who drove, as was her custom, in total silence as if to savour the pleasure to the full. At this moment he found her to be the perfect image of feminine grace: so pretty in her svelte outfit and so adorable in her slightest gesture.

'I'm dying to have a bath at the hotel and relax with a glass of champagne. Pierre …' She gave him the look that he knew only too well. 'We're not going out tonight, are we?'

'I hope not. Why are you asking?' he added mischievously.

'You know very well, silly.' She burst out laughing. 'Meanwhile, darling, give me a cigarette.'

He lit a Muratti and passed it to her. She brought it to her lips and drew a long puff. He gazed fondly at her. Her loose curls fluttered in the rushing wind. He noted the unconscious grace of her bare arms as she drove with one hand, an elbow resting negligently on the door, the other hand holding the cigarette up to her lips. All her thoughts and emotions seemed concentrated in the look which she focused on the road ahead. He noted the contrast between the seriousness in her eyes and the smile on her lips. There were times when he had the impression that she was trying to escape from him; moments he called her "thoughtful look." Anyone less in love would have suspected she was not thinking about anything at all.

She had been wearing that look when he had first seen her in profile, in the Romanesque manner, sitting in a bower of the enchanting garden inside the old walls of the Edgar Allan Poe museum in Richmond. With one arm draped nonchalantly over the back of the park bench on which she sat, she was drawing on a cigarette with the same concentration he could observe now. He had been surprised when she had suddenly addressed him in French, despite the fact there was nothing particularly French-looking about him. She had claimed to know nothing about the place; strolling around town while her husband, an engineer, attended a meeting in a local factory, she had simply seen the garden through an iron gate and been prompted by curiosity to enter. He had assumed that the unnecessary detail was intended to convey to him that she was not looking for romantic adventure and so, in all innocence, he had volunteered to show her the museum.

He would have been hard pressed to say exactly what had happened between them. It could have been the atmosphere of the place exercising its power over their subconscious, or maybe that afternoon he had been particularly brilliant – he was writing his thesis on Poe and she had certainly appeared to be hanging on his every word; whatever the reason, as they parted they exchanged addresses. She and her husband lived in Baltimore and he was in New York on a year's secondment to Columbia University. She had written first and seemingly with no ulterior motive; they had met two or three times.

After Pierre returned to Paris they continued to correspond, in an increasingly intimate manner. One day she stopped writing to him and two interminable months went by before he received a letter which he had frankly assumed would never come. She informed him of the death of her husband from gastroenteritis and of her intention to return to France once the estate was settled. He had gone to meet her off the S.S.Normandie at Le Havre and three weeks later they were married.

It had been barely a year, but in that short time his life had been transformed. He had been surprised to learn the day after the wedding that his wife, having inherited a number of important patent rights from her deceased husband, possessed a considerable fortune. On her initiative they proceeded to enjoy life at a level that he could never have afforded on his meagre salary as a junior lecturer at the Sorbonne: the villa near Versailles, her constantly refreshed wardrobe, gifts on the most trivial occasions, and now the Delahaye. He had accepted it all without asking himself too many questions, so dazzled to have been chosen – he who had always considered himself to be so average – by such a seductive creature, that nothing surprised him any longer. And so it was that, despite knowing so very little about his wife, his curiosity never prompted him to find out more. He knew she was the daughter of a diplomat (her parents had died in an accident several years earlier) and she had told him the occasional anecdote about her youth, but he had never thought much about it. Once or twice, when he had become aware of empty passages in Solange's past life, he had been tempted to ask her more, but he only needed to look at her as he was doing now for his curiosity to vanish and for him to think only about his present happiness. He was startled out of his thoughts by the imperious blast of a motor horn which caused him to turn sharply round. A large Mercedes had suddenly appeared behind the Delahaye and the driver was sounding the horn furiously. Her eyes fixed on the rear view mirror, Solange raised a wrathful eyebrow, threw away her cigarette and swerved to the right. The road was barely wide enough for the two vehicles and the wheels of the Delahaye were on the verge and almost over the edge of the slope as the saloon roared past, then slowed sharply to take the next bend, the driver, a huge man dressed in black to match his machine, making a vague hand gesture as he disappeared.

'Road hog!' shouted Solange into the wind, with little hope of being heard. Reading the licence plate, she added: 'Not surprising, they were *krauts*!' Pierre had just had time, while the other was overtaking, to observe the massive silhouette of the driver, a younger man seated next to him, and a very pale woman in the back with a velvet crimson hat crammed down over her blonde hair.

Solange had slowed down a little, as if to show she was determined, as befitted a cultured person, to take her time and enjoy the countryside. If she had wanted, the Delahaye Grand Sport could, with a tap of the accelerator, have left the Mercedes far behind. As it was, the two vehicles were almost at a crawl as they went through Minusio, the last village before Locarno. Lake Maggiore spread out below them, its waters blackened and somehow thickened by the huge shadows cast by the two mountains that dominated it, their slopes covered by a dark, funereal cloak of fir trees. The sun having disappeared behind the rocky crest, a cave-like chill was emanating from the dark liquid mass, and she shivered.

'Is that the famous lake you've been telling me so much about?' she muttered in a tone full of reproach, flicking her jacket back onto her shoulders.

He had been, like her, eager to contemplate in admiration this legendary site whose enchanting natural beauty had been so vaunted by the books he had read, but he was far more concerned about her disappointment than his own.

'It would seem to me,' he said, 'that a pilgrimage to Lake Maggiore, in the footsteps of Stendhal and Gobineau, should be treated as a kind of initiation, understanding also that every initiation must include certain tests. We have, perhaps, been in too much of a rush to find what we were looking for....'

And he launched into a eulogy about nature, that sly magician, so adept at hiding her charms, the better to seduce you when finally she decided to reveal herself, proclaiming it with that air of professionalism mixed with a dash of pedantry which so amused his wife, the more so because she knew he only adopted that tone when he was annoyed. But this time she blushed, bit her lip and fell silent for a moment; after all, he was right, and she cursed herself for having spoiled the moment – so she let herself be gently reprimanded, as it seemed to her that every good wife should, in such circumstances. And, truth be told, when he spoke like that she felt an almost sensual pleasure and pride in her husband's intellect. And so she said:

'I'm sorry, Pierre. I'm not very intelligent.'

Under his breath, he murmured:

'If you weren't driving, I couldn't have helped kissing you.'

After a moment, he said out loud: 'And all that because you aren't very intelligent!'

The road took them along the northern reaches of the lake, after which they turned towards the south, where the mountains receded into the background and the vast expanse of the lake took on a silver colour. They could discern terraces leading down to a port and a white boat anchored at its jetty. And there, at the end of their journey, they entered Locarno.

***

Many years later, when Pierre Garnier looked back on those days, he would remember with a nostalgia bordering on despair that period before the war when everyone could still believe that peace was not lost. He would recall the easy nonchalance of life, the bustling open-air cafés at the moment of the *mandarin-curaçao* aperitif, the ladies more beautiful than ever in their tailored suits, the songs of Lucienne Boyer and the novels of Pierre Benoit, the jazz orchestras in the casinos, the open sports cars devouring the empty roads. That era had passed, but the memory would be fresh enough in his mind for him to recall what happiness had been like despite the intellectuals' fantasies of a "better world."

In that late summer of 1938, he was tasting life to the full, despite the omens and forewarnings of disaster. But he noticed nothing and heard nothing; he was much too happy for that.

Before him lay the town, already illuminated. The blue streetlights of the port were reflected in the impenetrable waters of the lake. From the balcony of his room he had a superb view; his wife had been right to insist on staying at the Grand Hotel. Ascona, where the symposium was being held, was only a few minutes away from Locarno but still far enough for them to avoid the lack of privacy inherent in that kind of meeting.

'That way I can always find something to do while you're in your dull conference, and I won't be continually on your back when you're having your discussions. And anyway,' she had added, 'I find all that business about murder and all kinds of other horrible things just a little unhealthy. And I haven't got the morbid turn of mind that you and all those clever professors must have to be so interested in detective fiction.'

It was true that the symposium theme was detective fiction but, given that she had insisted on accompanying him, he had been startled to hear her talk like that. He had almost retorted that detective fiction was a branch of literature in its own right, and there was nothing unhealthy about reading Stevenson, Dickens or Chesterton; and if she was worried about his "morbid" tastes, she could attend his session where he was going to argue that Edgar Allan Poe, eaten up by neuroses and melancholy, had invented the genre in order to rid himself of his demons and to exercise his intellectual faculties dispassionately. But, having noticed his reproving look, she had immediately added: 'Darling, can't you see I'm teasing?' and, as happened each time she detected the glimmer of a disagreement between them, she had sealed his lips with a kiss.

'Do you know we're terribly late?' said Solange, emerging from the bathroom preceded by a strong whiff of *Shalimar* and laughing as if she didn't really care. On their arrival at the hotel they had found, waiting for them at the reception, an invitation to the inaugural cocktail party that same evening at the Albergo Monte Verita. She proposed taking the Delahaye, but he argued that it was already in the garage and, not knowing the route to Ascona, they would never find the Albergo; and anyway an omnibus had been arranged to take all the symposium participants staying at the Grand Hotel.

What Pierre didn't say was that he didn't want to draw attention to himself by arriving in such a luxurious motor car. He was afflicted with the modesty of the simple man who hates people talking about him. His wife was already too beautiful and too elegant – as was he in the dinner jacket she had insisted he wear – for this crowd of academics that prided themselves on their disdain for worldly things and paraded their ugly wives as if to proclaim the simplicity of their lifestyle.

In fact, although his scruples did him credit, they were, in the present circumstances, grossly exaggerated. Pierre Garnier should have known, having lived in the United States, that the stereotype only applied to Sorbonne professors and that things were quite different in foreign universities. For, at the reception, they made the acquaintance of a dashing *cavaliere*, none other than the eminent *professore* Umberto Lippi of Bologna, freshly arrived from Milan on the *vaporetto*. The professor, once he had set eyes upon them – or, more precisely, upon Solange – had sought them out and introduced himself, followed by a 'Dr. Garnier, I presume?' and a graceful bow, perfectly executed, to the young woman, with just the suggestion of a kiss to the hand.

Courteously, but with the familiarity that clearly indicates superiority of rank, he congratulated Pierre for an article he had published but had never imagined such a distinguished personage would have deigned to read, let alone show such an interest in. To understand Pierre's surprise it is necessary to describe in greater detail the distinguished Professor Lippi, recipient of more laurels than any literary expert since Aristotle. Inventor of the "neo-poetic", a science exclusively devoted to the structure of the narrative, from which he had derived a general philosophy, he had achieved fame with the publication of his masterful study of the influence of the Homeric epics on the Divine Comedy and the subsequent influence of Dante's work on Melville's Moby Dick, based on the incontestable facts that Dante had known nothing of the Iliad or the Odyssey and Melville had never read the Florentine poet.

The first thing Pierre noticed was the professor's relative youth; given the man's reputation, he would have expected someone of a venerable age. In fact, he barely appeared to have reached his fifties. Tall and slender, his skin was tanned, his teeth were sparkling white and, paradoxically, his silver hair made him appear younger. As a rule he was not particularly congenial, being somewhat haughty, as if he was aware of his superiority and expected others to acknowledge it as well. Pierre only realised that later, when he finally understood that Lippi's warm welcome had been due in large part to the presence of

Solange; she, on the other hand, had understood immediately, given her sensitivity and the fact that she was used to such attention. Having quickly sized up the brilliant charmer as one of those harmless men more infatuated with themselves than any woman, she amused herself promoting her husband by steering the conversation towards his supposed (and, as it turned out, real) admiration for the Italian scholar's work.

'"Let us admire the great masters, but let us not imitate them",' announced Lippi pompously, and paused to allow Pierre to identify the quotation.

'Victor Hugo,' said Pierre, calmly. 'But all he did was to adopt an idea from Horace: *"Virum magnum praecipio honore habemus, sed non imitamur".*'

'Book II of the Epistles, correct?'

Pierre nodded his head in approval.

Lippi seemed impressed and Solange shot him a look of victory. They were in the little omnibus which was taking them to Ascona and the Italian, sitting in front of them, was half turned towards them in an elegant pose, his hand dangling elegantly across the adjacent seat.

'Signora, I knew your husband to be an expert in Anglo-Saxon literature, but now I see he has conserved the tradition of the humanities.'

He smiled broadly and bowed slightly. He expressed himself in perfect French, fluently but with a slightly pedantic hesitation: as if he constructed the more complicated sentences in Italian before carefully translating them.

'I must confess, alas,' he continued, 'that I know far less about Edgar Allan Poe than you do about the Latin poets, and I am dying to hear what you have to say about the ingenious author of "Tales of the Grotesque and Arabesque." *À-propos* extraordinary tales…' Here he adopted a sibylline air so as to arouse their interest. '… I don't know if you are aware of the one about the strange place we're going to, which bears the bizarre name of Monte Verita. Which means, dear lady, for those that do not speak Italian – .'

'— The Mountain of Truth,' snapped Solange, annoyed that anyone would doubt her linguistic capability.

'My humble excuses. I should have realised it was self-evident.'

Pierre intervened, mischievously.

'"No truths are self-evident."'

Lippi raised a puzzled eyebrow.

'Pascal?' he offered.

'Poe,' replied Pierre, a note of reproach in his voice. The Italian shrugged his shoulders in a sign of helplessness and continued:

'Well, anyway, getting back to the name Monte Verita, I wanted to add that it's an anti-phrase, that is to say one containing a word in the opposite sense, given the mystery that surrounds this place. Since you know Poe better than I, you will readily realise that it's a sort of Domain of Arnheim, even though the Albergo, thank goodness, is more comfortable than the house of Usher. There couldn't be a better spot for us amateurs of puzzles and strange events.... '

'Here we go,' thought Pierre. 'This is what public speakers call the *exordium*, the enticing introduction. Next, he'll dangle the *fabula,* the raw elements of the story. Once he's got us hooked, unless I'm much mistaken, we're supposed to implore him to tell us the whole tale.'

'But I imagine,' continued the professor with a perfect note of disdain, 'that you didn't come here to listen to the old wives' tales of the region. In any case,' he announced, looking out of the window, 'it seems we're nearly there, so....'

'Oh, no, Professor!' exclaimed Solange, stepping into the trap with both feet. 'Please, be an angel and tell us the story.'

Lippi put on an air of surprise and made them wait a few seconds in order for them to appreciate the favour he was about to bestow.

'I warn you,' he said after a suitable pause, 'that it's a very strange business that has never been properly explained and where it has proved impossible to determine what's true and what's false.

'At the turn of this century these mountains, which at the time were deserted, attracted a small group of men from the north who were seeking a place where a new and happier society could blossom, based on an understanding of nature and a return to paganism. They established a small colony on a sunny outcrop situated between the black of the lake and the dark green of the pine forests and they called it Monte Verita. The men wore long hair, loose-fitting tunics and sandals; the women were draped in white fabric undulating freely in the manner of Isadora Duncan. They were vegetarians and lived in cabins, the better to remain in contact with the natural elements and they took air, sun and water baths. Innocuous stuff which represented little danger save that of ridicule which, unfortunately, is rarely fatal.

'The leader of these gentle cranks was a sort of wise man named

15

Henri Oedenkoven, a native of Anvers, a woolly-minded philosopher, self-taught, who had stuffed his head with esoteric theories. Well, this little man, who was one of life's perpetual failures, called himself Rosenkreutz."

He paused a moment to allow the dramatic effect of the name to sink in. Needless to say Solange asked, in a tone rather more passionate than was necessary, who exactly was Rosenkreutz.

'You've never heard of him?' replied the professor, feigning astonishment. 'Ask your husband.'

'To the best of my knowledge,' replied Pierre, 'the chevalier Rosenkreutz was an imaginary figure dating from the turn of the seventeenth century in what is now Germany, and to whom we attribute the founding of the secret Order of Rosicrucians.'

'Quite so,' sneered Lippi. 'So secret indeed that that nobody has ever been able to prove their existence. No follower has ever stepped forward to admit his membership in the brotherhood, because it is secret and real Rosicrucians must swear they do not, in fact, belong to the order. That means, *ipso facto*, that the one thing we can be certain about is that anyone who claims to be a member is almost certainly not. Consequently, not only is there no historical proof of the existence of the Rosicrucians, there can, by definition, never be one.'

'Well, just imagine that!' gasped Solange who, when it suited her, could play the nitwit to perfection.

Lippi shot her a suspicious look but, reassured, continued:

'Oedenkoven succeeded in persuading his followers that he was the reincarnation of Rosenkreutz, if not Rosenkreutz himself, and that they were the true inheritors of the original Rosicrucians. Immediately following the war, new disciples started to arrive: mystics, theosophists, followers of the traditional sciences and German visionaries who would later found the mysterious Thule Society that, we are told, played an occult yet decisive role in bringing Hitler to power.

'They borrowed a number of rituals and signs from classical magic (perpetual flames, nocturnal ceremonies by torchlight, the symbol of the red rose at the centre of the swastika) and they developed a sort of theosophical doctrine that announced the coming of an Unknown Superior who would decide the destiny of the world. It goes without saying that none of their sacred texts could be divulged to the outside world. As far as we can make out from the little we know, they promised their members – those of pure blood and preferably German – that, once they reached the ultimate stage of their initiation, they would acquire supernatural powers, such as the ability to transform matter, to travel instantly in space, to make objects move at a distance and to pass through walls.'

Pierre shrugged.

'Typical rants to keep the sect happy.'

'Yes, and that's why I became interested in the matter. It goes with their existence just as with other human activities. They all conform to a model that one could characterise as fictional, or, to put it more crudely, they reproduce incessantly a story established in advance. They all feature blind obedience, initiation rituals and secret evocations. Each secret society decrees protocols that form the basis of worldwide revolution. In view of their prophetic nature and their extraordinary resemblance to secret societies of the past, one is led to conclude that they are the work of people with a full understanding of the traditions of past societies and who know how to reproduce their ideas and their styles. Most of the time there's not much of note and they're simply following the same narrative formula that determines the fate of sects, always being persecuted and always being reborn. All of which led me, in an article I've just written, to analyse their history and each of their episodes just as one would analyse a fictional text; in other words, by applying the same method that the specialists of the narrative form apply to literature.'

That was Professor Lippi's big idea, which he had developed at great length in his works: that the world and the life of each individual had to be read the way novels were read; that reality and fiction obeyed the same narrative laws, so that from an analyst's point of view it was practically impossible to distinguish one from the other. Pierre had a sneaking suspicion that he was in fact rehearsing his speech for the following day. He glanced at his wife, who was trying to suppress a yawn, and was about to suggest to the professor that they continue another time, when the other picked up the thread of his story.

'Let us go back to Christian Rosenkreutz who was, as my excellent colleague has correctly observed, an imaginary figure, invented by a Protestant theologian who made him the hero of a novel written with the aim of ridiculing all sects. Here we have the opposite case: not reality read as fiction, but as fiction read as reality. This has given place to the well-known phenomenon, namely that of projecting the fictional world upon the real, in other words believing in the existence of fictional characters. The most famous examples of this phenomenon are the good people who believe that Edmond Dantes or Sherlock Holmes really lived and who visit the Chateau d'If or 221B Baker Street in the expectation of seeing some trace of their presence there. Well, good old Rosenkreutz, a fictional character who became an escapee into the real world, was reincarnated in poor Oedenkoven, who decided – or rather who was compelled by narrative necessity – to follow his destiny to the letter. The imaginary Rosenkreutz had ended his days entombed in a grotto; the real Rosenkreutz, or rather the one who saw himself thus, shut himself away in a natural cave that one can visit, not a hundred metres from the Albergo.

'Those are the facts, as recorded in the police report; as the sect faced a growing hostility from the citizens of Ascona, the authorities in the canton resolved to put an end to the disturbances and ordered the members of the sect to leave the region without further delay. The Grand Master gathered his flock and announced that he would henceforth seal himself in the grotto, which served as the site of their underground ceremonies, to meditate and to pray to the telluric powers to help him find a solution. The faithful formed a cortege to the grotto's entrance and saw him enter. Then, on a signal from him, they sealed the entrance with boulders. For three days and three nights they took turns standing guard outside. On the morning of the fourth day, having seen no sign of the Grand Master, several of the more audacious followers broke the seal and slipped into the grotto. They emerged in shock, shouting that they had found no one there. Others carefully combed the grotto which, as you will have already guessed, contained no other issue. I say "as you will have already guessed", because you cannot have failed to notice that this true story reproduces in a quite remarkable way another celebrated *fabula,* even though, unlike the Saint Sepulchre, there was no angel inside the tomb to announce the Resurrection. It has always surprised me, incidentally, that no writer of detective fiction has ever thought to cite the account of the Evangelists as the very first example, eighteen centuries before Edgar Allan Poe, of an impossible disappearance from a hermetically sealed chamber.'

He stopped after throwing that thinly-veiled barb and looked at each of them in turn, a malicious gleam in his eye. Pierre, who knew the professor to be an agnostic, felt he had gone rather too far with his allusion to the Evangelists, but he contented himself with a tight-lipped smile. Solange, feigning indifference, turned to look out of the window. The omnibus's gearbox emitted a series of screeching protests as the driver navigated a series of hairpin bends in almost total darkness. Despite her attempts to appear relaxed, Pierre sensed that his wife was feeling a great deal of nervous tension, which in turn made him ill at ease. By the side of the road, under the overhanging trees, menacing shadows seemed to move. Lippi chuckled.

'So sorry to have unnerved you. The end of the story is not quite so disturbing: the investigators' verdict, naturally, found collective hallucination, or false testimony, or both; the community was dispersed and the affair was quietly buried, so to speak. Nobody ever saw the alleged Rosenkreutz again and he was assumed, until the next reincarnation at least, to have departed the land of the living. In 1925, Baron von der Heidt bought the land and built a modern hotel, with rooms and exhibition galleries, designed by a Bauhaus architect. His idea was to attract writers and artists. He retained the cabins of the cult members and transformed them into luxury bungalows equipped with every modern convenience. You'll see what I mean. They're scattered around the grounds of the hotel and that's where most of our symposium colleagues are staying. That's where we would have been as well, had we not judiciously chosen the more modern conveniences of the Grand Hotel. They're actually quite disconcerting places to stay, particularly at night. Not that they're haunted, despite the rumours, but they are isolated in the midst of the trees and they're not for someone who fears being alone.

'I think we've arrived!' exclaimed Solange, a note of relief in her voice. Through the tops of the fir trees above them they could see twinkling lights and hear the sound of an orchestra playing *Stompin' at the Savoy*. It was as if Solange had awakened from a bad dream. She fluttered her eyelashes, pressed herself against her husband, and whispered in his ear:

'That story gave me the creeps. Will you dance with me, my darling?'

***

The cocktail party took place on the terrace of the Albergo which stood more than a thousand feet above the oily black mass of the lake. Constellations of light from the streetlamps of nearby villages formed an arc like a scattering of pearls, and a light breeze from the lake floated up to the warmer heights, bringing an odour of stale water.

Solange pressed herself harder against her husband. The orchestra was playing *September Song*, one of Pierre's favourites, and he felt as if time were standing still. Many years later, when he tried to describe it, he would be unable to capture the colour of that evening – the vibrant nocturnal sounds and the moonlight in which everything would forever be bathed in his memory. He would have to turn to Poe for that: the atmosphere of fragile happiness hiding fears and premonitions – an oasis in arid times:

Twas night in the lonesome September
Of my most immemorial year...

The trumpet sounded its last notes; he was vaguely aware of snatches of conversation and the occasional laugh above the tide of conversations. Already Professor Lippi was leaning over Solange and leading her towards an energetic jitterbug. Pierre was overcome by a wave of solitude and felt ridiculous standing there on the dance floor. He looked around. On the terrace, surrounded by palm trees, the waiters were circulating, carrying trays loaded with multicoloured drinks. Small tables lit with candles were scattered in the shadows and here and there the red tip of a cigarette could be seen. Some guests, seated in front of the long low line of the white concrete hotel, benefited from the light emanating from the salons and bars; he noticed, seated in a circle and obviously set apart from the rest, a group of men distinguished by their three-piece suits, whom he identified immediately as French academics. He recognised a few of them. They were the same faces that were to be seen at all the conferences – or at least those where the daily expenses were included in the invitation.

He approached their table, greeted them and sat down without being asked. Since the little group consisted entirely of academics, most of whom were professors, Pierre could reasonably have anticipated an interesting discussion in agreeable surroundings. On the contrary, he was obliged to listen to conversations that had nothing to do with literary matters. In the place of gems of erudition and critical insight, all he heard were complaints about government grants and guesses about who would be elected to which academic post.

After several years of purgatory in a provincial school, following his graduation from Normale Supérieure, Pierre Garnier had taken a university post, imagining life at the Sorbonne to consist of intellectual controversies and lengthy hair-splitting discussions beneath the ancient school's vaulted ceilings. But, their magnificent lectures aside, most of his colleagues could have been replaced by cost accountants or millinery salesmen without anyone noticing. Apart from the rare occasions when any of them turned up in the flesh for a class, they spent most of their time in interminable meetings where they decided complicated strategies for getting more assistants, or worked out subtle alliances for council votes, or sharpened old rivalries, or tried to find out what the dean of one faculty had said to the rector of another.

Since his presence at the table had aroused very little interest, which did hurt him a little, there was nothing to prevent him slipping away to find the table where Lippi had taken Solange. He found, seated with them, two individuals he had never seen before. One was an Oxford academic whom one could have easily mistaken for a major in the Indian Army – with his solid frame, clipped blond moustache and plump rosy cheeks – were it not for his exhaustive and sometimes exhausting knowledge of the labyrinthine detective novels of Conan Doyle and Wilkie Collins. He was in the middle of a somewhat disdainful discussion with a small person with a round head and bulging eyes seated in front of him, back hunched and eyes blinking nervously. Lippi presented the former to Pierre as Professor George Harvey, and the latter as Professor Mikhaïl Mikhaïlovitch Prokosch, a Russian scholar exiled in Switzerland, disciple of Vladimir Propp and analyst of fairy tales. The man exuded poverty, with his sparse grey hair seemingly covered in dust and his threadbare suit obviously several sizes too large for him.

Pierre sat down beside his wife who was pretending to listen while sipping on her Manhattan. She fished the cherry out with two fingers and, leaning tenderly towards him, placed it gently in his mouth; he blushed and glanced awkwardly at the others, but they appeared too absorbed in their discussion to have noticed the charming gesture of conjugal intimacy. They were talking politics: for the news of the events sweeping across Europe to have disturbed the tranquillity of their ivory towers, it must have been very grim indeed. The Englishman tried to be reassuring: he reminded them of Hitler's speech at the end of the Nuremberg Congress, wherein he renounced, in exchange for the annexation of the Sudetenland, all claims to other western frontiers. The little Russian prophesied that, after the Sudetenland, it would be the turn of the Czechs and, after that, the Poles. Lippi asked Pierre what he thought, which was not much because he detested offering opinions outside his sphere of expertise. His mind wandered. He wondered, looking at Prokosch, if he had come to the symposium to reveal who really killed Little Red Riding Hood and who had given a soporific to Sleeping Beauty. As they were clearly expecting a reply, and he tended to share the view of the Oxford professor, he took refuge in a quotation:

'"The wolf makes war with the sheep. The wolf does not make war with the lion."' And, looking at Lippi, he added: 'Fénelon.'

'*Telemachus*,' replied the professor. 'But please allow me to disagree: "The animals are perpetually at war; each species is born to devour another."'

'Well played,' conceded Pierre. 'Machiavelli?'

'Voltaire,' declared the Italian, triumphantly marking a point.

Prokosch regarded them with amazement, and the Englishman – unable to recall a quotation from Shakespeare that was just on the tip of his tongue – blushed in confusion.

'It's just as easy to predict Chancellor Hitler's next moves,' announced Lippi in a peremptory tone, 'as it is to infer from the prologue of a tragedy the events that will follow, "plausibly and necessarily" as Aristotle said.'

'How so?'

'Quite simply by considering that History, with a capital H, is constructed in the same way as a story, which one may consequently read as a fiction; in the same way – reciprocally – a fiction may be read as a historical reality. That's what I was explaining just now to friend Garnier here. The reader of a romantic novel is led by the functioning of the mechanics of the story to suspend his disbelief and collaborate in the construction of a universe with its own internal coherence. By the same token, he is led to believe in it by virtue of the celebrated formula: "All that is rational is real."'

'All right,' said the Oxford professor, wriggling in his seat. 'I haven't got a cut-and-dried opinion on the subject: "It is a tale told by an idiot, full of sound and fury." Shakespeare,' he added modestly.

'But it *is* a story, my dear Harvey, even if it's told by an idiot,' retorted Lippi. He made a dismissive gesture at the sound of the name Shakespeare, for he reproached the bard for having scorned Aristotle's precepts. 'Nevertheless, to please you and to try to avoid a confusion which, although it can sometimes be pleasant and innocent, would in this case turn out to be a tragic cause for concern, I propose to distinguish between *natural fiction* and *artificial fiction,* while keeping in mind that, since the beginning of time, both have obeyed the same laws.

'Thus any account I might produce of tonight's conversation would only differ from the same account written by a novelist by the trivial fact that in the one case it actually did happen, and in the other the writer is trying to make believe it really happened. But the result is exactly the same.'

'That doesn't hold water,' retorted Harvey, whom Pierre suspected of Platonist leanings. 'You're confusing the being and the appearance, the true and the false, the real and the illusory. Every thinking man is capable of making the distinction, and I don't need to pinch myself to know that I'm not a character in a novel!'

'You "don't like belonging to another person's dream," my friend,' said Lippi delicately, which Pierre translated for the benefit of Prokosch, who clearly hadn't understood.

'Ah, yes!' replied the Russian, '*Alice Through the Looking Glass.*' And he added timidly: 'I think Professor Lippi is right. The child hearing a fairytale projects the Ogre and Tom Thumb into his world, and, because of *mimesis* – the imitation of nature – to cite Aristotle again, feels the same fear and the same pity as if they really existed.'

'And it is not I but one of your compatriots,' continued Lippi, looking hard at Harvey, 'who said that the most painful event of his life was the death of one of Balzac's heroes.'

'Oscar Wilde. Damned Irishman,' growled the Englishman, gritting his teeth; at which point Pierre, sensing that the discussion was taking an ugly turn, decided to intervene.

'Could we get back to your ideas about Adolf Hitler?'

Lippi, clearly exultant, flashed a ferocious smile.

'Now there's a perfect example of a character from natural fiction! Not only can we understand, we can even predict all this fellow's historical events in terms of what I call a *readable text.* It is only politicians and blind men that imagine that History makes no sense – I'm not talking about you, dear boy – and no one can see what's going to happen.'

'I would very much like to know,' interjected Harvey scornfully, 'just what *you* make of it all.'

'Very simply,' announced Lippi with an amiable firmness, 'by attributing a fictional existence to this – alas, very real – person.

Imagine that an author of detective fiction invents a character that he calls X or Y – or Hitler, for that matter. In the first few pages, this character divulges his motives, announces the crimes he intends to commit and how he plans to operate. No reader will believe it, for the simple reason that he will discount anything presented to him as evidence and he knows that no real criminal would behave that way. The reader will only think about how the criminal will conceal himself and what insidious means he will employ to commit his crimes – methods so ingenious that the reader will only discover them at the end. Well, nobody believed it probable or possible that Hitler would spell out his projects in a book, under the eyes of the whole world, so as to reduce the chances of anyone ever guessing what he intended to do. But in my case, thanks to my theory, the more I read *Mein Kampf*, the more I was convinced that the author, in order to conceal his plans, had recourse to the deftest of expedients, namely to hide them in plain sight.

'Now, once we admit that our little corporal – a term often applied to Napoleon, even though he never was one – as I was saying, if we admit that our little corporal is a fictional character and that History itself unfolds as a novel, then I am in a position to expound – .'

Harvey groaned.

'Some other time. You've been expounding the whole evening.'

'I am in a position to expound,' the Italian continued, 'on the narrative model on which his development is based. History is an eternal and, I grant you, confused, tragic-comedy where only the roles and the masks change but the actors and the events stay the same....'

'Have you noticed the fat man at the next table?' Solange had placed her hand on her husband's arm and was now whispering in his ear: 'He hasn't stopped looking at me.'

Pierre took a discreet look and saw a corpulent individual in his fifties. It was too dark for him to see the man properly, but when he leaned forward for several seconds to light a cigar, the candle on the table illuminated heavy features with a snub nose, a lantern jaw and pale beady eyes that stared at Solange from behind steel-rimmed spectacles. Pierre felt as if a spider was lying in wait in a dark corner, and a shiver ran down his spine.

'He looks like the driver of the Mercedes,' he whispered back. 'I think he's recognised you.'

'Do you think so?' breathed Solange.

In fact, as far as Pierre could remember, at the moment of overtaking the driver hadn't even turned his head.

The man must have sensed he was being observed because he changed position and exchanged a few words with the blonde woman sitting beside him, who was holding a glass of champagne with an absent-minded air. Opposite them sat a tall, thin young man of an obviously weak constitution, but with a surprisingly sensual mouth.

'I'm sure,' murmured Pierre. And, to reassure her, he added:

'I hope the fat thug will come over and apologise.'

But in that he was wrong, as will be seen later. Lippi had loosened his dinner jacket and was continuing his discourse, rocking back and forth on his chair, his hands clasped together on his false shirt-front. Pierre felt that he was going to great lengths to dress up in scholarly terms and tortuous reasoning the old adage that History is constantly repeating itself.

'So,' proclaimed the professor in too loud a voice, as if in a pulpit, 'every great despot who sees himself as master of his own destiny is actually living a tale in which it's the historical myth that is the driving force for all his acts and decisions. Everything repeats itself, the crimes as well as the battles, the victories and the defeats, and each leader's destiny follows that of the one before. Caesar is a transcription of Alexander, Napoleon is a pleonasm of Caesar and even of Charlemagne, Napoleon III is an inferior copy of his uncle and our beloved *Duce* Mussolini follows in the footsteps of that same Caesar who, well before him, also marched on Rome. As for the illustrious *Reichsführer*, his story is so inextricably tied to that of the great Napoleon that one may predict without risk every step of his career, from his ascension to his decline, and from his decline into the inevitable fall....'

He paused and looked at each of his listeners in turn. Harvey was calmly filling his pipe. Prokosch, in the candlelight, wore an expression at once courteous and Mephistophelean, as if he knew more than he had let on, and was biding his time.

'Do you understand? We have before us a *readable text*. Now, if you're interested to hear what I've read....'

'It's what interests me as well,' announced a new voice.

Pierre hadn't seen the man approach, even though he had heard a chair at the next table scraping the floor. Perhaps it was the arrival of a stranger that surprised them. Or maybe it was his voice, harsh and imperious, with guttural undertones. In any case, they all turned to look at him. The man kept out of the light. His outfit, austerely military in style but luxurious in the choice of material, was too tight for him. He spoke again in formal, rather pedantic, tones:

'You must excuse me, my dear sirs,' he said, ignoring Solange, 'but I couldn't help overhearing your conversation. I would like to ask a question of the celebrated professor.'

'Well?' asked Lippi, coldly.

'Do you not believe,' continued the newcomer, taking a gloved hand out of his pocket to point at him, 'in the determining role played by the Great Men of world history and the inspiring example of their values? That they are the chosen ones, the heroes, the leaders, the true creators of History and that they bend men and events to their will?'

'No, I don't,' said Lippi, rudely. 'Do you?'

'I believe so, since the day the great Thinker and Visionary arose in Germany whose thoughts, formulated first in words and then in deeds, have made of him the guide whom we are all happy to obey blindly.'

This insane declaration acted on the group like a log exploding on a peaceful fire. It was getting late. A sudden gust of wind blew out most of the candles. On the dance floor the band had stopped playing and the guests were starting to leave the tables. The little group hardly noticed. Harvey cleared his throat and Prokosch looked about uncertainly.

'Listen, Lippi,' intervened Pierre, who sensed the almost palpable fear that had seized his wife, 'this fellow is off his rocker. Why don't we….' And he made a sign to the waiter that they were leaving.

'Let the professor speak before making a decision,' retorted the stranger.

Lippi looked at him with sarcastic irony.

'As you wish. But before I do, perhaps you will do us the honour of introducing yourself?'

With his gloved left hand, the man extracted from his pocket a visiting card bearing a clearly visible crest. On it, Pierre could read: *Baron Karl Hoenig* in gothic script and, below that, *Doktor der Kriminalwissenschaft*.

Lippi burst out laughing.

'Well, well,' he said, 'I guessed as much. So you're a criminologist? I suppose you've come to talk to us about the crimes of your beloved Führer?'

The man stood rigidly still, except for the muscles in his jaw, which transformed his mouth into a contemptuous arc.

'Now may I hear the rest of your dissertation?'

'With pleasure,' replied Lippi unexpectedly. 'Allow me to be brief, as we are all anxious to eat.

'Just as a mediocre playwright, never having read Aristotle, unwittingly applies the rules of *Poetics,* your brilliant Adolf Hitler will be forced to follow, *by the divine pressure of the story* – and I haven't got time to enter into detail – the overall scheme of the tragedy of Napoleon. As of now we're only at the prologue, in other words the introductory stage. The confrontation, may I say conflict, will inevitably follow. It will start with lightning victories. The Führer has already started to push the French into war and he's preparing to use the methods used to such good effect by Napoleon in Italy: forced marches straight to the target without worrying about the enemy's strategy, destruction of all means of communication, and combined cavalry and artillery operations. The Italian campaign lasted one year. With the rapidity possible with modern arms and combined operations between tanks and aeroplanes, I'll bet you anything you like that the *Wehrmacht* will be in Paris in less than three months.'

'Hold on a second,' protested Pierre. 'The French army is the most powerful in the world.

'So was the Austrian army. But, you see, all the campaigns will be repeated. The French are going to try and restart the 1914-1918 war, and the Germans will reproduce the Franco-Prussian war of 1870. You'll see they'll repeat the breakthrough at Sedan. Once France is liquidated –.'

'Ach!' exclaimed Hoenig, swelling with pride.

'Don't rejoice too soon. Conquering Europe isn't enough if England is still standing. Napoleon, to invade, masses his troops at Boulogne. Hitler, copying him slavishly, does the same. But, since proud Albion is mistress of the seas, the result is the same fiasco.'

'Good show, old boy,' said Harvey. 'Keep it up.'

'Both turn to Russia, with the major inconvenience that neither have been able to avoid: having to fight on two fronts at once. They are both in a hurry to finish. In both cases, a furious assault up to the gates of Moscow. Then, just as in our well-ordered story, a dramatic reversal of the situation. In other words: Berezina.' He sneered. 'Would you like me to go on?'

'That would be pointless,' growled the German. 'Napoleon was a charlatan with an Italian temperament and French boastfulness. His work was only a rough sketch, an unfinished work that our Führer will finally complete!'

He straightened up, and for a moment Pierre thought he was going to click his heels and give the Nazi salute.

'I bid you goodnight, my dear sirs. My respects, Herr Professor! Tomorrow morning I shall have the pleasure of attending your lecture.'

They were starting to get up and leave their table, when Hoenig, who was on the point of reaching his, changed his mind and, to Pierre's surprise, planted himself in front of Solange. He bowed stiffly from the waist and, fixing her with his glacial stare, muttered two or three rapid phrases in German. She replied briefly in the same language. Her face was like marble and it was impossible to read the slightest emotion, but it seemed to Pierre that she blanched.

***

'What did he say to you?' he asked her once they were in the omnibus taking them back to Locarno. And he added: 'I didn't know you spoke German.'

'Come, come, darling,' she replied, frowning. 'You know I spent part of my youth in Berlin.'

'So what did he say to you,' he insisted.

'Nothing. He apologised for the intrusion and politely invited me to attend his lecture.'

'The man's mad,' repeated Pierre. 'What's the topic?'

He turned to Lippi who, no doubt exhausted from having talked too much, was slumped down in his seat, his eyes closed.

'I don't really know,' he replied, yawning. 'I seem to recall from the programme that he's talking about criminal women or some such thing.'

'I'm dying for something to eat,' sighed Solange.

Pierre didn't feel the same way. Even though he had eaten nothing since the lunch at midday, he wasn't hungry at all. Already the illuminated mass of the Grand Hotel loomed over them, dominating the town from its elevated position. And they could see, behind the great bay windows, the crystal chandeliers of the dining room.

II

Professor Lippi's lecture was due to start at 10.30 in the morning. The large room in the Albergo was full at least an hour ahead of time. The local newspapers had given the session wide publicity and the public eagerly awaited the moment the speaker would mount the podium. He was delayed, however, by the customary and lengthy speech of the president who, in his introduction, announced that all lectures and debates would be in French, a language in which any self-respecting foreign academic should be completely at ease. He went on to congratulate himself for having, in such troubled times of international tension, managed to assemble so many eminent representatives of the elite European cultural establishment in an atmosphere of collaboration and peace, and he elaborated at great length on that theme. One of the attendees, seated near Pierre, interrupted the speech to ask whether it was true that Arthur Carter Gilbert, the celebrated writer of detective fiction whose participation had been announced with a fanfare, had declined the invitation, as was rumoured. The speaker stiffened and stammered that Sir Arthur was temporarily indisposed, but there was every hope he would recover in time. As the audience appeared far from satisfied, he cut his speech short and made a hasty sign to Lippi, who was sitting in the front row, not far from Pierre and Harvey. 'Professor Lippi, the floor is yours.'

Lippi slowly climbed the platform steps. An enthusiastic audience, composed mainly of academics from Switzerland and neighbouring countries, students in the throes of writing their theses, several passionate readers and numerous professional and amateur writers – not counting the perpetual curiosity-seekers at the rear of the hall – noticed that the professor had not brought any notes and applauded him the more for that, except for a dozen or so specialists who hunkered down in their seats in chagrin.

'Mr. President, ladies and gentlemen, my dear colleagues,' he started, getting immediately to the heart of the subject: 'the criminal is an artist, the detective is only an art critic....'

'Nothing new about that,' hissed a specialist to his neighbour, sufficiently loudly that all could hear. 'He took that from Chesterton's Father Brown.'

'... and the author of detective stories,' continued Lippi imperturbably, 'has to be criminal and detective by turns. He must be, at the same time, a Hyde who conceives the story of the crime and a Dr. Jekyll who writes the account. The former proposes the enigma and the latter provides the solution. For the novelist, that implies the necessity to penetrate the mentality of the criminal and the talent to do so; to enter truly into the criminal's brain and to stay there long enough to organise the story into a coherent whole, until he himself appropriates the criminal's plan. Once that is done, and only then, can he don the detective's outfit and switch over to the account of the investigation that reconstructs the original story. But one must never lose sight of the fact that the true author of the novel is none other than the criminal, the creator of the work of infernal art, of the diabolical machination which remains a mystery to the reader; and that the detective is only there to expose the inner workings of the crime to the light of day.

'If, as we were promised, the great Carter Gilbert were here amongst us, he would be able to explain better than I that he starts, before anything else, by working out the prodigious system of reasoning that allows a murderer to escape from a locked room – after which the novel is practically finished: from then on, the account will merely look for explanations of apparently impossible actions and situations; throw out more and more demented hypotheses; dangle red herrings in front of the reader; and provide him with clues sufficiently well concealed that he cannot find the solution before the final revelation of the story conceived beforehand. What sets the impossible crime novel apart as a genre of its own is that, contrary to other forms of literature, the account is not intended to tell the story but to disguise it until the last few pages. So as to –.'

'Excuse me, professor,' asked a soft feminine voice with a Swiss accent, from somewhere in the middle of the hall. 'May I ask a question?'

'Silence, madam!' remonstrated the president. 'The public may only ask questions after the talk.'

'Because the charming lady I can see in the third row asked me so disarmingly, I shall make an exception in this case and be happy to answer her question,' said Lippi, all milk and honey.

'I don't understand the distinction you make between the story and the account. Aren't they generally taken to mean the same thing?'

'No, madam, and I'll give you an example that will make it all clear. Perhaps you remember the story of the filmgoer who neglected to tip the usher. By way of revenge, she whispered in his ear: "The butler did it." She had revealed the end of the story, so he lost all interest in the account of the film. Let that serve as a lesson. If your husband, speaking about a book he's planning to read, asks you: "What's it about?" please don't tell him the story, unless you want to create a scene. Don't tell him it's about a giant ape that kills people in the Rue Morgue or, as in *The Mystery of the Scarlet Room*, the crime was committed by shooting a crossbow bolt through a keyhole....'

A wave of laughter rippled through the audience. Lippi looked up ecstatically. He proceeded to cite a long list of categories of methods of killing in hermetically sealed rooms, affirming that locked room mysteries were the most interesting subjects in crime fiction.

'But I do recognise,' he said, raising his voice, 'that there are a number of detractors including, no doubt, some of you. They don't appreciate that kind of story, claiming that: "That kind of thing can't happen in real life." They only like situations which they call "realistic" and brandish the word "improbable" to express their disapproval. Now, that's the very last word that should be used to express contempt for the impossible crime novel. Its devotees love the genre precisely because it *is* improbable. When B is found dead inside a lift he was seen entering alone and whose doors only open when the apparatus is at rest, it is indeed improbable that A could have killed him. When D is found stabbed at the top of a tower that nobody else could have entered, it is improbable that C could be the guilty party. If G has an alibi sworn to by a host of witnesses, it's improbable that, with his innocent air, G could have done it. Yet he turns out to be the murderer! One must agree that, in all those cases, the word "improbable" is completely meaningless.

'We are here in the domain of pure fiction where the events obey only the internal logic of the mechanics of the story, and the role of the writer – *magister dixit* – "is to tell, not what really happened, but what had to have happened in the order of narrative necessity." Asking a man who writes detective stories to pay heed to improbability is as ridiculous as asking a mathematician to use a ruler to verify the accuracy of his calculations on an ironing board.'

He paused briefly to assess the effect of the metaphor on the audience and, greatly encouraged, launched into further philosophical observations, all of which caused him to overrun his allotted time. The public was starting to become restless so he was obliged to cut short his peroration, and the applause that greeted the end of his speech was due more to relief than anything else.

It was time for the debate, to the general satisfaction of those that had not left the hall. It proceeded as is customary at such events, with each participant asking a question more for effect than from a desire to advance the cause of knowledge. When it became obvious the discussion was winding down, the president, anxious to end the proceedings, looked around and asked without enthusiasm: 'Would anyone care to ask one final question?' A sonorous voice asked to speak.

'Doctor Hoenig?' said the president.

The whole audience turned round to look at the criminologist, who was standing at the rear of the hall. So far, he had passed unnoticed by everyone but his immediate neighbours. What was he going to say? He walked down the aisle with a heavy tread and stopped in front of the rostrum.

'I believe I heard you say,' he started in a soft voice, 'that a locked room mystery is the *ne plus ultra* of detective fiction and those who take a different view in accusing it of improbability are making a grievous mistake. And you added, if I remember correctly, that such stories don't need to justify themselves by the fact that they could have happened in reality, in other words it's not important that these kinds of situations cannot occur in real life.'

'Quite so,' snapped Lippi. 'Your point being?'

'My point being,' repeated Hoenig, raising his voice, 'the following question: are you the same Professor Lippi who expounded in his works the famous theory that narrative fiction only differs from true fiction in negligible ways and that each imitates the other?'

Lippi did not answer straight away. He smiled as if secretly enjoying himself and nodded his head before replying.

'Any scholar worthy of the name must rejoice at being found in apparent contradiction by his peers,' he began, seeming not the least joyful. 'I forgive you, as you are clearly not a specialist, for not knowing that the impossible crime novel is a genre entirely apart, with its own *letters patent* of nobility in the same way as the fantastic and the fairy tale. It doesn't have to answer to reality, and its readers don't give a fig about adherence to the norms of daily life. I fear you're comparing it to the realist school of crime fiction, where murder is treated as just another fact of daily life amongst so many others. You are, of course, perfectly free to derive your pleasure from the penny dreadful, but, for my part, I am incapable of allowing myself to be seduced by vulgar accounts of human turpitude.'

'Leave my tastes out of it and answer the question: do you deny that a real criminal could perpetrate a murder in a hermetically sealed chamber?'

'I didn't say he couldn't, I said he wouldn't.'

'And why, may I ask?'

'Because it's a horribly complicated way to kill someone,' sneered Lippi, 'and there are far more simple methods. Let us assume there is a murderer sufficiently mad to decide to stab a victim barricaded inside a house in the middle of a clearing in a forest, surrounded by snow, illuminated day and night by searchlights and under constant police surveillance – and without leaving any traces.' He shot an amused look at the audience. 'Well, ladies and gentlemen, by great good fortune we have before us a specialist in criminal phenomena, and I'm sure he'll be able to explain how such an individual would have gone about it in *real life*.'

Laughter rang out on all sides of the audience, and the good doctor's face turned purple. He opened his mouth to reply, but remained utterly speechless. He looked desperately at the young man sitting next to the seat he had vacated. The latter's expression was inscrutable, but a close observer might well have concluded he was trying desperately not to laugh out loud.

'I thank you for your eloquence,' said Lippi, now playing shamelessly to the gallery. Pierre realised he was toying with the German, trying see how far he could goad him. It made him think of a thesis jury, unable to resist the pleasure of tormenting the unfortunate candidate.

'Tell us at least, Doctor,' continued the Italian, driving the nail home, 'whether, in the course of your long career, you have ever found yourself face-to-face with a murderer who stabbed his victim with a piece of ice, or who shot him with a contraption concealed in a telephone, designed to fire a piece of rock salt shaped in the form of a bullet into the head of whoever picks up the receiver. I'm only mentioning here – and I can see that everyone in the hall except you understands – a few of the diabolical schemes dreamt up by the eminent Carter Gilbert. So, I ask you, can you cite a single case when such an extravagant method was used?' He folded his arms and the audience held its breath. 'Come now, sir, you must answer.'

Hoenig squared his shoulders, folded his arms and, chin thrust out, announced in a firm voice:

'I shall do it. I shall do it on Monday morning, when I present my paper.'

'May we ask how you propose to answer?'

'I shall describe a number of impossible crimes I have had to examine, which have never been explained.'

'Why should we take your word for it?'

'I shall provide dates and facts and I shall cite names. Even if that causes problems for certain people here,' he added under his breath, so that only the attendees in the front row could hear, even though the words made little sense to them.

He looked defiantly around the auditorium and Pierre had the impression the man paused briefly to stare at him.

'And what then?'

'What do you mean?'

'You will merely be demonstrating the ingenuity of your interpretation. Nothing more. Didn't Aristotle declare that a theory must conform to the experience of things as they are?'

Hoenig's face went red with anger as he realised his tormentor had no interest in any discussion where reason played a role.

'Get to the point,' he snarled in a harsh voice.

'I'm getting there. Everyone here knows the endlessly repeated story of the miraculous grotto where poor Rosenkreutz disappeared… Well, because you claim that the same hocus-pocus can be performed in real life and that a man may indeed escape from a hermetically sealed area, are you prepared to submit to a conclusive experiment?'

'That is to say…?'

'Shut yourself in the grotto.'

'And then?'

'Disappear!' shouted Lippi, guffawing helplessly. Hoenig unfolded his arms slowly and, with his hands shaking, marched at a glacial pace out of the hall, his long steps pounding the floor. On the way, he took the hat handed to him by the young man and rammed it down on his head without looking back. Although Pierre tried to convince himself it was all theatre, he thought of the menacing words the big man had uttered. In any case, Lippi had almost certainly not heard them; he appeared, quite the contrary, to be satisfied with his petty victory.

III

It was only towards the end of the morning that it dawned on Pierre that a catastrophe was about to occur. The previous evening he had left before the last lecture, so eager was he to find his wife. She had, in fact, spent an excellent day, having risen late and strolled around the town window-shopping. ('It's amazing, the number of jewellers here. I've never seen so many watches in my life.') After lunch, she had taken the funicular up to the shrine of the Madonno del Sasso: 'A very Italian church, everything gilded, with some marvellous *trompe-l'œil* paintings that I'm sure you'd have loved. And guess who I met? The beautiful Madame Hoenig! Well, I admit she's not as beautiful as all that, unless you like the valkyrie sort, but I found her very pleasant. Much more so than her husband, anyway. We stopped for tea at a charming little inn further up the mountain, with an absolutely sublime view of the lake....'

While she was babbling in her bath and he was dressing for dinner, he decided he would not breathe a word about the dispute between Hoenig and Lippi and the unseemly way the latter had treated the former. These locked room stories were starting to get on his nerves and he was starting to believe that Solange was right: there was something unhealthy about the subject.

Earlier that day, when the morning session had finished ahead of schedule, he had thought of going back to Locarno to join her, before remembering that she had arranged to meet Freyja Hoenig for lunch. He wasn't all that happy with the idea of Solange pairing up with the woman, but after all she wasn't responsible for her husband's loutishness and it was hardly surprising if two bored spouses tried to find things to do together. So he headed to the bar and ordered a dry martini to fortify himself for the monastic custom of the communal meal.

A noisy good humour reigned in the bar. Professor Harvey, moustache ruffled and tie askew, was brandishing his pipe and fulminating. A young French philosopher, squinting horribly behind round spectacles, addressed acerbic remarks to him over a whisky soda. The subject of their apparent disagreement seemed to be the new form of American crime novel to which Professor Lippi had referred the day before, and, in particular, stories dealing with gangsters and private eyes. In an unguarded moment, Harvey had allowed himself to be convinced by an ill-intentioned friend to read a couple of "hard-boiled" novels and had selected the works of one Dashiell Hammett. Harvey was not a tolerant man. His attempts at book-burning – he had managed to sprinkle the books with lighter fluid before throwing them on the fire – had fortunately not burnt his library down. Aside from a fire in the chimney, there had been very little damage.

As Pierre listened to the taunts of the philosopher, his mind wandered elsewhere. He smiled serenely as he savoured his martini: he hadn't a worry in the world. His paper tomorrow, which he had so carefully prepared, was bound to be a brilliant success and Solange would be there to see it. And yet… problems had a habit of appearing suddenly like bats out of a cave, just when least expected.

All that stuff about disappearance from the grotto… Bah! Lippi had simply wanted to embellish a good story. All the same….

'A Perrier citron and a lemonade, please,' said a voice behind him, then added: 'Would you care for a refill, Monsieur Garnier?'

He knew without turning round who was speaking. Dr. Hoenig hauled his heavy weight up onto the barstool. Despite the broad smile on his face, a malignant gleam lurked in his eyes. Pierre noticed that he was wearing a dark brown suit far too heavy for the time of year and was sweating profusely beneath his iron-grey hair.

'No, thank you,' he replied curtly.

'My congratulations, you know how to limit yourself. Personally, I do not drink alcohol and I practise vegetarianism. It's consistent with the hygiene we're trying to instil in our people. Is that not so, Strahler?' he said, turning towards the young brown-haired man who, were he not so thin, one would have said followed him like his shadow. The latter agreed without enthusiasm as he morosely contemplated the glass of sparkling water that had been placed in front of him.

Hoenig presented him as his assistant, a psychiatry student who helped him in his work. That work, he added for Pierre's benefit – even though Pierre had not enquired and was becoming suspicious of this new-found affability on the German's part – was about the genetics of criminology and, specifically, the presence of a dominant gene in criminal pathology; the objective of this vast research, he explained passionately, being to eliminate pathological factors by a rigorous selection process and thus create a healthy race, rid of all moral tumours in the same way one eliminated physical tumours. Pierre, who was not gifted in scientific matters, listened politely and nodded his head. Having received a Catholic education, he did not believe in innate evil, but was not about to enter into a controversy on the subject.

The German must have realised this, for he gave Pierre a hard stare and changed the subject abruptly.

'*À-propos*,' he said, and Pierre's first thought was that he had mistranslated, for what followed was a complete non sequitur. '*À-propos*, my wife told me she'd had the pleasure of making the acquaintance of your charming wife. It's fortunate for her to have met someone who speaks such good German, because she herself doesn't speak anything else.'

'Yes,' said Pierre. 'She was brought up in Germany.'

'Her father was the consul in Berlin, I believe?'

'Yes, I believe so,' replied Pierre.

'I may have known her parents. What was her maiden name?'

Pierre couldn't remember her ever having told him, but he recalled seeing the name on the marriage papers. It was an easy name to remember.

'Duvernois, I think. Solange Duvernois.'

'Do you think so? Tell me, Monsieur Garnier, how long have you been married? Trust me, I have reasons for asking that.'

'We were married last year. It will be just one year next month.'

'Just one year,' repeated his inquisitor in a thoughtful voice.

Pierre racked his brains to try and understand the reason for all these questions and cursed himself for not having had the guts to send this fellow packing. The bar was starting to empty, with small groups of guests now wandering into the dining room. Strahler had done the same, leaving his glass untouched on the counter. The only other person in the bar was a nondescript individual of modest physique, wearing a ready-to-wear suit who was obviously not part of the crowd. Pierre sensed that he was observing them but, when he turned to look, the fellow was staring fixedly at his half-empty glass of beer.

'I seem to recall having read a number of articles....' The doctor's gaze fell upon the unknown man, registered curiosity, then returned to Pierre. 'A number of articles by a certain Monsieur Garnier, written by someone with a keen analytic mind. One in particular, regarding *On Murder, Considered As One of the Fine Arts*, by De Quincey, a fundamental work on the psychological anatomy of character and the motives of those –male or female – who commit such crimes. Is that correct?'

'What if it is?'

'And, if memory serves, you also expounded on criminal schizophrenia in a penetrating analysis of *Dr. Jekyll and Mr. Hyde*. Where did you obtain the material necessary for your diagnosis?'

In any other circumstance, Pierre would have been more than happy to answer; he would have been flattered, even, to reveal his knowledge. But he saw that the man was toying with him, so he replied coldly:

'I've read two or three books on the subject.'

'Freud?'

'Among others.'

Doctor Hoenig gave an exasperated chuckle and looked at the ceiling. Then he turned again to Pierre with a disapproving air.

'I can see, young man, that you're no more astute in your private life than you are in your lectures.' He adjusted his position on the bar-stool, which groaned in response. 'One final question: would you remind me of your wife's name?'

At this point Pierre, already highly exasperated, lost his self-control and exploded:

'For heaven's sake, where are you going with all this?'

'I haven't expressed myself very well,' responded the doctor, a look of immense sadness spreading across his face. He looked away as he asked:

'Do you know who the woman calling herself Solange Duvarnois really is?'

Pierre, unable to speak, looked at him in fear and amazement.

'I think,' continued Hoenig, in a voice tinged with both distress and benevolence, 'that I'm going to have to tell you sooner or later.'

He sighed deeply and climbed carefully down from his stool. Pierre sat frozen in place for several seconds, trying to make sense of what he had just heard, while the man, with his heavy tread, walked slowly out of the bar. Pierre was too shaken to be angry. He told himself the fellow must be mad, and shrugged his shoulders as if trying to force himself to be indifferent.

***

Pierre Garnier found an empty seat next to the young philosopher, whose name was Albert Mestre, and whom he had met before. They had both graduated from the Ecole Normale Superieure, although Mestre was from a later year, and this had formed something of a bond between them. Long tables had been installed in the vast dining-room and there was a hubbub of lively conversation as the attendees sat bathed in the sunshine from the great French windows.

Mestre reported what he had heard on the radio. Germany continued to demand the annexation of the Sudetenland, the Czechoslovakian army was on a war footing, and the French were waiting on Premier Daladier's dithering regarding troop mobilisation. Among the small group of Frenchmen at that end of the table, the talk was of whether and how soon they would have to pack their suitcases. Some declared that war would be a crime and were hoping for a miracle; those over fifty years old were confronted with the memories of their frightful youth; one of them, who made no attempt to hide the fact he was communist, argued that it was the fascists and the "two hundred families" – as Daladier had described the top industrialists in France – that wanted the war, as well as the Jews and the Americans.

Mestre, the only one of an age to be mobilised, listened to them argue with a scornful smile on his face. He had nothing in common with them, which brought him closer to Pierre. In an aside, he confided that France no longer had an air force since the Popular Front had come to power, and very few tanks, so any confrontation with Germany would be over in less time than it took to describe it – Pierre remembered that Lippi had made the same prediction – and frankly he didn't give a damn. He thought that the world was absurd, that existence had no sense other than that imparted by a pure act without ulterior motive, and there was no point in fighting for liberty because everyone was free anyway.

Even though it was not in his character to be cynical, Pierre had a certain sympathy with his friend's views. He didn't pay much attention to contemporary calamities and displayed a studied indifference to events in the material world, provided they didn't threaten the cocoon he was curled up in. During his military service he had been afflicted with acute sciatica complicated by heart murmurs and had been

41

discharged after a long convalescence in a military hospital. During his time as a student, he had been cloistered with culture and books, and if he had chosen university life it was because he thought it would offer him a sort of monastic harbour from which he could serenely contemplate the storms that troubled the rest of humanity. He was ten years old in 1914 and thirteen when his father, a patriotic teacher, died from a bullet in the head at the battle of the Aisne. Watching his mother waste away from grief, he formed the impression that the world had been plunged into chaos and that humanity wasn't worth the effort to understand, now that bestiality had taken over. His chance encounter with Solange had only served to accentuate his desire to shut himself away and he was only too happy for the two of them to confine themselves in a microcosm of shared love, with their own happiness as the only law.

Nevertheless, he couldn't help thinking that behind the outrageous comportment of Dr. Hoenig lurked evil forces, certain statements hinted at a background full of obscure threats and menaces, and some kind of plot was being hatched in the shadows.

Although he was, happily, seated at a distance from the big man, he was able to observe his repugnant eating habits, with mayonnaise sauce dribbling down his chin as he devoured a plate of Kartoffeln. Meanwhile Strahler, sitting next to him, profited from the occasion, downing two glasses of white wine in rapid succession.

'Who exactly is that fellow?' he asked under his breath, but loud enough for Mestre to hear and look up.

'Ah! The Nazi,' he replied, his voice full of disgust.

'Who is he?'

'I'll tell you as long as you keep it a secret. He's one of Alfred Rosenberg's closest advisers on the matter of racial anthropology.'

'So what?'

'You might not think of it to look at him, but his research is about how best to preserve the blond Aryan strain and eliminate hereditary defects that could spoil its purity. If you ask me,' he sneered, 'if they were serious about their aesthetic criteria, the Nazis would have disposed of him a long time ago. And not only him,' he added fervently.

'Have you any idea what he's doing here?'

'That's a good question, old boy. He also happens to be one of the greatest living authorities on criminal matters.'

'An authority on criminal matters,' repeated Pierre. He was impressed and frightened at the same time.

'Yes, Baron Karl Hoenig. Until 1933 he was the medical expert attached to the Berlin police headquarters. He played a decisive role in the arrest of Hans Beckert, the celebrated child murderer, which is no doubt why the Swiss invited him.' He lowered his voice: 'Don't tell anyone I said so, but my friend Saussure, one of the symposium organisers – no relation to the linguist – told me in confidence that they were under great pressure from the German ambassador in Berne. He's all the more furious that Hoenig was invited because Carter Gilbert, who is a die-hard conservative but an antifascist, decided not to attend when he found out Hoenig would be here.'

Mestre blinked his eyes, took off his glasses, pinched the red mark they had made across his nose, and put them back.

'But, hang on, didn't I see you talking to him just now? What was all that about?'

'Nothing important,' replied Pierre, lying through his teeth and shrugging his shoulders. 'The organisation of the symposium, the lack of hygiene in Swiss cooking, and he also asked me what I thought of this morning's local newspaper, which he had found absolutely pathetic.'

'What an absolute ass!' said Mestre, by way of summary.

***

The evening of that same day, around six-thirty, as the sun disappeared behind the mountain and an early twilight descended under the trees, Pierre Garnier and Professor Lippi walked rapidly down the winding path through the park forest. The afternoon had been very trying, with a provocative paper by a Marxist academic on class criticism in the novels of Agatha Christie. They had decided not to wait for the shuttle and to walk down to Ascona where they could catch the bus to Locarno.

The path took them through a grove, in the middle of which stood a fountain where they stopped for a brief moment. It was in the Egyptian style; the dry basin, full of climbing plants and dead leaves, was surmounted by a black marble stele on which the image of the goddess Isis had been carved in bas-relief, decorated with hieroglyphics *en cartouche* to indicate royalty.

Down the slope from the fountain, and linked to the main path by

43

gravel tracks, they could see a number of bungalows scattered under the thick canopy of fir trees. They were quaint little buildings, each surrounded on all four sides by a strip of lawn, with shingle roofs and walls made from logs joined by thick planks. Each had a front porch, a pair of double-windows along one wall at waist height, and flagstones leading up to the porch. Most of the bungalows were occupied by conference attendees and through the branches they could see, here and there, light filtering through drawn curtains. As they passed one of the bungalows closest to the path they could see Harvey in the shadow of the porch, sitting in a rattan chair, taking in the evening air. He saw them and raised his pipe in salute.

Beyond the Englishman's bungalow, the path became suddenly steeper and then curved around the foot of a steep escarpment standing amidst a mass of fallen rocks. At the base was a narrow fissure roughly the size of a man.

'That's the entrance to the famous grotto,' said Lippi over his shoulder. 'The locals call it the Sorcerer's Grotto. In fact, it's nothing more than a simple cavity, only a few metres deep, just big enough to shelter from the rain or to frolic with your lover. Alas!' he sighed, 'when reality tries to imitate art, the result rarely lives up to expectation.'

Pierre wasn't listening. He had stopped, unable to take another step. It was possible that the old wives' tale Lippi had served up had affected his judgment. But the unkempt nature of the site in the middle of such a well-maintained park seemed both incongruous and sinister. Black conifer trunks seemed to stand guard over rocks covered with wet moss, and shoots of ivy escaping from the dark fissure looked like fingers clawing at the stone.

He shuddered as his mind filled with images: a whispering multitude all dressed in white; a small man in a billowing robe turning towards them to make an enigmatic sign before entering the grotto; naked arms rolling and stacking rocks to seal the natural sepulchre....

And suppose, entering the dark chamber and groping around, one's fingers touched something soft, a face with rotting skin or a half-decomposed corpse, pressed against the rear wall...?

He turned to see the Italian looking at him with amusement.

'You can't get in there any more,' he said, as if he'd been following Pierre's morbid thoughts. 'After Rosenkreutz's disappearance, the authorities installed a steel grill to bar access to the site. Whatever is left in there, it is highly unlikely it will ever see the light of day... I have to admit I was a little hard on that cretin of a doctor when I challenged him to shut himself up in that hole,' he added when they recommenced their walk. 'The grill is solidly embedded in the rock and not even Houdini could get out.'

The path descended once again and followed another curve. The fir trees were thinning out. Soon they could see below them the low wall that bounded the property and the gate beyond which they could see, above the roofs of the village, the black mirror that was the lake.

To their left was a bungalow – the last before the wall – which seemed, as they walked past, to be abandoned. The roof was covered with a tarpaulin and a small scaffold stood against the log wall. Looking back up the slope to their right and through the trees they could see another bungalow about fifty meters away, connected to the main path by a narrow track and not far, it seemed, from the pale patch of the grotto escarpment. In the gathering darkness around the little building its lines were no longer visible and all that could be seen was the rectangle of a lighted window.

The door of the bungalow they had just passed was wide open. Without thinking, Pierre went back to take a look. It was pitch black inside but he had a vague impression that something was moving and it seemed to him that he could make out a point of light (the tip of a cigarette, perhaps?) which went out abruptly. A labourer who had stayed behind? What would he be doing in the dark? 'I'm hallucinating!' he thought. But why let himself be affected by the atmosphere in this part of the property – of sinister tree trunks and damp undergrowth, giving off a sickly odour of decomposing mushrooms. That would be childish! No doubt. Ridiculous! Certainly. At that moment he spotted two abandoned cigarette butts under the porch – which a real detective would not have failed to examine closely, he told himself ironically, shrugging his shoulders.

He was about to rejoin Lippi, who had stopped to wait for him, when he looked back up the slope and realised that, from where he was standing, there was a perfect view of the double-windows of the other bungalow. A man, of whom he could see only the upper part, was sitting in the middle of the lounge. The view was so clear that, even from afar and through the glass, Pierre could recognise Dr. Hoenig. The medical expert's huge head could be seen in the glow of a standard lamp. He was wrapped in a violet dressing-gown and was holding a cigarette in his hand, and was looking in the direction of the window but not at the window itself.

And, standing in front of him with her back to the window, was a woman, a petite woman in silhouette, backlit by the lamp. She was wearing a dark suit of an unfashionable and severe cut, her hair was tucked inside a felt hat with the rim down and she carried a large bag equipped with a shoulder strap.

Later, Garnier and Lippi would be unable to provide a more detailed description. The one thing they were sure about was that the woman was not Freyja Hoenig, who was much taller and whose abundant blonde hair which she wore in a voluminous chignon would never have fit under the hat. What puzzled them was the absence of any intimacy between the two figures, which ruled out the possibility of a tryst. The woman did not move and made no gesture, yet she must have spoken because the man appeared to listen with a cold calculating look on his face. All of a sudden she became more agitated and opened her bag to take out some papers which she offered to him at arm's length, and Hoenig put on his glasses to examine them.

'This Hoenig is a very strange character,' observed Lippi while they were walking away in the direction of the park exit. 'One always gets the feeling that he's involved in some dubious scheme or other. In any case,' he added with a satisfied chuckle, 'it would seem that something's going on. We may have stumbled on the beginning of a secret and complicated intrigue. In the first place, why is Hoenig in a bungalow so far from the Albergo and set apart from the others? And who is the mysterious woman visiting him when his wife isn't there? Also, I remember seeing his wife at a table on the terrace, in a *tête-à-tête* with a thin fellow, who I would swear was making eyes at her. What are they all up to? What kind of show: comedy or tragedy? I daren't hope for a tragedy with, as Aristotle said "an action causing pain and destruction and murders committed on stage".' He turned abruptly to his companion. 'Tell me, Garnier, what do you think?'

Pierre pulled himself together, suddenly aware that he was expected to show some sign of interest and propose a theory, even though he hadn't the faintest idea.

'I think,' he replied, weighing his words carefully, 'that Dr. Hoenig chose the bungalow simply for its view of the lake. I also think there's a good chance that the mysterious woman was a journalist who had come to interview him or submit an article. As for the hypothesis of an idyll between his wife and his assistant, it's too much of a literary cliché to be taken seriously.'

'"Interesting, although elementary",' quoted Lippi, looking at him ironically. 'But: "I am afraid, my dear Watson, that most of your conclusions were erroneous."'

'"Some people,"' responded Pierre, '"without possessing genius, have a remarkable power of stimulating it."'

'Good,' said Lippi, approvingly. 'Very good! *Baskervilles*, first chapter, I think?'

'Exactly,' replied Pierre.

And conversing thus, they took the road to the bus station.

***

Lippi went up to his room and Pierre joined his wife who had been reading the evening newspaper in the hotel lounge while waiting for him.

'Have you seen the news?' she asked anxiously, frowning charmingly. 'It looks as though there's going to be war. I'm beginning to wonder if we wouldn't be better off staying in Switzerland.'

'And what would I do?' he asked with nervous smile.

'I don't know. Whatever you want. You could write detective stories, for example.'

'I thought you didn't like detective stories?'

'No, but it seems to be profitable,' she replied with a knowing look. 'Look at Arthur Carter Gilbert: he has a beautiful villa in Lausanne, a boat and a charming wife much younger than he is.'

It was his turn to frown.

'Do you know him?'

'Of course. Didn't I tell you? I knew him when I was very young. He was a great friend of my parents when my father was posted to London. He used to sit me on his knee and call me his little fairy, and I used to call him Uncle Arthur.

Pierre was stunned. It wasn't the first time she had unexpectedly revealed a part of her past, but he still found it hard to get used to it.

'At the time, he hadn't yet published anything. He was working in the Foreign Office, and that's how he and Papa....'

The sentence tailed off and she stared at him wide-eyed.

'Why are you looking at me like that? What have I said?'

'Nothing. I didn't know you knew him, that's all.'

47

He had promised himself never to question her, but he couldn't help asking her, rather too sharply:

'Why didn't you tell me when you knew we were coming to the symposium?'

'You didn't tell me he was going to be here. I found out from Freyja Hoenig this afternoon. Anyway, he's not coming. He's an old bear; he has a horror of appearing in public.'

He changed the subject and adopted a lighter tone.

'Listen to me, darling. It's probably nothing, but you must have shared some confidences with that woman, and I have very good reason to believe she told everything to her husband.' He forced a smile. 'It's hardly surprising, but he appears to be interested in you. He asked me certain questions and –.'

'What are you talking about?' she replied angrily. 'I chatted with Madame Hoenig, as women will do. You're acting very strangely this evening.' She hesitated, then burst out laughing. 'What makes you think I shared any confidences?'

'Nothing,' he confessed, shaking his head. 'I just have a bee in my bonnet.'

'If we're talking about confidences,' she continued, 'she was the one confiding in me. In any case, I can tell you two things: that woman does not love her husband, and she doesn't share his views.'

'Who doesn't love her husband?' whispered Lippi who had suddenly appeared in front of them. He took Solange's hand and brought it to his lips. 'Certainly not you, dear Madame... Sorry to interrupt, but as we're all a little tired of the hotel cooking, I thought I would take you to a restaurant in the old town to try a genuine Swiss *fondu* accompanied by a delicious local wine.'

With the Italian's arrival, the atmosphere relaxed a little and Pierre, already won over, turned to his wife, who looked doubtful.

'It wouldn't be reasonable, darling. You have to give your paper tomorrow morning.'

She finally gave in and the evening turned out perfectly. The light from the candles on the table brought out the smoothness of Solange's skin and accentuated the silky highlights in the chestnut hair curling around the nape of her neck. The décolleté of her green dress displayed the graceful line of her throat and shoulders to perfection. She had never looked more beautiful. Lippi put himself out for her and was at his scintillating best with a stream of sparkling witticisms. But, although she laughed heartily at his jokes, Pierre noticed that she chain-smoked nervously and the only time her innocent grey-green eyed met his, he believed he could detect a secret anxiety.

IV

Pierre, on the podium, was in a lively debate with an admirer of the hammer and sickle and follower of a doctrine that professed internationalism but was nonetheless driven by an inflexible chauvinism. He railed against "Anglo-Saxon imperialism" and the idea that an American had invented detective fiction seemed to him to be yet another impudent reactionary lie. As far as he was concerned, the genre had been created by the French, along with the Rights of Man and the guillotine, and had been inspired by the activities of the secret police under Fouché – Napoleon's partner in crime; Balzac's novel *Une Tenebreuse Affaire (A Murky Business)*; and Gaboriau's serialised tales.

Pierre replied courteously that the conjecture, while not exactly erroneous, was – and here he deliberately used English words – *unconvincing* and *irrelevant* ; for, while it was clear that each moment in history had inevitably followed all the preceding ones and so – put that way – nobody could deny a connection between Fouché's snitches, the gigantic ape of the Rue Morgue, and the phosphorescent mastiff of the Baskerville family, he himself, not being a specialist in dialectic materialism, was unable to see it. Particularly since *Une Tenebreuse Affaire* was written in 1841, the same year as *The Murders in the Rue Morgue,* and the first novel of the so-called precursor Gaboriau, *L'Affaire Lerouge,* didn't appear until 1863.

This brilliant rejoinder ended his session with a flourish and earned him hearty applause from everywhere but the ranks of the speaker's colleagues. '"To win without risk is to triumph without glory",' Lippi whispered in his ear, his appreciative smile belying his words. Pierre, momentarily dizzy with his success, did not consider the effect the incident might have on his *cursus honorum* – his academic future. For now, he was just deeply happy to have been a success in front of his wife and couldn't wait to be alone with her to listen to her congratulations.

From his position on the platform where he was holding forth on

51

the enigma of *The Scarlet Letter*, he had finally dared to glance in her direction. She was sitting modestly to one side at the end of the third row, dressed for the occasion in a dark brown suit with a matching beret, which gave her the air of a student. She listened with that innocent, almost too innocent, expression she wore when she was bothered: her eyes, under their long lashes, held that look of rapture which subtly hinted at sexual arousal. When she had realised he was looking at her, she blushed and lowered her eyelids.

She left the auditorium at the end of the debate and went to wait for him on the terrace. He caught sight of her standing not far from the door, in the full sunlight that was beating down on the flagstones. Trying to make his way towards her while avoiding the attendees wishing to ask him questions, he bumped into Albert Mestre who insisted on congratulating him and wanted to ask permission to publish his talk in the review he edited.

He answered him distractedly, keeping his eye steadfastly on his wife and waving to her discreetly. At that very moment his feeling of euphoria vanished. In the middle of the terrace, among the groups of chattering attendees, he could see Dr. Hoenig walking towards Solange, with his heavy tread, jutting jaw and disdainful mouth, and the air of someone who knew exactly how to get what he wanted. Pierre saw him speak to her. She, initially startled, smiled with a forced ease that fooled no-one: the smile was like a mask. She fiddled nervously with the clasp of her handbag and, when the doctor leaned towards her to emphasise his words, recoiled instinctively and looked around for help.

It seemed to last an eternity. Mestre had been replaced by a cackling swarm of Swiss students who bombarded him with compliments and trivial questions. He tried to push them away but they kept returning and he felt paralysed and impotent, as if trapped in a bad dream.

In fact, the whole scene lasted only a few minutes. He managed to free himself and stepped forward with clenched fists. 'If that repugnant thug speaks to her for one second more,' he said to himself, 'I'll punch him in the nose.' As if he had heard the threat, Hoening bowed curtly and turned on his heels. Suddenly, Pierre found a radiant Solange in front of him, throwing herself into his arms. And he suddenly felt so good that he wondered, laughing at himself, whether his imagination had once again played tricks on him.

***

Solange stayed for lunch at the Albergo and the conversation, with Pierre, Mestre, Prokosch, and Professors Harvey and Lippi at the table, was very lively. There was no discussion of detective fiction, locked room mysteries, dark sorcery, or even politics. Instead they talked about trivial yet essential things such as gastronomy, wine, the new painters in vogue, the latest Paris craze, the recent Paul Morand novel and the annual Giraudoux play. Amid a general feeling of well-being, Lippi raised his glass and cited the prophetic phrase from *La Guerre de Troie n'aura pas lieu*: 'A minute of peace is always worth seizing,' and Solange captivated Prokosch by telling him about *Snow White and the Seven Dwarfs,* a full-length cartoon that she had just seen on the Champs-Élysées. All present went out of their way to be witty and frivolous, helped greatly by the charming local Tessin wine. The young woman was amazed that so many serious and erudite people could behave like tipsy students.

As soon as they left the Albergo by the door to the parking space where the Delahaye was parked, Pierre gathered her to him and kissed her at length and lovingly. It reminded him of the first time he had held her in his arms, on the quay at Le Havre just after she had disembarked from the ocean liner; they had held each other as if the world was about to end, completely oblivious to the crowd milling around them. 'You won't be back too late, darling?' she asked imploringly as she slid behind the wheel and looked up at him with eyes welling with tears. And, as he stood there alone, he felt the trees and the landscape spin around him.

'I've had too much wine,' he thought. He steadied himself and walked resolutely back down the steps leading to the Albergo. Just as he was about to step onto the terrace, he froze. A valet was opening one of the great French windows and Dr. Hoenig appeared. He was wearing his customary thick woollen suit, out of the top pocket of which he produced a cigar, which he stopped to light with an almost maniacal attention. Once again Pierre felt extreme unease. He saw in a flash the incident earlier that day, and felt the same surge of anger. But instead of stopping to think, as he would have done in his normal state, he marched straight towards the fat man and stood defiantly in front of him.

'What did you say to my wife?' he said, almost spluttering. His

53

mouth was dry and his throat was tight and he didn't know why.

Hoening looked him up and down.

'What do you want, Monsieur Garnier?'

'I demand to know,' he repeated, 'what you said to my wife.'

Hoenig raised his eyebrows to show astonishment.

'What I said to your wife? Nothing important, I can assure you. I just reminded her of two or three episodes in her past. Murky businesses she was mixed up in, which had sparked the interest of my country's police force.' He paused and took a long and exasperatingly slow pull on the cigar. 'Listen to me carefully. I couldn't care less about justice as you understand it, which is a pathetic invention of decadent democracies. Whatever you may think, I have great admiration for her; I mean for her intelligence, obviously, for she is a woman of superior intelligence, which of course you already knew. No, no, rest assured I have no intention of reopening the files.'

Pierre stood thunderstruck. Hoenig looked at him with a scornful pity. He removed the cigar from his mouth, considered the tip thoughtfully, and started to leave. Mechanically, Pierre followed him as if under the pull of an invisible magnet.

'Look at it this way,' continued Hoenig, descending the stairs towards the park with a measured step. 'Intellectually, I'm very curious. I wouldn't want to leave this world without discovering the solution to one of the rare criminal problems that has defeated me.' He stopped to look patronisingly at Pierre. 'I like you, Garnier. If you agreed to help me, I could help you in return. Otherwise….'

Pierre found his voice, but he was so confused that his anger had subsided.

'I don't know if you realise it or not,' he replied dully, 'but I have absolutely no idea what you're talking about.'

'That doesn't surprise me, Monsieur Garnier. To borrow the illuminating distinction that your friend Professor Lippi makes between the story and the account, you find yourself in the position of the hero of the novel, to whom all kinds of things happen without him having the faintest idea of the story he's living. At least until the dénouement, which generally occurs right at the end. But neither you nor I have the patience to wait until then, no?' It was a rhetorical question and he continued: 'However, as it's a long story, I suggest you come with me to my bungalow where we can take all the time we need and sample an excellent cognac to boot. Oh, yes,' he sighed, 'I have been known occasionally to break the strict rules I impose on myself. Don't worry, it will be our secret. My wife and my assistant have gone to do a little shopping in Milan where, incidentally, cigars cost less than half of what they do here in Switzerland. By the way, your charming wife has asked mine to bring back some cigarettes.'

'No,' said Pierre, and stopped dead.

Hoenig turned round.

'No, what, Monsieur Garnier?'

'I'm not going a step further. I've already heard enough of your rant.'

The doctor opened his hands palms up in a conciliatory gesture.

'Just as you wish,' he replied calmly. 'I expected as much. But, if I may be permitted an indiscreet question, what do you earn outside of your university salary?'

The question was so incongruous that Pierre burst out laughing. He told himself his first hypothesis was correct: the eminent Herr Doktor was completely off his rocker. It felt as if a great weight had been lifted from his shoulders. Hoenig, however, observed him with a clinical eye and repeated imperturbably:

'Let me put it another way: are you rich?'

'Of course not! How can you possibly think – .'

'So, consequently, she is the one with the money. Obviously. In that case....' He frowned and nodded his head as if the revelation had opened new avenues of thought.

'In that case, it isn't altogether out of the question that she's in love with you. It's true that it's fairly frequent with this kind of pathology....'

In his mind's eye, Pierre could see Solange's imploring look as she took leave of him; Solange who couldn't bear for him to be away, even for a few hours; Solange who professed not to be very intelligent and who admired him so much; Solange and her lack of common sense; Solange who spent hours making up and dressing up to please him; Solange so gentle and so innocent. That innocence shone out of her as rays from her sensual nature, and when Solange was in love she had absolutely no idea what she was doing or saying.

He smiled and became so absorbed in his reminiscences that it took him a moment to realise they were walking past the rocky face at the foot of which lay the sinister crevasse. The interplay of light and shadow in the sunlit undergrowth intensified the dark places. He was vaguely conscious, as if in a fog, of Hoening's impersonal and interminable droning.

'… for that reason, Monsieur Garnier, I don't think you are in any danger, at least for now. But be very vigilant, your wife –.'

'Leave my wife alone! If I see you near her once more, I'll kill you!' He breathed in deeply to try and calm himself. 'That's enough. I'm going.'

'Go in peace, Monsieur Garnier,' replied Hoenig with a beatific smile. 'Your wife's real name is Simone Lantier. And she's a murderess.'

***

'Her parents were both from the French working class. The father, Maurice Lantier, was a carpenter who married a domestic servant, Marthe Vatard, in 1907, and a year later she bore him a daughter they named Simone. Two or three years before the war, Lantier, who was involved with a number of anarchist groups – you've heard of the Bonnot gang, no doubt – participated in an attack on an armed security guard. Things went wrong and the guard was killed in a fusillade of gunfire. In 1913 several of the gang members were caught and four of them, including Lantier, were sentenced to death and guillotined shortly thereafter. All of that is historical fact and can be easily verified.

'At the time of her husband's death, the mother was working for the Duvernois, a wealthy childless couple of rather liberal leanings, who showed great affection for the little girl. When Marthe died in 1919, a victim of the Spanish flu, the Duvernois adopted the orphan and changed her name to Solange, which they presumably found more distinguished. They took her to London, where the husband had been made an attaché in the French embassy. She was already exceptionally pretty and they raised her as their own child. However, she was also rather a handful and she ran away at the age of sixteen with a small sum of money. By that time the Duvernois were in Berlin, where the husband had been posted. She got into trouble again two years later when she pilfered a diamond brooch from a jeweller's in Potsdamer Platz. The Duvernais used their connections and the jeweller dropped his complaint, but the *Stadtpolizei* referred her to me for a psychological examination. Hers seemed to me to be run-of-the-mill case and I recommended she be placed in a specialised institution

56

where, according to her teachers, she turned out to be a brilliant and hardworking student.'

Dr. Hoenig placed on the table the file which, to hear him tell it, the Berlin police had expedited to him by aeroplane. He took off his glasses and his pale eyes looked up at Pierre, who was listening expressionless and with apparent detachment.

'Even supposing all that to be true, those are trifling matters,' said Pierre, shrugging his shoulders.

Having decided to hear Hoenig out, he was sitting in a wicker chair opposite the German, who had his back to the window and against the light, his massive head silhouetted by the dazzling glare from the sun-drenched lake in the background. What passed for the bungalow's lounge was an inelegant room furnished in pseudo-rustic furniture. On one wall were framed photographic enlargements illustrating the daily life of the early inhabitants of Monte Verita. Men in tunics and women in white dresses could be seen eating a meal of rice and vegetables around a communal table, or, arms reaching for the sky, performing some kind of pagan dance in a sunny clearing. In the nearest photo Pierre could see a bearded, emaciated, vaguely Christlike figure standing outside a log cabin. In the background, between the trees, could be seen a lake and he wondered if it wasn't in the same cabin, transformed and modestly improved, that they now found themselves.

'You're not paying attention,' sighed Hoenig, 'and yet we're just about to get to the heart of the matter. I didn't hear any more about the young lady until 1931 when chance again caused our paths to cross. At the time I was at the Ministry of the Interior as the principal medical expert. One Friday morning – it was in the month of March, but I don't remember the exact date – we were notified that a businessman named Käutner had been found dead in his office on the top floor of a building in Kurfürstendamm Avenue. I went there accompanied by Commissioner Lohmann, now Deputy Director of the *Geheimestaatspolizei*. The body, which was already cold, lay behind the victim's desk next to a chair that had been knocked over, and there was a dried trickle of blood from a bullet wound situated behind the right ear. The weapon – a military revolver that Käutner had brought back from the war, and which he kept in one of the desk drawers – had fallen onto the carpet less than a metre from the body. Only one bullet had been fired.

'There was no doubt it was suicide. The door had been locked from the inside and the key was still in the keyhole. The windows, also locked, were in any case completely inaccessible. The locksmith sent to open the place had had the devil of a job to get in.

'We questioned the widow who, according to the servants, had spent the entire evening and night at home. She had gone to bed without waiting for her husband after he had notified her he would be late. She shed such torrents of tears that even we, hardened investigators that we were, could not fail to be moved. She was so young and so delicate – and so seductive!'

'And that woman,' Pierre heard himself ask in an expressionless voice, 'was....'

'It was Simone Lantier, alias Solange Duvernois, who had become Frau Käutner. Yes. She had married a friend of her adopted father whom she had met after leaving boarding school. The inquest was concluded rapidly, even though no motive for the suicide was ever determined. Käutner's business was booming, despite the economic crisis, and his marriage, despite the difference in ages, seemed to be a happy one.

'The pretty widow, now in possession of a tidy fortune, disappeared. Vanished from the face of the earth. Then, two years later, one of those coincidences occurred that one imagines, wrongly, are more frequent in fiction than in real life.

'Lohmann and I found ourselves in London for an international conference on criminology, during which someone had arranged a visit to Scotland Yard for us, under the auspices of a certain Inspector Parker. He told us, by way of conversation: "We're working on a rather intriguing case at the moment: a man who killed himself in bed by stabbing himself in the chest with a kitchen knife. Really very curious. And yet, we're going to have to close the case soon because there's no doubt it was suicide." Lohmann, naturally, asked him how they arrived at that conclusion, given that suicide candidates normally chose rope, the gun, or poison in preference to such a painful method.

'The chief inspector replied that the room had been sealed from the inside, which ruled out any other hypothesis. "Really closed?" "Hermetically." He explained that the man lived in the suburbs in a really isolated cottage and had a phobia of burglars. On the massive oak door there were two deadbolts that were absolutely impossible to manoeuvre from the outside. The only window had solid shutters, also made of oak, which had to be broken down with an axe to get in. And that wasn't all....'

Dr. Hoenig took the time to serve himself two large fingers of cognac and asked Pierre, who shook his head, whether he had changed his mind. Hoenig swirled the liquid in the glass in thoughtful contemplation.

'You see, Monsieur Garnier, the officers at Scotland Yard found themselves in a dilemma impossible to resolve. On the one hand they had a suicide without a motive, and, on the other, they had a suspect with a motive but without any proof.'

'What suspect?' asked Pierre, afraid he already knew the answer.

'The wife of the alleged "suicide," much younger than he and the sole beneficiary of his will.' He took a large sip of the cognac and rolled it around his tongue. 'I don't need to tell you that I asked to see her. Nothing could have been simpler: she was in one of the nearby rooms, being questioned. Inspector Parker opened the door and I shall never as long as I live forget the expression on Lohmann's face as he turned to me and whispered: "*Grosser Gott!* It's the same woman!" A cigar, Monsieur Garnier?' he asked.

'And naturally,' growled Pierre, ignoring the offer, 'you would have me believe –.'

'I'm not asking you to believe anything, my poor friend. Those are simply the facts.'

He selected one of the Havanas and removed the end with a small silver knife.

'And?'

'And so the police interrogated her once more.'

'And what did she say?'

'She opened her beautiful eyes in horror and said she didn't understand anything. She acknowledged her previous marriage but, according to her, it was nothing but a dreadful coincidence. Needless to say, nobody believed her and the police started over again.'

'And?'

'With the same result as in the Käutner case. She had passed the weekend with some friends and had returned on the Monday morning. Finding the door locked, she had called the police.'

'So she had an alibi?'

'If you want to call it that, but it wasn't even necessary. We examined the problem from all angles and nobody could explain how that clever little lady had managed to fool the police of two continents.'

He stopped and looked around for a box of matches. Not finding one, he heaved himself out of the chair and went over to search the pockets of his jacket, which was hanging on the window knob. The window was wide open and, when he straightened up, he appeared to have seen something, for he took the cigar out of his mouth and looked for a moment at the bungalow situated further down the slope. Then he closed the window and drew the curtains.

'What is it?' asked Pierre.

'Nothing,' replied the doctor, lighting the cigar and returning to his seat.

'Fine,' said Pierre, shrugging his shoulders and sinking down in his chair, which squeaked in protest. 'Whichever way you look at it, they were suicides after all.'

'It's possible,' conceded Hoenig in a conciliatory tone, 'but it's by no means certain. Naturally, Scotland Yard continued to observe her discreetly. But in early 1935 she applied for and received a visa for the United States. They tried to find a reason to prevent her leaving, but in vain. She hadn't broken the law in any way. Inspector Parker, who was keeping me abreast of events, acknowledged that for his colleagues it was almost a relief. Let her get hanged somewhere else!' He tapped the ash of his cigar so it fell on the carpet. 'Do you think I'm inventing all this to amuse myself? Get that idea out of your head. I've studied enough criminal psychology to know that that woman is fundamentally bad. I knew she would never stop, just as I knew that our paths would surely cross again. She belongs to that species I call recurrent murderers: those that cannot help themselves. For them, it's a pathological need. The power over life and death... *Ach!* You can't imagine what an inspiring feeling that is!'

A host of objections sprang to Pierre's lips but he was unable to articulate any of them. He could not rid himself of the idea that she had known other men and had pretended to love them. In his confused state, the fact that she was supposed to have killed them was not all that important. If only she hadn't told him all those lies about her past....

But she hadn't told him any lies. She simply hadn't told him anything.

Hoenig was looking at him as though he could read his thoughts, with the same kind of interest and professional pleasure shown by a doctor at the bedside of someone with a complicated complaint. He was the first to break the silence:

'Now try to see things from my point of view. I come here for the symposium, of course, but mainly to get away from the crushing daily burden I must carry in my own country. Also, because it's an opportunity to study human nature and the behaviour of imbeciles.'

Pierre was about to protest, then decided the German simply didn't realise he could have given offence. To him, it was simply a matter of excising a malignant tumour as if he were a surgeon.

'And then what happens? I suddenly see a criminal I've lost sight of since that business in London. Not only is she married, but she happens to tell my wife in casual conversation that her "first" husband (actually the third by my reckoning) was a brilliant chemist who died shortly before she married you. So please don't tell me,' he said, eyes rolling heavenward, 'that, after everything I've said, the possibility that she's gone back to her old ways hasn't even crossed your mind.'

'But he died of an illness,' protested Pierre, feebly.

'What kind of illness?'

'Gastroenteritis, I think.'

'Exactly the same symptoms as arsenic poisoning!' sneered Hoenig triumphantly. 'I can cable Baltimore and get all the details in less than twelve hours. Ach! She changes her *modus operandi*: first the revolver, then the knife and lastly poison. I wonder what scheme she has in mind for the next one, namely *you*,' he concluded, pointing his cigar at Pierre and looking him straight in the eye.

No answer.

'You don't believe me? Or do you think she'll make an exception for you?'

Pierre tried unsuccessfully to take control of the situation, but regretted the words as soon as he had spoken them.

'That's ridiculous. She wouldn't benefit in any way from my death. I haven't got a penny.'

Hoenig looked at him condescendingly, with a mixture of pity and disdain.

'If that's true,' he said, 'it's possible that this time she really is in love. But what happens when her amorous sentiments start to wane?'

Pierre stood up. The room was unhealthily hot. The shabby furniture, the thick curtains, the horrible photos on the wall and Hoenig braying like some infernal creature: all combined to make his head spin. He wiped his hand across his brow. All he could think of was escape from the stifling atmosphere and from the voice tormenting his spirit and draining his mind of all thought.

'You have the choice of two solutions,' the German continued inexorably. 'And your natural inclination will be to choose the first. You'll try to get to the bottom of things, yes? You'll tell her everything I've said and you'll beg her on bended knee to deny the evidence, yes? And she will deny it, of course. And then you'll find yourself facing a dilemma, given that either way you have nothing to gain. For, if I'm right, she'll know she's been discovered and you'll lose her. And if I'm wrong, she'll detest you for having suspected her and you'll also lose her.'

'What's the other solution?'

'The one that your good sense should tell you, if you have any left. The one I would choose in your place. Try to discover exactly who she is. Observe her closely. And stay on your guard. It's a sort of bet, to which one of your great thinkers gave a quasi-mathematical form. If you bet on telling her everything, you lose – whatever happens. If you bet on keeping quiet, you might lose but you also might win. There is a slight possibility that I'm mistaken. So, if you bet on her innocence, you have nothing to lose and possibly everything to gain.'

He crushed his cigar in the ashtray and got to his feet. He unbuttoned his shirt collar and breathed a sigh of relief.

'When I say you have nothing to lose, I'm not talking about your life, of course. It's up to you to decide how much she means to you. And as for me, I might have the opportunity to discover how she carried out her crimes!'

V

At nine o'clock on Sunday morning the speakers and attendees assembled on the Ascona pier, the Swiss having organised an excursion to the Borromeo Isles. Pierre was not thrilled. He had been planning to go alone with Solange once the symposium was over, and the idea of visiting the enchanting spot – "created for the happiness of lovers", to quote his beloved Stendhal – in a group of tourists filled him with revulsion.

For a moment he had thought about pleading sickness as he had sometimes done during his military service to avoid some particularly tiresome or repellent chore. But Solange, no doubt with happy memories from college days, had declared it would be "wonderful to go all together," and that "in any case, my poor darling, everything is closed on Sundays and we're not going to spend the whole day in the hotel, are we?"

'What's wrong?' she had added, a hint of concern in her guileless eyes as she had searched her husband's face. 'Why are you pulling that face? You're not plannin~ *t*~ ~n~il *th*~ f~un, I hope?'

He didn't know wh   ased or upset by her attitude. Surely she wasn't wishing not to be left alone with him! On the other hand, being together in a group would hopefully allow the awkwardness there had been between them since the day before to dissipate. It would allow him to collect his thoughts without feeling he was being deceitful. He had promised himself not to say anything even though he was burning to do so. So he hastened to assure her that all was well, that he had just been a little tired and that the boat trip would probably do him a lot of good.

It became seared in his memory as an unmitigated disaster.

The morning was fresh and clear as they boarded the *vaporetto* and just chilly enough to wish for the sun to climb into the sky. But it was not so much the sun that rose, but the mountains that appeared to fall away in its presence. As they crossed the liquid frontier separating Switzerland from Italy, its rays illuminated in magnificent clarity Lake Maggiore, stretching out before them in an almost infinite expanse to the south. Solange stood in the bow, her arms raised to clutch the rim of her hat. The gusts of wind moulded her white dress to her body. The fragrance of her perfume wafted as far as the two men perched in front of the deckhouse, prompting Lippi to joke: "'The Perfume of the Borromeo Isles,'" referring to Boylesve's beautiful novel. Freyja Hoenig came over to take Solange's arm and steer her towards the stairway to the bridge. 'We're going for a coffee,' said Solange as she walked past her husband, and he noted with surprise that she didn't invite him to join them.

The air was now gentle and warm, to the point that the infrequent breaths of wind felt like human caresses on his neck. Some girls who had worn light shawls and scarves because of the morning chill now removed them and stretched their necks with undulating movements. Pierre suggested to Lippi that they join the ladies but the Italian, eyes half-closed, shook his head nonchalantly and stretched out in the sun like a lizard. Pierre got to his feet and climbed the steps briskly.

Freyja and Solange were standing in front of the bar. Strahler had joined them and the three had their heads together as if sharing confidences. He noticed how cheerful his wife looked. Strahler was talking quietly to Freyja who seemed to thrive on the attention.

Solange sensed she was being watched and looked up directly at her husband, only to look down again immediately and emit a laugh as clear as a bell.

He slipped away discreetly and went for a walk around the bridge. He passed close to a man with his back to the handrail who was trying to read a newspaper despite the pages flapping in the wind. Without attaching much importance to it, he recognised the nondescript individual he had first seen in the Albergo bar and then several times since, roaming around the terrace and between the buildings. The man gave him an expressionless look and Pierre had the impression he was following him with his eyes.

64

He went towards the stern. As he was going around the poop he noticed Hoenig huddled in a deckchair up against the bulkhead to protected himself from the wind, a thick muffler around his neck and chin. He was either sleeping or pretending to, manifesting a complete disregard of the scenic landscape that was unfolding along the capricious contours of the lake.

Pierre went to find shelter under the drum of one of the great paddle-wheels throwing up spray. He looked without seeing at the hotels with their jetties, by the side of which, on the esplanades, elegant folk nonchalantly took refreshments as they lounged on wicker seats; at the resplendent lakeside villas with their pink-flowered laurels; and at the bell-towers calling the faithful to Sunday service from one bank to the other. It felt strange not to have his wife at his side. The boat entered the magnificent channel in which lay the Borromeo Isles, steaming past the opulent green dome of Isola Madre behind its great pink palace. Almost immediately a handsome young Italian, at whom several muscular young German girls had been smiling, announced the name Isola Bella. And to Pierre it was as if he were suddenly confronted by the dazzling mirage of a pleasure boat anchored peacefully in the azure waters of the gulf.

The raised stern of this strange vessel was composed of staggered terraces forming a pyramid, adorned with great urns containing orange and lemon trees and bordered by hedges of laurel and box, the parapets surmounted by obelisks and baroque statues. Below, the lawns and parterres, covered with camellias and azaleas, among which circulated white peacocks, simulated bridges and decks. The gardens extended as far as the Borromeo Palace itself, which played the role of forecastle of this fantastic vessel. In any other circumstance, Pierre would have been beside himself with joy and elation. He had planned to spend at least one entire day here with Solange and – who knows? – maybe the rest of their lives. But at the moment he felt dreadfully alone and he felt she had gone forever.

During the hours that followed, it seemed to him that she was studiously avoiding being left alone with him. Lunch was served under the trees in front of an inn on Isola dei Piscatori. To his chagrin, he saw her sit down next to Mestre among a group of students that gathered eagerly around her. He in turn found himself among a group of academics who spoke with their mouths full and were quite incapable of holding their white wine. They ogled the bare-armed waitresses and made suggestive remarks. He ate practically nothing, emptied a few glasses, and stared at her all the time. She responded by making faces and opening her eyes wide in feigned astonishment. The young men around her flirted harmlessly and she gave every sign of being completely at home in their company.

He left the inn and made a perfunctory and listless tour of the island. On his return he found most of the tables empty. The boat's bell was ringing. He followed the late leavers as they hastened towards the jetty. As the *vaporetto* cast off with a great roar of its paddle-wheels, he looked for Solange on the bridge. But it was packed to capacity and he couldn't see her.

Once on Isola Bella, he searched all over for her, including every room of the palace. After standing for a while contemplating paintings and statues in order to appear composed, he ran into Freyja and Strahler at the door of the great hall. "If you're looking for your wife," the young man said amiably, "we saw her going to the grottos." He was even helpful enough to indicate the way down at the end of a long corridor.

When Pierre reached the foot of the stairs, he saw in front of him a series of interconnecting vaults, inlaid from floor to ceiling with mosaics depicting seaweed, shells and marine creatures. The bizarre structures, reminiscent of baroque *rocailles*, were lit by small oval windows almost at the level of the lake itself, and just wide enough to allow the changing reflections from the shimmering water to penetrate. His footsteps made no sound on the mosaic paving; advancing as if in slow motion, with the half-light and the sensation of underwater freshness, he had the impression of walking at the bottom of the sea.

He lost count of the number of rooms he went through without meeting a soul and was just about to return when he heard the echo of a conversation reflected off the vaulted ceilings. At first, it was just two voices whispering in a language he guessed was German. As he got closer, he first recognised that of his wife, false and hypocritical as it appeared to him; then the other, dry and without anger, that of Dr.

Hoenig who spoke with a calm authority. He approached as far as he dared, slowly and carefully – like a spy, he thought to himself regretfully.

Framed by the doorway, he witnessed a strange scene, played in a language he didn't understand by two people whose shadows were thrown on the shellfish wall by the ethereal light. The reflections from the lake caused them to flicker but it was possible to distinguish their movements with an eerie precision. How long they had been here he had no way of knowing, but it had to have been quite a while. The man had the air of someone patiently giving instructions and the young woman responded as someone who had already submitted: briefly, and in monosyllables. Suddenly the man pulled an oblong object from his jacket which, projected on the illuminated wall, appeared longer than it actually was, and tendered it to the young woman; she in turn extended her hand, but recoiled as if to place herself beyond the door. He had the impression she was about to rush out of the room and, seized by panic, he ran away.

When he reached the top of the stairs he was assaulted by the intense heat. The visitors had scattered. He caught a glimpse of the solitary individual from the boat wandering about with an anxious air, a folded newspaper tucked under his arm, as the rooms of the palace emptied. It was surely past four o'clock, maybe closer to five. The tour guides were organising their flock for the return trip. Despite the semi-torpor that seemed to smother him like a blanket it seemed to Pierre that he could hear a distant rumbling of thunder as if in response to the ringing of the *vaporetto* bell.

Once on board again, he waited for his wife on the bridge, feeling a sudden pang of anxiety that she might miss the boat. Amidst the crowd of passengers hurrying towards the jetty he could see Hoenig and the tall silhouette of Freyja, followed by the ever-attentive Strahler, who gallantly offered her his arm to help her onto the gangway. As the stragglers hastened to get on board and the bell clanged out its last appeals, Solange suddenly appeared on the bridge, swinging her handbag. She was alone and ran quickly to him. 'I was looking everywhere for you,' she said laughingly, as if it were of no importance. She was slightly out of breath, beads of perspiration flecking the roots of her hair. He found her so alluring and so captivating, and he was so relieved to see her, that he wanted nothing more than to hold her in his arms. But he could not help answering her coldly:

'That was what I was going to tell you.'

She stepped back to look at him. Her eyes were glistening and it seemed to Pierre they held a hint of anxiety, maybe even fear.

'Pierre,' she said calmly, 'what's wrong?'

'What's wrong? I haven't seen you all day.'

She looked at him, horrified.

'You don't think it was deliberate, do you?'

He knew in advance all the reasons she was going to give: that they couldn't always keep to themselves; that everyone was so charming and so kind to her; that she had no intention of being rude and ungracious simply to please him .... He was suddenly aware of a chasm opening between them: a chasm of lies and things left unsaid.

As the boat was leaving the shelter of the bay a cold wind sprang up and swept violently across the bridge, causing her words to vanish and obliging her to clutch her broad-rimmed hat with both hands so that it, too, did not disappear. 'Storm!' shouted Lippi, suddenly next to them. He nodded to the north where thick black clouds were approaching, projecting an immense moving shadow over the countryside and lending a nightmarish quality to everything: something distant and sinister coming slowly towards them, before which they stood momentarily petrified, unable to make the slightest movement. A woman's scarf, swept up by a violent gust, blew over their heads. On the already foaming lake, sailboats, almost flattened against the water, fled to whatever shelter they could find, their sails clattering under the onslaught of the wind.

By now the sky was as dark as at twilight. A blinding shaft of lightning bathed everything in a pale glow. It was swiftly followed by a deafening clap of thunder. Every detail was captured as if in a flash photograph: in the background, the mountain tops with their cloak of fir trees undulating in the turbulence; the superstructure of the boat and the bridge, all deserted of passengers; in the foreground, Solange's face like that of a drowned person, her eyes seeking Pierre's with a silent cry for help so moving that he knew he could no longer resist taking her into his arms.

Two or three heavy raindrops fell and then suddenly water poured onto the deck as if the lightning had punctured the clouds and opened a reservoir. Solange made no attempt to move. She appeared paralysed, but Pierre could see her body was trembling. He wrapped his arms around her waist and she collapsed limply against him as he dragged her to the nearest doorway.

The lounge, the bar and the stairs had been invaded by a crowd of people surprised by the storm, their light clothing bearing traces of water stains. It was hot and humid and there was a stench of wet clothes. The downpour lashed the window panes and hammered the sheet-metal roof. In the midst of all the din and confusion several elderly Englishwomen, seated by the windows and looking out on a landscape under deluge, took out their thermos flasks and cardboard cups and calmly proceeded to take their five o'clock tea.

Pierre removed his arm from around his wife's waist. Her dress, clinging to her body, dripped water down her naked legs. He took off his vest and draped it around her shoulders. She had removed her hat; her beautiful chestnut hair was tousled and glistened from the water drops. Pierre, pressed against her, inhaled her scent and her breath and the intense emotion that seemed to possess her made her more desirable than ever. Never had he felt such a profound sadness.

Little by little, as the *vaporetto* made its way, with the puffing of its engine and the din of its big wheels, through waves as huge as to those at sea, the lightning became less frequent and the thunder receded. As the deluge was replaced by a fine, persistent drizzle, they could see the lights of Locarno shining in the distance through the deep black night.

VI

The rain continued through most of the night and it was only in the early hours that a warm wind from Italy cleared the clouds and the sky assumed its customary limpidity once more. When Pierre woke up the sun was throwing golden stripes on the wall through the louvered shutters. He had a hangover and a migraine which refused to go away when he covered his eyes and shook his head. He had slept like a log. His dreams must have been dreadful but he couldn't remember them now. He looked across at his wife who was still in a deep sleep, stretched out on her stomach, with her head buried in her pillow.

Even so, they had gone to bed early the night before. As soon as they reached the hotel they had gone up to their room without dinner, each avoiding talking to the other. Pierre was cold and feverish. Solange had run him a very hot bath and ordered a hot grog which had almost burned his tongue, after which his body had languished in a torpor which had mercifully cut him off from the world about him.

It was almost nine o'clock by his watch. He dressed hastily and was still fiddling with his tie as he left the room. He didn't wait for the lift but ran down the stairs two at a time and crossed the hall at a gallop. In front of the hotel, in the clear, calm warmth of the morning, he felt ill at ease. He had neither washed nor shaved and he ran as fast as he could in the direction of the bus whose motor had already started.

'No need to hurry,' said Lippi in a calm voice as Pierre slid next to him on the bench seat. 'Apparently Dr. Hoenig's lecture has been cancelled.'

'If that's a joke it's in bad taste,' said Pierre, giving him a dark look.

'It's not a joke,' retorted Lippi, complacently. 'We found out at breakfast. Someone had apparently telephoned from the Albergo. In any case, as you can see,' he continued, indicating rows of empty seats, 'the majority of our dear colleagues have decided to return to their rooms for a lie-in.'

71

'What happened to Hoenig? Is he sick?'

Lippi sneered.

'You may well ask. Is he really sick or is he suffering from what the French call a *maladie diplomatique*? That is the question.'

'I don't follow,' said Pierre.

'Think about it: the illustrious *Herr Doktor* announced sensational revelations which would demolish my arguments and pin me to the wall. It was, of course, pure bluff. When it came time to put his cards on the table, he lost his nerve.' He gave a contemptuous laugh. 'A typically German attitude. Look at their Führer: he's the very height of arrogance. On words alone, he's a braggart. But when his bluff is called....'

Lippi was obviously enjoying himself. He rubbed his hands and continued gleefully:

'I have another piece of good news. French radio has announced that the British Prime Minister has flown to Berchtesgaden and *Il Duce* has proposed a peace . The rest, as you will see, is simply a question of procedure. To be frank, it's what I expected. *Tragediante, comediante.* Everything turns to farce and ends, according to the rules, in general kissing.'

He gave himself a modest pat on the back.

'It's exactly what I predicted.'

Pierre started to open his mouth to point out that, as far as he could recall, he had never heard such a prediction; in fact, he was ready to swear that Lippi had said the exact opposite. But he was so relieved to learn that Dr. Hoenig would not take the podium – the only matter that concerned him – that he refrained from throwing cold water over the Italian's euphoria.

He promised himself that, once he reached the Albergo, he would bid the organisers farewell and then telephone his wife to pick him up in the car. There was, after all, nothing further to keep him at the symposium. He was pretty well through and his presence was no longer necessary. They would return to the hotel, where they would pack their suitcases before fleeing like criminals to Italy. They would spend a few days in Venice before returning to France via the Riviera. Once they were alone in the long voyage in the sun, the torments he had endured would be blotted out of his memory, in the same way bad dreams vanished in the clear light of day. His departure would signal he was slamming the door on the spirits that were haunting him, and consigning them to oblivion.

The door closed on Pierre before he had time to organise his escape; it closed as well on the sequence of events leading up to the night of Sunday to Monday. Everything else was but a nightmare series of fleeting images, like a chaotic puzzle whose scattered parts would later be assembled by Sir Arthur Carter Gilbert.

During the night in question, while a fine drizzle fell on Lake Maggiore and created a light mist on the leafy slopes of Monte Verita, someone proved the feasibility of an impossible crime in Dr. Hoenig's bungalow.

***

'Dr. Hoenig is dead,' said Mestre.

And Prokosch added, in a solemn and lugubrious tone to which his heavy Russian accent added a comic note:

'He was murdered.'

'Stabbed,' specified Mestre. 'Last night. In his bungalow.'

Pierre looked at each of them in turn, with such an expression of disbelief that the philosopher appeared amused.

'That's the way it is, old man,' he observed, phlegmatically. 'What are you having?' he added, beckoning in vain to the waiter who, seated behind the bar, failed to notice him.

'Who did it?'

'Calm down,' said Mestre. 'But, first of all, let's get out of here. There's too much of a crowd and you can't hear yourself speak. ' He put some change down on the bar and finished up his scotch. 'Let's go out on the terrace.'

As they left they ran into Lippi who had seen all the police cars as he stepped down from the bus and had talked to one of the drivers in Italian.

'Well!' he said. 'This is a fine state of affairs.' He adopted a suitable expression for the occasion and followed the others to an empty table.

Pierre chose a seat in the shade. The strong sunshine bothered him. He felt sick and there was an acrid taste in his mouth.

'I could use a coffee,' he said offhandedly.

Prokosch took it upon himself to get the refreshments and Lippi ordered an expresso. Mestre, having settled on a further dose of whisky, leant back too far and fell off the back of his chair. The sound of a police siren could be heard from afar.

The silence that followed was broken by Lippi:

'All right, my friend, bring us up to date. How did it happen?'

'I prefer to tell it from the beginning,' replied Mestre, taking his tobacco pouch out of his pocket and rolling himself a cigarette, as was his custom. 'But I don't want you to think I know the whole story. I can only tell you what I saw with my own eyes.'

'Perfect!' exclaimed Lippi enthusiastically, in an attempt to get them to relax. 'That's always the best way to tell a story: from your own viewpoint, but not omitting any detail.'

'So, last night I was at the bar, finishing one last scotch before turning in. I suppose it must have been a little after eleven, although I didn't check my watch. There must have been about a dozen of us, drinking and talking man-to-man stuff. There had been some good news on the radio and someone had suggested cracking a bottle of champagne. There were several Frenchmen, two or three Swiss and a completely pie-eyed Spaniard who insisted on drinking a toast to Franco. We sent that one packing. I was forgetting: there was also the lovely Madame Hoenig sitting at a table in the far corner, accompanied by the inevitable Stahler and they were whispering things while looking into each other's eyes.'

'I told you so,' announced Lippi triumphantly, looking at Pierre. 'There's something going on between those two.'

Pierre ignored him. He asked Mestre:

'Where was Hoenig while this was going on?'

'He had stayed behind in his bungalow to prepare his lecture. At least, that's what Stahler said when we asked him the question. Hoenig wished to be alone and the dear boy had devoted himself to keeping his wife company.'

'Aha!' cried Lippi.

'I admit I find it hard to believe myself,' admitted Mestre, 'but it's their business and I don't like gossip. Anyway, we had finished one bottle and were about to open another.'

He paused as Prokosch returned with the refreshments and placed them on the table.

'I wasn't there,' said Prokosch, 'but Monsieur Mestre told me everything.'

'Where were you?' Lippi asked him.

Prokosch opened his eyes wide and dropped down in his chair.

'In my room, on the first floor. But I didn't hear anything. I was asleep.'

'Well,' continued Mestre, 'things were proceeding merrily enough when a fellow walked in through the terrace door. I'd never seen him before. It was raining hard and his raincoat was soaked. He asked the barman where the telephone was and ordered him to get the manager. When the barman protested, he pulled out an official card of some kind, thrust it under the fellow's nose and told him to get a move on. Then he picked up the phone at the end of the bar. He spoke quietly and in German, but it was clear that something serious had happened and he was asking for instructions.

'The manager arrived, half-asleep and dishevelled, still putting on his jacket. The intruder told him to get a passkey to open Hoenig's bungalow and not to ask any questions. The manager went to his office and returned with a key, excusing himself for having taken so long, due to the necessity of opening the safe. They went quickly out together, taking with them the concierge who was carrying an electric torch. We followed suit.'

'All of you?' asked Lippi.

'All of us. There was even one of the hotel bellboys who had squeezed in amongst us, but when the manager noticed him he was turned back. We tried to dissuade Madame Hoenig from following us, but we could do nothing to stop her. She was there on the arm of Strahler who had somehow got hold of an umbrella.'

Pierre had a clear, almost cinematic, image of that night scene: the group hurrying soundlessly down the path in the darkness; the drizzle forming a spectral halo around the rare streetlamps; the black silhouettes of the firs caught in the wavering beam of the flashlight. And Freyja Hoenig bringing up the rear, clinging to her companion's arm and stumbling in her high heels.

'In front of the bungalow,' continued Mestre, 'stood a second man in a raincoat, the twin of the first. He had a torchlight in his hand and appeared to be on guard. He came towards his colleague and whispered a few words. The first man told him to stay in place and keep an eye on the surroundings; he then led the hotel manager to the bungalow door. The manager took out the key and put it in the keyhole. Everyone got closer to get a better view. By then there were quite a few people because it seemed that others had joined in along the way. It was difficult to see who: it was pitch black and, away from the streetlamp next to the door, you couldn't see two meters in front of you. The policeman told us to stand back, but of course –.'

'He wasn't a policeman,' Prokosch interrupted timidly.

Three pairs of eyes turned to him. But the little Russian waved his hand and said softly:

'I didn't say anything. Please go on, Monsieur Mestre.'

'Thank you,' replied Mestre. 'I must tell you that I was right at the front of those standing on the porch and I saw everything immediately the door opened. But I must first explain the lay of the land. Every bungalow, including the one where I'm staying, is built on the same model. There is a relatively spacious entrance hall which also serves as storage space. Behind that is the lounge and, at the rear, the bedroom which has in one corner a partition, behind which are the bathroom and the toilet. In the lounge there's a window and –.'

'Let's keep it short,' said Lippi impatiently. 'What did you see?'

'I'm getting there.' Mestre put on an air of detachment which was far from what he was actually feeling. 'The door to the lounge was wide open and the room was flooded with light. All the wall lights were on, as well as the standard lamp. The window on the wall to the right, which was framed by heavy velvet curtains, was shut. The shutters were closed and held in place by metal hooks. Opposite the window was a table piled with a sheaf of papers in disarray with a pen on top. A chair had been turned over and, next to it, a burnt-out cigar stub lay on the carpet. There was a smell of tobacco and burnt wool in the air, mixed with the persistent aroma of an expensive woman's perfume.'

'Now we're getting somewhere,' said Prokosch. Once again, the others looked at him quizzically but he merely whispered, with a mysterious smile: 'I'll explain later.' Mestre continued:

'Of course, I only registered those details later. At the time, all I could see was Dr. Hoenig lying on his stomach at the foot of the standard lamp. There was nobody else in the room. The body was wrapped in a dressing-gown tied at the waist. His cheek was pressed to the floor and, with his head turned towards the door, he looked at us with those little beady eyes. His glasses had been broken in the fall and one lens had gashed the left eyelid, causing a thin trickle of blood. The

76

knife had been planted between his shoulder blades and the wooden handle pointed straight up in the middle of a bloodstain that the material had absorbed. The downward stroke of the blade must undoubtedly have caused instant death.'

'You could have been a detective,' said Lippi drily. 'I've never heard such a precise report, certainly not from the mouth of a metaphysician. Now, you said he was dead. How could you be sure?'

Mestre shrugged his shoulders.

'His eyes were rolled upwards, his mouth was wide open, and it was obvious he was no longer breathing. But please let me go on. The "policeman" – I don't know if he really was one, but he certainly seemed like one to me – was the first in the room and he rushed straight to the door in the rear; he opened it and disappeared into the bedroom, only to reappear three minutes later with a completely baffled expression. He then set about searching every inch of the lounge; he looked behind the curtains, he wrapped his hand with a handkerchief from his pocket before opening the window and thoroughly examining the shutters. Then he moved to the table, where he examined the papers without touching them. That was when he noticed an object that was partially covered by one of the papers.

'He asked for a pencil and I stepped forward and gave him mine, which he used to bring the object towards him. From where I was standing, I could see it clearly: it was the key of the bungalow. They're all made the same way, including mine. The bungalow number is cut rather crudely into a copper tag that's attached to the key by a solid metal ring. There's no way to detach the tag from the key. In this case the tag bore the number 12, which was Hoenig's bungalow.'

'Let's keep it short,' growled Lippi. 'All the cheap hotels use the same system.'

'You asked me to tell you every slightest detail and that's what I'm doing,' said Mestre, obviously miffed. 'To continue: the man passed my pencil through the ring to pick up the key which he then wrapped in his handkerchief and placed in his pocket.

'While this was going on, the people outside came onto the porch to get out of the rain and a number of them squeezed into the entrance hall. They jostled each other to try and see what was going on behind the wide shoulders of the manager who was blocking the way into the lounge. A voice, which turned out to be Strahler's, cried out "Give me some room. Let me pass." He finally announced he was a doctor and the manager let him through.

'He knelt down in front of the body, lifted the eyelids, examined the pulse and generally did everything that's done in such cases, before finally turning to the crowd and shaking his head in an exaggerated mime. But it wasn't really necessary because it was obvious Hoenig was dead.

'At that point someone moaned. It was Madame Hoenig, who had managed to push her way to the lounge door, and who now collapsed into the arms of the hotel manager. Everything after that happened very fast. People rushed to her side without really knowing what to do. It was almost comical: some rubbed her hands, others patted her cheeks; the manager threw a fit when he saw that the bellboy he had sent back to the hotel earlier had returned, so he ordered him to the Albergo again to fetch a cordial for Madame Hoenig. Finally, after the man in the raincoat had managed to get everyone back outside the bungalow, the widow recovered thanks to Strahler's diligent attention.

'What else can I tell you? After a final look at the inside of the bungalow, the man in the raincoat asked the hotel manager to double-lock the door and place the key in the safe from whence it came. His colleague entered the names of everyone who was there in his notebook. He told us to go back to our rooms and stay there. We were all soaking wet and shivering with cold, so we didn't need telling twice.

'Everyone, including the two men in raincoats, went back to the Albergo. The hotel manager asked timidly whether it was prudent to leave the bungalow without surveillance. The one who had made the phone call, and who appeared to be in charge, said there was little likelihood their "customer" would sprout wings. "Perhaps we should alert the authorities," the manager suggested. The man retorted that he and his colleague *were* the authorities. According to him, the death of Dr. Hoenig was an affair of state, involving issues of national security and their instructions were not to touch anything, leave things where they were and await the arrival of a highly-placed official from Berne, who was already on his way and would be there by the morning. He concluded by asking us not to talk to anyone about what we had witnessed. After which, needless to say, the news spread like wildfire.

'There. Now you know as much as I do. I can't wait to hear your suggestions. What's your reaction to all this?'

He sat silent, staring at his hands while he rolled himself a new cigarette. Everyone had so many questions that no one knew where to start. Lippi stroked his chin.

'I wonder,' he said slowly, 'how long a cigar takes to burn down to the stub.'

'That depends,' replied Harvey thoughtfully. He had just joined them and so had missed much of Mestre's report.

'Where have you been?' asked the Italian brutally.

'I was in my bungalow. It's crawling with policemen down there. They're hanging around Hoenig's bungalow. Apparently they're waiting for someone – no doubt the big cheese from Berne that Mestre mentioned – and they're in a perfectly foul mood.'

'Put yourself in their place,' said Prokosch mildly. They're called to the scene of the crime and then they're told to stand there and do nothing.'

'You'd never see that in England,' growled Harvey. 'These Swiss don't do anything the same way as everyone else. I have to say, however, that the inspector who questioned me seemed like a gentleman. He was a tall fellow, blond and very correct, and he obviously had his suits made in London.'

Prokosch gave an approving smile.

'Superintendent Brenner of the Lugano police. He's an ace detective.'

'He asked me if I'd seen or heard anything. In fact, as I told him, I was awakened in the middle of the night by the sound of footsteps on the path and voices murmuring. I got up and put a trench-coat over my pyjamas. There was a crowd gathered in front of the German's bungalow. When I tried to get closer a rather disagreeable individual told me to go back to bed. Which is what I did.'

'You don't seem very curious,' observed Lippi acerbically.

'I don't poke my nose into other people's business and there was no cause to suspect the doctor had been killed. Of course, if I'd known there was a corpse in one of the nearby bungalows, I wouldn't have slept so soundly. In any case, I had a dreadful nightmare which I don't wish to remember.' He shivered and shook his head. 'But you were asking about cigars....'

'Quite so. Mestre was telling us about a cigar which was just about to go out, lying on the carpet next to the body. So I was wondering....'

'How long it would take? That depends.'

'On what?' asked Mestre, suppressing a giggle.

'On where the tobacco came from, the make of cigar and, of course, its length. Let's see, Hoening smoked Havanas, fat ones. Basing my calculations on the work of dear old Holmes, I'd say between twenty and twenty-four minutes.'

Lippi thought hard.

'How long does it take to walk from the Albergo to the bungalow'

'At a brisk walk, less than ten minutes.'

'And ten more for the return plus two or three minutes for the man to make the telephone call. So that means that Hoenig had been dead for just over twenty minutes when his body was found. From which I deduce that the man in the raincoat who came into the bar must have been a witness to the murder.'

'Quite so,' said Prokosch, approvingly. 'But I could have told you that immediately if you'd only asked.'

'And furthermore,' continued Lippi, ignoring him completely, 'that raises another question. We don't know anything about that man or his colleague. Who exactly were those two?'

'Why don't you let Prokosch speak?' suggested Pierre, who was becoming irritated by all the chatter. 'He has something to tell us.'

'Oh!' exclaimed the little Russian apologetically. 'I just wanted to clarify a couple of obscure points in our friend's report.' He cleared his throat. 'I'd gone to bed early, so I was up early too and went to the bar. It was not yet open but I saw the two men the professor was talking about. They're I expect you've guessed already – Secret Service agents. It turns out I know them, or more precisely I know their boss in Berne, whose name I'm afraid I can't give you. But he's highly placed in the Bureau Fédérale de Surveillance de Territoire: the Swiss equivalent, Monsieur Mestre, of your Sûreté Générale.'

Mestre dropped his matchbox in surprised and stared incredulously at the Russian.

'You're joking! How do you know him?'

Prokosch cleared his throat again and his embarrassed smile seemed more like a grimace.

'Well, you see, I had to deal with him when I applied for political asylum in Switzerland. He helped me to get it and, in return, he required me to perform certain services. Nothing very serious: reports on the situation in the Soviet Union, translation of a few documents, passing on trifles of information. When he found out I'd been invited to this symposium, he entrusted me with a mission that I couldn't refuse: my naturalisation depended on it, you understand. I was to observe what Hoenig said and did inside the symposium, while the other two agents looked after what happened outside.'

'But what for?' asked Mestre.

'He had good reason to believe that the conference would serve as cover for a meeting between Hoenig – who, it's no secret, is the assistant director to Rosenberg in the Foreign Affairs service of the Nazi party – and an emissary of Molotov, the Soviet Foreign Minister. The Swiss, as far as I could make out, had been told about it by French Intelligence.'

He paused and looked around the table with his soft, myopic gaze. His habit of stooping while batting his eyelids gave the impression he was about to apologise profusely at any given moment. The others could not believe their ears. The very idea that beneath the mask of a dreamer lost in the clouds lurked a first-class intellect – a man sufficiently important to be entrusted with state secrets – had never crossed their minds. Nevertheless the "specialist in fairy tales" spoke five languages fluently and knew all the secrets of international politics; he had, after the revolution, been a member of Trotsky's inner circle and had followed him into exile. The four others, sitting at the table in the morning sunshine on the terrace at Monte Verita, knew none of this – and didn't know any more when, two years later, the inoffensive little scholar was killed by an unknown assailant shortly after his master's assassination. But that, as Kipling would say, is another story.

'I say, old man,' said Harvey, breaking the long silence that had descended on the conversation. 'Why are you telling us all this? Surely divulging this kind of information is a serious offence?'

Prokosch sat for a while with his head bowed and his bony hands gripping the table. Then he looked up and they were astonished to see him smile gently.

'A serious offence,' he repeated. 'Really? Quite frankly, gentlemen, there was no other way to make you understand what really happened. As for divulging secrets – .'

'It's just another of your fairy tales, Prokosch,' Lippi declared affably. 'A deal between Hitler and Stalin ! It's about as likely as Bluebeard and the fairy Carabosse.'

'Why not?' commented Mestre as an aside. But nobody heard him.

'There you have it!' exclaimed the little Russian with a gleam of amusement in his eye. 'You've just heard the reaction of our narrative specialist. It goes without saying that because of the rules of the art form, he holds this situation reversal to be inadmissible... even thought it's used frequently in fairy tales which do not, any more than the history of the universe does, submit to Aristotle's rules. Very well. I will now lay out for you the facts as described to me by the two agents this morning and you can draw your own conclusions. I need to warn you that, though true, they are utterly improbable.

'Last night, around eleven o'clock our two men were at their posts in the bungalow under repair, which is downhill from Hoenig's and about fifty metres from it. One was sleeping on a camp bed; the other, sitting in darkness, was observing the bungalow opposite through the door opening. The lounge shutters were wide open and he had, despite the rain, a clear view of the interior – which was brilliantly illuminated as Monsieur Mestre has verified. Hoenig was sitting behind the table, facing the window, his head down peering at his papers. The light from the standard lamp shone right on him. He was writing.'

'A perfect target,' observed the Italian. 'A good marksman –. '

'Yes, but that wasn't the case.' Prokosch cut Lippi off with an authority that surprised those who thought they knew him. 'As I was saying: at some point Hoenig looked at his watch, put down his pen, stood up and went into the bedroom where he stayed several minutes. Forgive me for boring you with all these details but the agents are trained to note the slightest incident. Hoenig sat down again at the table and started to write.

'The man who was watching him was starting to get bored. He was sleepy. He went to fetch his thermos of coffee which he had left inside in a corner. It was pitch black in there and some time elapsed before he could locate it. When he finally found it and got back to his post, Dr. Hoenig was no longer alone. He was standing next to the lounge door and the person who had just come in was in the middle of the room.

'The agent has excellent eyesight. He has been able to retrace all the details of the murder scene with a remarkable clarity. He had – and these were his own words – the impression of being at the theatre. He swore to me that he had never seen anything quite so horrible.'

'Damn it, man,' barked Harvey. 'Get on with it. As an eye-witness to the crime, he must be able to describe the murderer.'

'He did,' replied Prokosch with an ominous calm. 'Only it wasn't a murderer, it was a murderess.'

***

The sun had moved in the sky and now it shone directly into Pierre's eyes, so he saw the terrace, the palm trees and his friends' faces through a dazzling glare. His metal chair made a scraping noise on the flagstones when he moved it. He had the impression that everyone was looking at him. Until then he had listened with a certain detachment, not asking any questions, with the polite attention of someone with no direct involvement. Yet at the same time he had had the feeling that there was the risk of immediate danger. Nevertheless, he was completely unprepared for the crushing blow which hit him now and which tore him from the reality to which he had been clinging – a reality based on intelligence, reflection and reasonable convictions – and plunged him again into nightmare. The most horrible aspect of the nightmare was that it wasn't based on false terrors, on a chaos of confused sensations. What made it particularly frightening was its total coherence. It was accompanied by the certitude that all the pieces of the puzzle fit together with an implacable logic. He remembered his meeting with Dr. Hoenig, the strange discussion between the doctor and his wife in the grottos of the Borromeo Palace, the confusion and the disarray of Solange, her bizarre behaviour towards him, and the truths which she kept from him.

He remembered their short time together the night before, the bitter taste of the drink she had made him take, his sudden desire to sleep and the bottomless pit into which he had then fallen. The memories rushed into his brain with the automatic rapidity of an association of ideas, and it took a determined intellectual effort on his part to interrupt the flow. "You're becoming delirious, old chap," he said to himself. "Your delirium has a certain logic to it, but it's time to remember that logic is directly instigated by delirium, as your master Edgar Allan Poe, was in the habit of claiming." And, assuredly, although reflection and intelligence told him to desist from his frightful thoughts, it was precisely because of them that he could not.

From where he sat he had a view of the staircase leading to the park below. A small group of uniformed police officers was climbing the stairs. At their head was a tall thin man carrying a raincoat over his arm and a leather briefcase in his gloved hand. He was impeccably dressed in a grey flannel suit and a brown felt hat. His fair complexion

83

made him appear younger than he was, for his temples were greying. As he crossed the terrace, he glanced with studied indifference at the table where the five men, more embarrassed than they tried to appear, sat stiffly and silently.

'Who's that,' whispered Lippi.

'Superintendent Brenner,' replied Prokosch. 'The policeman I was telling you about.'

Pierre followed him with his eyes. The man seemed all the more dangerous for not looking like a policeman. "He must play his cards close to his chest," he thought. The superintendent joined one of the organisers who had been waiting for him at the door and disappeared into the Albergo.

'We're certainly going to be questioned,' announced Lippi solemnly. 'In the novels, the chief inspector or the superintendent gather all the suspects together and warn them not to leave the area before the end of the investigation.'

'Are you serious?' exclaimed Harvey. 'I have to get back to England. I have a magistrate's court in Oxford on Friday.'

Mestre burst out laughing. He looked at Harvey and then at Lippi, still giggling.

'You're both the same. We aren't in a detective story. And we aren't suspects. If what Prokosch just said is true, Hoenig was killed by a woman. And, unless I'm much mistaken, there isn't a woman amongst us.'

'Actually, there is,' said Harvey thoughtfully. 'In fact there are two: Madame Hoenig, whom we can eliminate because apparently she has an alibi, which leaves Madame Garnier.'

'*Cherchez la femme*,' chuckled Lippi.

Pierre had seen it coming, in a vague sort of way. But now it had been said. Mestre rushed to his aid:

'Stop pretending you're Dr. Watson, Harvey. And as for you, Professor, you're not funny. Look at poor Pierre.'

'I merely wanted to point out ....' protested Harvey, weakly.

'What? That you were all alone in your bungalow, a few steps away from the scene of the crime, and you haven't an alibi? You could quite easily have disguised yourself as a woman and killed Hoenig.' He tilted his chair back and look at them quizzically. 'I'm sorry to disappoint you puzzle lovers, but the whole business seems exceedingly simple to me.'

'Exceedingly is the *mot juste*,' agreed Prokosch, in an even tone, and they all turned towards him. It was only now that it dawned on them that he had been speaking without an accent for quite some time. Putting the tips of his fingers together, he contemplated the sky just above the trees.

'I told you that the crime was committed in front of witnesses and they had seen the murderer. Nothing could be more simple, in fact. Well....'

'Well, all that remains is to arrest her and put a rope around her neck!' exclaimed Lippi, cheerfully.

Prokosch coughed gently.

'Well, at least you're not shy in expressing yourself,' he said with obvious distaste. 'Er... may I go on? But first I would ask you to envisage the scene as I did when the two agents described it to me. Let's start with the woman. She was a head shorter than Dr. Hoenig, which puts her height at about one metre fifty-eight – five feet two inches in English terms. She wore a very ample brown raincoat, without a belt, and a scarf knotted under her chin in place of a hat. What disconcerted the witnesses is that she didn't remove either the coat or the scarf, even though they must both have been soaking wet.'

'But surely,' exclaimed Pierre, forcing himself not to betray the anxiety he was feeling, 'they must be able to provide more detail? Was she blonde or brunette, for example?'

'That's the trouble,' replied Prokosch. 'They couldn't even tell us that much. The scarf covered her hair and part of her shoulders. Under the circumstances –.'

'Hang on!' said Mestre. 'There was plenty of light in the room. Don't tell me they didn't see her face.'

Prokosch shrugged his shoulders.

'At that distance, behind the window glass and through the rain? You can't be serious. The agents only saw a shape: that of an individual of the female sex, fairly short, and who seemed quite young. At the time, they thought they recognised her, for it was not her first visit to the doctor.'

'Wait!' said Lippi, brusquely. 'The other evening, as Garnier and I were strolling near Hoenig's bungalow, we saw a woman with him. We couldn't make out her face either, but it's probably the same woman.'

'I was going to say the same thing,' added Pierre, hardly able to contain his relief. 'I think we should report that to the police.' He turned to Prokosch, who put on a polite expression. 'A woman in a badly cut suit, wearing a shapeless hat. Apart from that, she fits the description,' he added lamely, trying to convince himself.

'Irena Samoïlova,' the little Russian announced, placidly. 'She's the Molotov envoy I spoke about before. There's no need to notify the authorities. They already know.'

'You don't seem very surprised,' said Lippi in astonishment.

'Surprised about what? The woman has been under surveillance since she arrived in Switzerland. I can understand why you want to look at all the possibilities, but that's not the answer.'

'Why not? She's about the height and build of the person who killed Hoenig. What are the police waiting for?'

'Yes, she's about the right height and build,' admitted Prokosch. 'But the description – if you can call it that – fits a multitude of women. Madame Garnier, for one,' he said to Pierre with a friendly smile as if he were joking. 'Although, having had the opportunity to admire her wardrobe, I can't imagine her rigged out like that.'

'Too true,' agreed Pierre, attempting to maintain the light banter. 'Even more so as she spent the entire afternoon in the company of Madame Hoenig.'

'Careful!' joked Lippi, in the same vein. 'You can't get away that easily! If we're talking alibis, Monsieur Garnier, where was your wife last night?'

'She was with me,' replied Pierre, a little too quickly. 'We never left the room and we went to bed early.'

'At what time, exactly?' asked Lippi, still in the spirit of things.

'Eleven thirty exactly,' replied Pierre.

It was the first actual lie he had told and it seemed to him as though his voice betrayed him.

'How do you happen to know the time so precisely?'

'That's enough, Lippi!' Mestre intervened. " I don't think we should be playing at detectives, even if it's only in fun. And that goes for you, too, Prokosch.'

Prokosch made a half-hearted protest.

'I'm sorry,' he said, 'I merely wanted to show that it was as absurd to suspect La Samoïlova as to suspect Monsieur Garnier's wife. What motive would she have? She was sent from Moscow to negotiate with Hoenig, not to assassinate him.'

'I still think she should be interrogated,' muttered Lippi.

'That's impossible for two reasons. One being that the Swiss are supposed to be unaware of her activities and it would create an international incident. The other....'

'Well?' said Mestre, impatiently.

Prokosch hesitated.

'The other being that she has disappeared. She slipped through the net last night and didn't return to her hotel. They've been looking for her for twenty-four hours.'

'Well, there you are!' announced Lippi, triumphantly. 'No need to look any further.'

'She had all the time in the world to kill Hoenig,' added Mestre.

'And so the Russkies set a trap with that story about a secret treaty which, as I said, made no sense at all. I'm truly surprised, my dear Prokosch, that you didn't recognise the signature of that Machiavellian playwright The Little Father of the People, who weaves his innumerable assassinations with the hand of a master.'

'You can't make an omelette without breaking eggs,' announced Harvey sententiously and somewhat incongruously, motivated not so much by any support for Stalin as a desire to show off his familiarity with French sayings.

'You can't make... Oh, that's a good one!' Lippi said loudly and with ill-concealed sarcasm, slapping Harvey on the knee. 'Did you just make that up or did you hear it somewhere?'

'Come, come, gentlemen,' interceded Prokosch in the manner of a schoolmaster admonishing unruly students. 'Instead of constructing all sorts of wild hypotheses, you'd be better off hearing the end of the story, even though I'm reluctant to tell it. It's quite likely you won't believe me. And I might as well tell you I don't know what to believe myself.

'Here's the rest of what the agent told me. Normally, he would have watched such a scene as a matter of routine importance, had he not sensed something bizarre about it. As I said before, the woman was standing in the centre of the lounge without making the slightest effort to take off her scarf or the brown oilskin covering the rest of her clothes. She even kept her gloves on (did I mention she was wearing gloves?): the cuffs were covered by the sleeves of the raincoat. At no time did her host invite her to sit down and he, too, remained standing. It was she who spoke most of the time, animatedly, it seems. The he started to reply and the discussion quickly became very heated. At least, that's what the agent deduced from the movements of the two participants which appeared confrontational; from Hoenig's gestures he was evidently furious.

'Seeing that things were taking a turn for the worse, the agent went to wake up his colleague and they both took up their observation posts. The woman had planted herself directly in front of Hoenig and drawn herself up to her full height. She appeared, according to the agent, to be "telling him a few home truths," and then she slapped his face. Hoenig didn't flinch. He adjusted his spectacles and laughed at her. The woman turned and walked to the door, which she opened and then disappeared from view. Both agents swear they heard the other door slam, the one leading to the outside. I must stress that, from their observation posts they could only see the side of the bungalow with the window; the front door and the porch remained outside their field of vision. Nevertheless, they would have seen her once she started to walk on the path, for there is a streetlamp not far from the bungalow. The fact is they did not see her, so they assumed she had worked her way round to the rear of the bungalow, which seemed a curious route to take.'

'And they didn't try to follow her?' asked Lippi.

'Why would they? Remember, they were more than fifty metres away and they would never have caught up with her in the darkness. And besides, they were under orders not to intervene in any way. So they went back to watching Dr. Hoenig.

'After the woman had left, he shrugged his shoulders and went back to the table, as if nothing had happened. He took his time lighting a cigar, then picked up his pen and continued writing. Then the woman reappeared in the room.

'She was moving very slowly, with her upper body entirely motionless. It was as if she were approaching her prey, gliding imperceptibly along the ground. Her right hand was tucked inside her raincoat. When she reached a spot behind the doctor, with his curved back presenting a clear target, she pulled out her hand. It was holding a knife. She was holding it at chest height, with the blade pointing slightly downwards, as the professionals do. The blade was aimed at the part of the body below the left collarbone. "Exactly the way we are taught in training," as one of the agents observed.

'At the time, everything seemed to be happening in slow motion. Without the slightest hesitation, the woman drove the knife in as far as the handle, putting all her weight behind the blow with, as one agent put it: "surgical precision." Hoenig keeled over on the table, his hands attempting to grip the edge. Because his face was directly under the lamp, the two agents saw his face almost distinctly, despite the distance. It held an expression of immense surprise.

'The woman took one step back and let go of the knife. Hoenig was seized with violent convulsions that brought him up out of his chair, which then tilted over and crashed to the floor, taking him with it. In the process, his body left the agents' field of vision. Then the woman did something extraordinary.

'She walked round the table to the window, which she opened. She then leant out of the window to grab the shutters. She pulled them towards her and closed them tightly. Curtains. The show was over.'

'Let's see,' said Mestre. 'When she leant out of the window, the agents must have got a look at her face, I assume?'

'Of course not,' sighed Prokosch. 'You can be sure I asked them that. The woman was seen in silhouette, backlit by the lamp. All they could make out was the colour of her hair. In that position, if it had been blonde or light chestnut, there would have been a halo around her head, despite the scarf. They didn't see anything, so they deduced she must have had black or very dark hair. By the way, La Samoïlova is a natural blonde.'

He paused for a moment, while the rest looked at each other in silence.

'Keep going,' said Pierre, brusquely.

'Our two heroes, both young and relatively inexperienced, stood rooted to the spot at first. One of them had the sense to look at his watch. It was 23 17. The other picked up a flashlight and they both ran out of the bungalow. They ran quickly up the path leading to Hoenig's bungalow and straight to the door which they tried to open, without success. One of them tried to barge the door down, but only managed to bruise his shoulder. Meanwhile, the other tried to open the shutters of the lounge and bedroom, to no avail. The door was bolted, the shutters were hermetically closed, and there was no other way in.

'Yes, there was,' objected Harvey. 'There was one at the back: the skylight in the bathroom ceiling.'

'You're quite right. There's one made of frosted glass, just wide enough for a small person to squeeze through. But it was also locked on the inside. Moreover, there's a grassy border all round the bungalow which was very soggy due to all the rain. Anyone dropping from the bathroom window couldn't have failed to leave footprints. And there weren't any.

'You see, these bungalows are set apart from each other and are protected by pretty effective locks so as to discourage cat burglars, for – despite what the natives may tell you – there are robberies in Switzerland just like everywhere else.

'So, to conclude, one of the agents went up to the Albergo and the other stayed behind to stand guard, in the unlikely event that the murderess had stayed behind in the bungalow. Their theory was that she had slipped out of the bungalow closing the door behind her and she had managed to escape by keeping herself out of sight. You know the rest, thanks to the excellent account given by Monsieur Mestre.'

'This is all terribly banal,' said Lippi, affecting a yawn. 'The villain has disappeared and all that remains is to find her. So what? Where's the mystery?'

'So what? But it doesn't hold up!' retorted Harvey, indignantly. 'Think about it: whether the woman shut the door behind her or let it shut by mistake – as has happened to me – all she had to do was to turn the handle. If the door didn't open when the agents tried it, it was because it had been locked with a key.'

'Thanks for your help,' sneered Lippi. 'I'd never have worked that out by myself.'

'There's nothing to laugh about,' said Prokosch, obviously irritated. 'Harvey has put his finger on an important detail. I hope you can see the implications. First of all, she took the trouble to lock the door. Why did she do that? For the same reason she closed all the shutters? We have no idea. Secondly, she must, as a consequence, have had a key in her possession.'

'O.K. She had a key. So what?'

'Nothing. Except she didn't have one.'

'Could you please explain?'

'Willingly,' replied Prokosch amicably. 'Remember what Mestre told us: the bungalow key, which agent Fantoni found, was lying on the table in the lounge.'

'Dammit!' exclaimed Lippi, totally exasperated. 'Let's agree there must have been another and get this whole business over with.'

Prokosch shook his head.

'That's the first thing we thought of. But the hotel manager is adamant: there are only two keys per bungalow, one for the clients and the other shut up in the safe in his office. The concierge hands it out every morning to the maid doing the cleaning and she returns it when she's finished. I know what you're going to say: someone could have made a copy. Dismiss that idea from your mind: they're specially made keys and the only way to get a duplicate is to contact the manufacturer.

'Now, about the lock: it's double-action and practically burglar-proof, activated by a key on the outside and a knob on the inside. If you're thinking of some of the tricks familiar to readers of detective fiction, like the string through the keyhole or under the door which turns the lock, let me inform you that: a) there's no keyhole on the inside of the door, just a knob and b) the door, which is made of heavy wood, fits so tightly in the frame as to be hermetically sealed. It's the same for the shutters in the lounge and bedroom – even though that's irrelevant because the agents never took their eyes off the windows.'

'I don't wish to be a bore,' ventured Harvey, 'but there's still that bathroom window....'

'I thought of that as well and I interrogated the agent who examined the bathroom. There's a simple latch inside the window. Simple, but the same problem: impossible to lock from the outside.'

'I know one trick that would have worked,' said Harvey, more than happy to display his knowledge. 'I read about it in one of Edgar Wallace's books. You break the window, activate the lock, then simply replace the broken pane.'

'I can see it in my mind's eye,' scoffed Lippi. 'The murderess perched on a stepladder with her little bag of glazier's tools.'

'Don't laugh!' Mestre fired back. 'You claimed in your lecture that this kind of thing couldn't happen in real life. Well, reality just threw a cream pie in your face. Can't you see what's happened? A murder has been committed in a room from which escape was impossible. Like it or not, we are well and truly faced with a locked room problem!'

Pierre stayed silent. He had felt the intrigue enveloping him inexorably, as if predetermined by some evil guiding hand. And now the moment of truth was on him and he felt the noose tightening. Nevertheless he managed to view the scene with a certain detachment:

the backdrop of the lake above the trees in the park; the sun-drenched terrace; the five people – including himself – grouped around the table. He watched the others out of the corner of his eye and asked himself which author had written the words they were speaking. Mestre was wrong, this couldn't be reality. Everything fit so perfectly: the action was too calculated, too logical. It was as if they were all in a novel. That's it, he said to himself, I'm reading a novel. All I have to do is close the book and step back into my life.

He didn't hear the roar of the car coming up the ramp, nor the sound of the tyres on the gravel, nor the heavy silence after the motor stopped. He didn't hear the clicking of high heels on the flagstones. But the scent of the familiar perfume reached him and enveloped him. And when he looked up, Solange was standing there.

***

Pierre Garnier was the person most directly affected by the events. He knew he would never forget the moment his wife appeared before him. Solange's expression reflected a genuine emotional upheaval, but he couldn't help thinking that, had it been calculated, it would be no less convincing. She looked distraughtly at each of the five men who had stood up at her approach. Her lower lip was trembling.

'So the bastard's dead,' she said, slowly and clearly. 'Someone managed to bump him off.'

She had never spoken so roughly. Harvey winced. As a well-bred Englishman, he detested hearing women uttering vulgarities. Pierre felt his heart skip a beat. He wondered if she was about to burst into tears. He moved forward and instinctively took her hand. Just as instinctively, she clung to him and allowed herself to be led to the chair Lippi was offering her.

'For heaven's sake,' she implored them, 'don't all stand there looking at me. Tell me what's happened.'

They sat down and Mestre, in a measured tone which seemed to calm her, recounted all that had happened. She shook her head from time to time as if to chase the cobwebs from her brain and repeating: 'I don't understand. I don't understand anything at all.'

Pierre noticed that Prokosch had kept quiet ever since she had arrived. He watched through narrowed eyes as if he were studying an egregious example of incomprehensible behaviour. The others affected detachment in a vain attempt to hide their embarrassment. It was obvious they didn't know what to think of her attitude and were asking themselves why she was behaving in that manner.

"Let's keep calm and think about this," Pierre told himself. "If the unthinkable had happened and she really was guilty, she wouldn't be behaving in such a way, drawing attention to herself in front of everyone." And yet… It was impossible to be absolutely sure. Maybe she was a very good actress. Maybe she marched to her own drum and didn't allow her sentiments, whatever they were, to get in the way.

But it was futile to torture himself this way he thought, yet again. The most important thing was to take her away and shelter her as much as possible. As if she had read his mind, Solange turned in his direction.

'Pierre,' she said in a low voice, 'I don't know what came over me just now. What I said was dreadful. I'm sorry, truly sorry.'

He leant over and gently put his arm on her shoulder.

'You're at the end of your tether, darling. We all are this morning. Would you like me to take you to the hotel?'

'Thank you,' she replied, pulling away from his grip, 'but I can find my own way back. Stay with your friends and don't worry about me. I'll be fine, I assure you.'

She stood up, nodded at everyone and, without another word, left.

He stood up. Deciding to go after her, he was just about to leave when he saw two men come out of the Albergo. The first was Superintendent Brenner. The other, a shortish individual, was the man he had glimpsed several times and whom he now knew to be one of the two agents charged with the surveillance of Hoenig.

What took place next happened so fast that Pierre wondered whether his anxiety had sharpened his eyesight. The agent had just stopped and was peering intently at Solange who, because she was walking diagonally across the terrace, didn't see him as she went by. He gave a slight cough to attract the superintendent's attention and whispered something in his ear which caused him to turn and look quickly at the young woman. They exchanged a few words more as she took the gravel path that skirted the Albergo.

If Pierre hadn't been holding on to the back of his chair, his legs would have folded under him as the policeman made his way to the table, where he stopped and looked at each of the five men in turn. In a polite voice he announced:

'My name is Brenner and I'm a police officer. Which one of you is Monsieur Garnier, Monsieur Pierre Garnier? I'd like to talk to him.'

***

The two men had just sat down face to face at a table at the rear of the bar. Pierre looked around and noted that they were alone save for the barman, standing motionless in front of several shelves of liqueurs with multi-coloured labels. The indirect lighting gave a spectral air to Brenner's fair complexion and accentuated the dark rings around his clear blue eyes. He seemed to have slept badly or not at all. His hat and briefcase were next to him on the bench. He removed his gloves slowly and took a packet of oriental cigarettes out of his pocket and offered one to Pierre, who refused, whereupon he lit one for himself with a silver lighter that clicked when he closed it. Florentine Brenner, top criminal investigator and idol of the popular press, looked at the younger man sitting opposite him with a mixture of amiable cynicism and benevolent irony. He seemed to be deciding how to start the discussion and, noting that Pierre was waiting with an almost palpable anxiety, he began to laugh quietly.

'I've no intention of submitting you to a full police interrogation, Monsieur Garnier. To be frank, what I'd really like to do at the moment is shave and take a bath. I landed here at dawn and I'm completely disorganised. Please understand: I haven't been here long enough to have formed a clear idea of the situation. Can you imagine that I haven't even been inside the crime scene? It's most unusual, but I'm under instructions to await a high-ranking official from Berne before opening the bungalow. And, on top of everything else, I've lost my watch. Have you the time, please, Monsieur Garnier?'

'It's almost eleven thirty,' replied Pierre.

'Thank you. He's arriving on the noon train and, given the time he needs to get here, that leaves us three quarters of an hour to kill. Let's use the time to talk things over. You need to be aware that it's a complex business involving powerful interests, and I tell you frankly, from where I'm sitting now I don't understand very much.' He shook his head despondently. Then he looked pleadingly into Pierre's eyes. 'Now you know why you're here: I desperately need your help.'

'You're a funny kind of policeman,' said Pierre, laughing despite himself.

Brenner laughed in turn.

'Yes, I understand what you must have felt when I asked you to follow me. You probably expected me to shine a floodlight in your eyes and heap abuse on you, all the while blowing smoke in your face.' He exhaled and elegantly waved away a thin filament of smoke that escaped from between his pursed lips. 'No, believe me, that is not my custom – at least not when I'm dealing with a member of a prestigious university who's a guest of my country, as you are, Monsieur Garnier. Did I make myself understood?'

Pierre nodded, but remained wary. He had rarely witnessed such a polished performance. Florentine Brenner was a clever man.

'But why me?' asked Pierre. 'And how can I help?'

Brenner appeared nonplussed at the question. He opened his briefcase and pulled out a sheaf of papers covered with a hasty scrawl, which he consulted as he spoke:

'I could say: why not you? One has to start somewhere. But there must be a better reason.' He pulled out a piece of paper and attempted to decipher the scribble on it. 'Here – I made note of a remark by Agent Fantoni. It seems that of all the attendees, you're the only who had any dealings with Hoenig.'

'"Dealings" is too strong a word,' replied Pierre. 'I bumped into Dr. Hoenig a couple of times and we talked of one thing and another. What's unusual about that?'

'Nothing. That's exactly what I told myself. But then why would Agent Fantoni take the trouble to report an unimportant fact? That's the kind of question I'd like your advice on. Why?'

Pierre shrugged.

'I don't know. Haven't you asked him?'

Brenner searched through his papers again.

'I should have done that, of course. Ah, yes. I did ask him that. I crave your patience, Monsieur Garnier. Here: he says that it struck him because he had the impression that the victim, Dr. Hoenig, had been ostracised by his colleagues. A sort of quarantine. Nobody would talk to him. Except you.'

Pierre couldn't see where this was going. He was bemused by the convoluted approach this "funny kind of policeman" was taking. He decided it was time to get to the point, even at the risk of playing into his interrogator's hands.

'I didn't approach him,' he said, in the firm tone of someone who has nothing to hide. 'He approached me. I have to say he was remarkably friendly, rather to my surprise. Should I have turned my back on him? I had no reason to treat him rudely. I confess that when he invited me to have a drink in his bungalow, I couldn't think of a reason to refuse. Now, if you want to know what we talked about....'

'Tut, tut,' replied Brenner, waving his hand as if to dismiss the thought. 'I'm not asking you to say anything, Monsieur Garnier. But, since you brought up the subject....' This time he didn't go through the pantomime of consulting his notes. 'It's true that you visited Dr. Hoenig on September 24th, a little after two o'clock, apparently for a drink. I imagine you chatted for over an hour about this and that: stories about your colleagues, or the political situation, or else subjects way above my head such as literature or philosophy. Is that what you were going to tell me?'

Pierre forced a smile. Brenner stared at him with his blue eyes.

'More or less.'

'I take it you have nothing conclusive to tell me about Dr. Hoenig's personality?'

'Nothing beyond what everyone already knows. You've certainly got much more information about him than I could provide.'

'Undoubtedly,' agreed Brenner, with a sigh. 'To tell you the truth, I never expected you would be of any great help, but I had to try. Hopefully, I'll have better luck with your colleagues.' He looked at a list which he had just pulled out of his briefcase. 'Professor Umberto Lippi, for example. We know he had a violent disagreement with the victim.'

'Oh, it was purely academic,' exclaimed Pierre, more enthusiastically. With the change of subject he felt a great load had been lifted from his shoulders.

'That is to say...?' prompted Brenner.

'The argument – this will make you laugh – concerned locked room murders. The professor claimed in his lecture that they were a purely literary invention and couldn't happen in real life. The doctor argued the opposite and promised to bring the proof to his forthcoming presentation. Lippi defied him to do it and –.'

'And killed him the day before to prevent him revealing what he knew. Your friends are very amusing Monsieur Garnier: I've never laughed so much in my life. However, I mustn't leave any stone unturned, so I shall ask him if he has an alibi. I don't suppose anyone could mistake him for a small woman but it's a matter of principle. And, as for yourself, I'm sure you have a solid alibi for the whole time....'

'Quite so,' replied Pierre, looking him in the eye. 'I was with my wife in our room at the Grand Hotel and we went to bed early.'

'So, a mutual alibi,' observed Brenner with satisfaction. 'I'll make a note of that.' He tapped his pockets and looked up with an embarrassed air. 'I seem to have left my pen in my raincoat. I don't suppose you have one you could lend me?'

Pierre handed him his Waterman and, while Bremmer was scribbling something on one of his bits of paper, he felt obliged to add:

'You should make a note that we had a hot drink sent up to the room. The hotel must have a record of that.'

'But I believe you, Monsieur Garnier, I believe you.' He replaced the cap of the pen and handed it back. 'That's a very elegant pen you have there. Now, regarding the young person I saw on the terrace a short while ago....'

'That's my wife.'

'Congratulations, she's charming. Well, I shan't keep you any longer. Thank you for giving me so much of your time.'

Pierre stood up. Brenner remained seated, his hands in his pockets, his eyes still on Pierre. His face was expressionless. He simply said:

'My reason for asking for your help was that, if you'd been able to assist, I wouldn't have found it necessary to ask someone else.'

He paused briefly, then continued:

'I'm given to understand that your wife – it is she I'm talking about – has made friends with Madame Hoenig. They were seen walking together. It's quite possible they've confided in each other – you know how women are....'

'That's ridiculous,' exclaimed Pierre angrily, falling back on to the chair. 'If you need intimate details of Hoenig's life, why not ask his wife instead of bothering mine?'

'There's nothing I'd like better,' said Brenner, wearily. 'But she's had such a shock, or so I've been informed, that the good doctor's assistant, a certain Strasser or Stratter who claims to be a doctor himself, has had her transferred to a clinic in Locarno and has remained at her bedside. It happened just before I arrived. The police let them go, and I can't blame them because neither of them was under suspicion. For now, Madame Hoenig is under sedative and can't be questioned. What time is it?'

Pierre glanced at his brand new Cartier watch.

'Five to twelve.'

'That's a very elegant watch you have there.'

'It's a gift from my wife,' said Pierre, almost blushing.

'And also a very elegant wife. My congratulations again. So, our man from Berne will be here in twenty minutes. While we're waiting, shall we have a drink?'

Pierre spoke firmly.

'I have to go back to the hotel. My wife is expecting me for lunch.'

'Tut, tut. You're not going to leave me all alone?' He gestured to the barman. 'What'll you have? It'll be a Scotch for me. How about you? Would you care for a cigarette?'

He held out the packet with an engaging smile. Pierre hesitated. He wanted to get up and leave. One the other hand, the policeman seemed so friendly that he was afraid of hurting his feelings. 'I'll make an exception,' he conceded, taking a cigarette. Brenner leant forward to light it. The smoke, warm and mild, tasted vaguely of roses. There was an almost palpable silence, broken by the clinking of the glasses the barman placed in front of them. Brenner drew on his cigarette and leant back on the bench seat with a look both dreamy and ironic in his half-closed eyes.

'Do you know what happened last night?' he said in a calm, collected voice that conferred an affirmation on the question. 'I presume that Monsieur Prokosch, with whom you were speaking a while ago, filled you in on all the details? We find ourselves presented with a pretty little problem which I'm supposed to solve, even though nothing remotely similar has ever crossed my path. Not only am I expected to show how a murderer can have escaped without trace from a double-locked site but it turns out the site itself is not your run-of-the-mill locked room: it's an isolated house with oak shutters secured by solid steel hooks, plus an oak door as well, with a lock that's absolutely impossible to activate from the outside without a special key. I've questioned Agents Mangin and Fantoni at length and they're absolutely convinced nobody could have got out of that bungalow without passing through the walls.

'Now, if you've been imagining something like a trapdoor in the floor or an opening under the roof, you can wave that idea goodbye. Every one of the bungalows is built on a concrete slab and the shingles of each roof are nailed directly to the battens. I've checked. And please don't suggest there are secret passages. You can rest assured there are no hidden exits and yet more than a dozen people are willing to swear nobody was in the bungalow when the door was opened. Do you follow me so far?'

'No,' said Pierre.

'I see. You have a theory, I suppose?'

'Well, yes. It seems to me that you ruled out the only plausible explanation: that the murderer simply walked out of the door and locked it behind him.' He preferred to refer to the perpetrator as masculine.

Brenner shrugged.

'Impossible.'

'Why?'

'Because there were only two keys in existence. That gossip Prokosch must surely have told you that much. We found one in the bungalow. The other –.'

'— was locked in the manager's office. I know. All the same, you can't rule out a third key.'

'That would suit you just fine, wouldn't it? Only I telephoned the workshop where they make the keys just this morning. They only make two originals of each key and they are guaranteed impossible to forge. In any case, even if there were a master key and the killer managed somehow to get hold of it, that still wouldn't be the answer. In the first place there are no marks of a break-in on the exterior lock. Secondly, the individual in question would never have had time to use it. Nor – and this is going to surprise you – would he have time to lock the door with a duplicate key, supposing by some miracle he'd managed to get hold of one.

Pierre looked at him wide-eyed.

'In heaven's name, why not? On the contrary, he would have had plenty of time, from what I understand. The door was out of sight of your agents for quite some time.'

'That's where you're wrong. We performed an experiment with a stop-watch, a sort of reconstruction of the crime. We took as the starting point the instant that Mangin and Fantoni saw the woman lean out of the window to close the shutters. It took them thirty-four seconds to get hold of their flashlight, leave their observation post and run the distance between the two bungalows. Let's add ten more seconds because of the rain and the darkness.

'Now listen carefully: it turned out that the entrance porch of the second bungalow came into view less than fifteen seconds after they left the first. That's because the path connecting them isn't straight but curves at that point. From there they could clearly see, from the light of the streetlamp, the porch and under it the door unquestionably closed. From which we can deduce that the murderess would only have had fifteen seconds – let's say twenty at most – to finish closing the shutters, to fasten them with hooks, to close the window itself, run to the door, open it, take the time to double lock it and then disappear.

'Agent Fantoni, a very agile fellow, has been timed performing the same sequence in the bungalow next door, which is identical to that of the crime scene. His best time has been twenty-four and six-tenths seconds. Believe me, this business is a real brain-teaser. Whichever way one looks at it, one always runs into a dead end.'

With a resigned air he lit another cigarette. Pierre looked at him with secret amusement. It was an understatement to say he was relieved. The more Brenner floundered around, the further the danger was removed. Why not try and confuse him even more?

'Superintendent, may I ask you a question?' he asked, with an air of innocence.

'I'm all ears.'

'You've based your findings so far solely on the word of your agents. What makes you think they aren't lying, at least about some of the details?'

'And why would they do that?'

'Who knows? That's for you to find out. But in the work they do, lying is second nature, isn't it? It's like the woman they imagined they saw.'

'Imagined?'

'How can they be so sure it was a woman? The description they gave – if you can call it that – could just as well apply to a man. A man wearing a raincoat, with a scarf tied around his head. At night, in the rain, tens of metres way....'

'They could have been mistaken, eh? You're really a great help,

Monsieur Garnier. All we have to do now is look for a short, thin man who's in the habit of wrapping a scarf around his head and wears size thirty-seven shoes.'

'Why thirty-seven?'

'Because they found traces of footprints on the flagstones in front of the door. Prints of a woman's shoe. The porch protected them from the rain. They went towards the house; there were none coming the other way. These prints – of flat-heeled shoes, by the way, size thirty-seven according to Agent Mangin, who is married – could have helped us identify the murderess. I say murderess because I can't see a man wearing woman's shoes to go and kill someone.'

He raised his glass calmly to his lips, but it was clear he was seething inwardly.

'Dammit, would you believe those two idiots allowed a crowd of onlookers to trample around outside the bungalow. Do you know how many people wear size thirty-seven shoes, Monsieur Garnier? The answer is most women! Yours, for example.' He gave an apologetic grimace. 'No offence. I couldn't help noticing her ankles.'

He extinguished his cigarette and added casually, as if joking:

'Could you believe that Agent Fantoni – who probably doesn't have much of a memory for faces – claimed to find a vague likeness between your wife and the woman in the bungalow?'

He paused to scratch his neck and continued:

'You'll think I'm being funny: do you know that, if your wife had dark hair and wasn't quite a bit taller, I might also have asked myself the same question?'

He looked at Pierre's glass:

'You're not drinking, my friend?'

'Yes, yes,' replied Pierre, whose heart had started to beat faster. He took a gulp and the alcohol burned his throat. Brenner kept his eyes on him and he wondered what that strange expression on his face could mean. What exactly did he know? But the policeman made a dismissive gesture and continued, lowering his voice:

'I'll tell you something in confidence: we're making a mistake if we allow ourselves to be preoccupied by this business about a disappearance. That's exactly what this woman wanted: to stop us asking pertinent questions. For example: why did she take the trouble to show us all that hocus-pocus? Why did she stab her victim in plain view, in front of the window, when she knew she was being observed by two men on the other side of the glass, just a couple of dozen metres away?'

'Wait a minute! What makes you think she knew they were there?'

'For three reasons: she wore an outfit that hid her body and her hair; she was careful to keep her face partly covered while she was in the room; she closed the shutters in her spectators' faces, just as a magician shuts out his audience when he steps into the cabinet from which he's going to vanish. Believe me, this woman is an artist and she's given us a performance. I'm beginning to wonder if....'

He raised his glass to eye level and studied it dreamily. There was a silence that appeared interminable to Pierre, broken occasionally by the sound of ice cubes swirling in the glass. Then Brenner emptied it in one gulp and placed it back on the table.

'Would you like to know what I think? This is not the first time she's done it. It's risky, but she's done it more than once already. And, so far, she's got away with it. She likes the challenge; she likes playing with fire. Look at it this way: we have an idea of her height, her weight, and her shoe size. We could easily expose her, and yet... Relax, Monsieur Garnier, I'm simply telling the truth.'

Pierre had the impression of lying full length on his back, with an enormous pendulum that made a whistling sound as it gradually descended lower and lower as it got closer to his heart. He could already feel the bite of the pendulum's blade but mustered the strength to respond.

'The fact is your analysis is absurd. You're trying to get me to accept there's a killer out there who sets the police impossibly complicated problems for the express purpose of being caught.'

Brenner shook his head.

'You're not following me. The problem for me is that of the likelihood of prosecution. You think that the culprit, duly identified and brought into court, will inevitably be found guilty. But, in practice, no judge will sentence a criminal if the investigation cannot explain how the crime was committed; a crime, if you will, that the culprit could not have physically committed. In the present case, I'll bet you anything that any jury would prefer to believe – just like you, a few minutes ago – that the witnesses have either lied or lost their minds, rather than accept that the murderess could have dematerialised before their eyes. We know it and she knows it. The challenge isn't to arrest her, but to prove how she did it.'

'So when are you going to arrest her?' asked Pierre, feebly.

For some time now he had been unable to think of anything else. How warm it was in the room! He could hardly move. Out of the corner of his eye he saw the door opening and a breath of fresh air caressed his neck. He turned to look. A uniformed policeman stood in the doorway. Brenner got up and went to talk to him. Pierre sat motionless, as if anaesthetised, his hands gripping the armrest of his chair.

He hardly noticed that the superintendent was coming back towards him, shouting something at the man at the door: "Find the manager and tell him to come with the key." Brenner reached across the table to collect his hat and his briefcase; "The man from Berne is here," he said to Pierre. "We're finally going to be able to open the damn bungalow."

'When are you going to arrest her?' he repeated, more firmly.

'When? Oh, it's just a matter of hours. Her description has been sent to the whole district. We'll get her when she tries to cross the frontier.'

Brenner was already walking away. Pierre moved his head and blinked his eyes, as if he had suddenly been exposed to a blinding light.

'So who are you talking about?'

Brenner turned and gave him a puzzled look.

'Who do you think I'm talking about? The NKVD agent who was in contact with Hoenig. She's one of the Soviet Secret Service's professional killers. Didn't Prokosch tell you?'

***

Pierre stayed slumped in his seat, first staring fixedly at the glass that he had barely touched, then emptying it quickly. He should have felt relieved, but he could feel from the tightness in his throat and his accelerated heartbeat that the anxiety was still there. One part of him said that the danger had receded; the other, more visceral and less reasoned, told him that the suspicions which tortured him would not easily go away. He could have sworn that Brenner had toyed cleverly with him, had amused himself, letting Pierre think that he knew more than he was saying; and he couldn't forget the last look the superintendent gave him as he closed the door: the cunning, insidious, heavily ironic gaze of the predator contemplating the prey it held at its mercy.

The terrace was deserted under the torrid midday sun and he wondered vaguely where everyone had gone. He hastened to cross it. "I have to stop thinking," he told himself. He felt utterly confused. His head was bursting with so many questions he couldn't decide where to begin; moreover he was reluctant to do so because of the shame he would feel in formulating them. "You've read too many tales of fantasy. How can you think such monstrous things about the woman you married?" And, anyway, what was there to back up his preposterous assumptions? Everything was based on the exaggerated claims of a half-crazed individual… and also the feeling that Solange had kept certain things from him. (Why hadn't he asked her to explain?) But that was all.

All of a sudden, there was but one idea in his head: to find her and hold her in his arms. He needed comforting and, above all, calming. He ran as quickly as he could down the path through the trees, towards the park exit. In the half-light of the overhanging foliage the slightest noise took on a significance of its own: the twittering of a bird, the rustling of a breeze in the branches, the flat sound of his own footsteps in the soggy ground. As he was running he could smell the heavy, wet odour of the lichens and mosses. Passing in front of Hoenig's bungalow, where the two agents had been posted, he looked up and saw people bustling about, examining the soil and searching in the bushes, to the accompaniment of muffled exclamations.

He was so eager to see his wife again that he failed to pay attention. In the village, one omnibus passed right in front of his nose, and the wait for the next one seemed interminable. He wondered if Solange had waited for him for lunch. With its window blinds down, its empty lounges, and an empty conference room, the Grand Hotel was taking a siesta. A clinking of cutlery and dirty dishes came from the dining room. He looked through the glazed panels and couldn't see Solange among the handful of guests. She must be waiting for him in their room. He stood frozen in front of the door and knocked. There was no reply, which he took as an omen.

The door had been left on the latch. All he had to do was to push it to enter. Streams of light, filtered through the Venetian blinds, illuminated the room. There was no noise except the tick-tock of the travelling clock on her bedside table. The hands pointed to a quarter past one.

'Solange,' he called out.

There was no answering voice. With a growing alarm he went into the bathroom. Above the washbasin was the usual disorderly cluster of pots of cream, lipsticks, eye make-up and bottles of perfume. The sweet fragrance of Shalimar was everywhere, wafting up from the silk undergarments thrown hastily at the foot of the bathtub.

When he went back to their room, he noticed that the mauve robe she had worn that morning had been thrown on the bed. He sat down on the edge and caressed the soft, light material.

That was when he saw the envelope placed against the pillowcase.

My Darling,

I know you're going to torment yourself but I have to go away. I beg you to trust me, our happiness depends on it.

You can't have any idea what's happening and it's horribly difficult to explain. I'll be back tomorrow evening and I hope everything will be clear then. Please don't get the wrong idea. IT'S NOTHING LIKE WHAT YOU IMAGINE.

I love you,

SOLANGE

P.S. I'm taking YOUR car. I've sent the suit you were wearing yesterday Sunday to be cleaned. The maid will bring it to the room. Please don't wear the polka-dot tie with it. The striped one goes much better. And don't put too much butter on your toast at breakfast. Think of your figure!

***

On that same Monday, 26 September, an event occurred that was even more extraordinary than anything that had occurred thus far. By virtue of its supernatural nature it put all of Monte Verita's previous mysteries in the shade. If Pierre Garnier, during his journey across the park, had resisted the mad urge to see his wife and instead had, out of curiosity, approached Hoenig's bungalow, what he would have found would have plunged him into the same state of bewilderment as those who had witnessed the drama – described by the police themselves as an abominable piece of devilry.

Here are the facts, as described in Superintendent Brenner's report:

105

I arrived at 12h 31 in front of the crime scene, accompanied by Superintendent Füssli of the Department of Security, Agents Mangin and Fantoni, and Dr. Calgari, medical examiner for the Tessin district. The bungalow, as seen from the exterior, was in the same condition as the two agents claim to have left it and as I had personally noted at 6.25 a.m: shutters closed, door closed. I unlocked the door with the key given to me by the hotel manager and let in Superintendent Füssli who had asked to be left alone inside. It was my understanding that he needed to be personally responsible for the highly classified documents in Hoenig's possession.

*A few seconds later the superintendent came out again, in a state of extreme agitation. He asked – and I quote – if this was our idea of a **** joke". Seeing my evident amazement, he invited me to step inside and I was able to ascertain that the body was no longer in the lounge or any other part of the bungalow.*

Dr. Calgari then drew my attention to a bloodstain on the carpet at the spot where, according to the witnesses, the body had lain. He took a sample which he dispatched immediately to the medical laboratory, along with a pair of broken spectacles found near the body.

A preliminary inspection of the premises established that the windows and shutters remained locked from the inside, as was the bathroom skylight which was, in any case, too narrow to allow a corpulent individual like Dr. Hoenig through. I can personally testify that the front door was double locked when I inserted the key. The second key, which had found been on the lounge table, had been given to me by Agent Fantoni who had kept it in his possession in order to have fingerprints taken at some point.

I concluded that the disappearance of the body occurred under the same circumstances as that of the presumed murderess from the interior of the same building, and remains equally inexplicable in the current state of the investigation.

I felt it necessary to inform Superintendent Füssli of the regrettable fact that Agents Mangin and Fantoni had left the bungalow without proper surveillance for one minute thirty seconds at 5.00 a.m., the time at which the Locarno police arrived.

I personally deplore the delay introduced by Department of Security before calling in the police, as well as their refusal to allow them to enter the crime scene. It seems quite apparent that these arrangements delayed the start of the investigation and compromised the proceedings.

The park and the adjacent hotel buildings are being searched, but without result at the time of writing.

VII

Tuesday 27 September

At nine thirty in the morning Superintendent Brenner gathered the principal witnesses together in a small room at the Grand Hotel that he had taken as his headquarters. The five: Lippi, Mestre, Harvey, Prokosch and Pierre Garnier were all warned not to leave the Locarno area and to remain until a new order regarding the investigation was issued, even though the tragic events had sounded the death knell of the and the other participants had already started to pack their bags.

Pierre stood away from the others, his back to the window in order to hide his haggard features and his tired eyes. Unlike the previous night when he had slept like a log, he had felt extremely tense and anxious, and his sleep had been troubled. He had woken up several times, groping the empty place next to him in the darkness and trying to persuade himself it was all just a nightmare.

No longer able to contain his restlessness, he had risen around six o'clock. The faint rays of daylight had already penetrated the room. He had started to search his wife's things. He had rummaged through her suitcases, inspected her clothes and explored the contents of her pockets. What exactly was he looking for? He would have been hard pressed to say, so much had his sense of shame clouded his judgment. At the back of a drawer filled with underwear, his hand had touched a hard object which he had brought out cautiously. It was a small bottle half full of blue pills. He had known what it was even before reading the label. He had put it back in its hiding place and, overcome with dizziness, had fallen back on the bed.

The little room tucked away at the rear of the Grand Hotel must not have been used often, for it smelled stale. The only window overlooked a dimly lit interior courtyard. Lippi was seated, legs crossed, in an armchair looking decidedly Mephistophelean. Next to him on a sofa sat Prokosch, eyes half-closed, which made him appear asleep. Harvey paced up and down on the threadbare carpet, muttering for the hundredth time a scathing remark about bringing the wrath of His

Majesty's embassy down on the heads of the local authorities. And Mestre was leaning against the panelling under a painting of sunset on the lake, casually rolling a cigarette, his perpetually sceptical smile on his face.

Brenner dominated the group by his sheer presence. He was leaning on the upright piano, having raised its lid, and was picking out an unrecognisable tune with one finger. Ash was falling on his jacket from a half-smoked cigarette that dangled from his lips, but he made no effort to dust it off.

'Do you really need to torture us with that bloody noise?' exclaimed Harvey, in exasperation.

Brenner stopped and allowed the lid to fall with a thud. Prokosch awoke with a jolt and the room fell silent. If the policeman had intended to play on their nerves, he had succeeded admirably.

'We're waiting for Herr Strahler,' he announced calmly, checking his wrist-watch. 'So. We'll start without him, if Mister Harvey would be good enough to sit down.'

The latter grumblingly obliged, taking a position adjacent to Prokosch. The superintendent looked slowly round his audience.

'So. I called you here because you are all avid readers and eminent specialists in those novels mistakenly called detective stories. I'm a detective myself and I confess I don't hold that form of literature in very high esteem. I simply can't appreciate stories whose only justification seems to be that they could never have happened in real life. In real life, may I remind you, a murder is a relatively straightforward act, brutal and even sordid, generally committed by someone pretty stupid, and there isn't a criminal alive who would amuse himself setting insoluble problems solely for the purpose of giving some poor detective a headache. Having spent twenty years of my life conducting criminal investigations I can assure you I've never once had to deal, directly or indirectly, with the situation known to the rest of you as "a hermetically sealed room." You, however, are all too familiar with the problem. So I ask you, in all humility: what advice could you give me that would help me solve it?'

'My advice is threefold,' replied Lippi tartly. 'The first is to get it our of your head that any of us is involved; the second is not to jump to conclusions before clearly setting out all the facts; and the third is to understand that the solution always depends on a trick cunningly hidden in the statement of the problem.'

'Thank you,' retorted Brenner, 'but I think I've correctly posed all the questions. For the last twenty-four hours, I've turned the problem over and over in my head and examined every angle. I've –.'

'Very well. If you've done all that you should have discovered the trick.'

'If I'd found it,' replied Brenner testily,' I wouldn't have needed to ask you for help.'

'The superintendent is right,' interjected Harvey. 'In a truly special case, one has to involve the specialists.'

Brenner nodded approvingly.

'Precisely. And, as far as I understand, you're among the best. I'm just a local *flic*; I'm used to working with the real and the possible. But in this case, the impossible has happened. We have irrefutable proof that no human being, living or dead, could have got out of that bungalow. And yet the murderer escaped and the corpse vanished! I'm telling you, it's a wretched business and we're nowhere near the end of it.'

Pierre stepped forward.

'And yet,' he exclaimed, 'you told me as recently as yesterday that you were about to make an arrest!'

'Did I say that? I may well have done. But that was before someone managed to whisk away the corpse. I may as well confess now that I never believed in the trail we were following. And I don't give a damn about those stories of political deals and secret agents. That's Superintendent Fussli's territory. He found what he wanted and the documents are now in the hands of the authorities in Berne. It's their business, not mine.'

'Speaking of documents,' said Mestre, 'what's become of the notes of the doctor's speech?'

'What notes? Are you talking about the papers on the lounge table? The superintendent handed them back to me. After examining them, he felt they were of no use to him. Here they are.' He opened his briefcase and showed them some papers. 'You all thought he was writing the draft of his speech. In fact, they're notes scribbled higgledy-piggledy and they're completely meaningless as far as I'm concerned. If you want to take a look....'

'Pass them over,' said Lippi.

'Don't jumble them up: the pages are in the order we found them in.'

Lippi consulted them rapidly, muttering incomprehensibly as he did so. Then he announced his verdict:

'It's a form of *aide-memoire* which he was, apparently, the only one to use. There are a few dates and events which he presumably was going to cite... "1925: Kaiser affair; 1927 ..." – I can't read what he's written. On the first page, which should in fact be the last, there is an interrupted sentence – which is probably due to him being stabbed right then: *"In truth, all external events only have their roots in our own interior: thus, all chance is deliberate, every accidental meeting is a rendezvous, every crime – ."'*

'"—*a suicide",'* completed Mestre. 'It's Schopenhauer.'

'Well, that's a great help,' sighed Brenner.

'However, it's interesting: it tells us where the doctor turned for inspiration.'

'Fair enough. I'll leave you to your philosophers; I've got a murder to solve. What interests me is how it was done. In any case, I'm sure of one thing: the Soviet special envoy had nothing to do with it.'

'She was seen in Basel yesterday morning,' explained Prokosch. 'She was boarding the express to Moscow which leaves at five forty in the morning. Note there is no night train between Locarno and Basel. As for a car, forget it. To cross Switzerland in six hours you need a flying carpet.'

'Or an aeroplane,' observed Pierre, his heart pounding.

Brenner shook his head.

'Bad weather. No aeroplane could have taken off that night. So,' he added after a short pause, 'I'm listening. Let's assume we are in a detective story. Explain to me how one goes about escaping from a hermetically sealed room.'

'There's a multitude of ways,' began Lippi ponderously.

'Sixty two, to be precise,' interjected Harvey. 'They're all listed by Arthur Carter Gilbert in his *Treatise on Impossible Crimes*. The book's in my suitcase. I can get it if you want.'

'That won't be necessary,' said Brenner hastily. 'Just tell me the ones that apply to the present case.'

'None of them,' observed Mestre wrily. He was obviously amused

112

by the proceedings. 'They're all about blocks of ice that melt; keys turned using string and knitting needles; magnets used to slide bolts and other poppycock. Not to mention idiotic schemes such as the murderer locking the door from the outside before sounding the alarm, then being the first to break into the room, where he pretends to find the key in the door.'

'Precisely what I said in my lecture,' said Lippi approvingly. 'All those tricks and illusions only work in the minds of detective story writers who, as Coleridge put it, require "the willing suspension of disbelief" on the part of the reader. Not one of them has ever invented a scheme that would work in real life.'

Brenner shot him a dirty look.

'If you say so, Professor. However, I seem to remember that one of your eminent colleagues – Doctor Hoenig, who shall remain nameless – took the opposite view. And, unfortunately for him, the facts appear to have proved him right.'

'"Facts are stubborn things",' Harvey declared, scratching his head in the vain hope of finding the source of the quotation; luckily, nobody asked him for it.

'Come now, Superintendent,' said Mestre indulgently, blowing smoke out of his nose the while. 'You're not going to find the solution in those boring old stories. Let's think logically about this. The scientific mind starts with simple, verifiable facts. If we're all agreed that it's absolutely impossible to escape from a hermetically sealed room without violating the laws of nature, one can logically infer that it's highly improbable for the woman with the knife to have done so. From which a child of four could deduce that she stayed inside.'

'Certainly,' agreed Brenner. 'But a child of four would also have seen that she wasn't there.'

'Allow me to proceed,' replied Mestre, imperturbably. 'Logic does not bother with phenomena. As far as our main problem, the disappearance of the body, is concerned, since no-one could have got into the bungalow, the body must have got out on its own. And since that couldn't have happened without witchcraft, it follows that we have to disregard the evidence of our own eyes. Hence the victim, whilst appearing to be so, was not in fact dead when we went into the place.'

'That is, however, what you maintained previously,' purred Lippi.

'It was only an impression. I'm not a doctor.'

'Dr. Hoenig was dead,' said a solemn voice. 'I can vouch for it.'

All heads turned to look at the emaciated figure framed in the doorway. It was Strahler. He must have been there for several minutes and heard what was said.

'I studied for eight years at the University of Leipzig,' he added, advancing towards Mestre, 'and I was assistant to Dr. Hoenig for four more. Don't tell me, Monsieur, that I can't recognise a dead body when I see one. Death appeared to have been caused by an internal haemorrhage. The victim's eyes were rolled up, there was no sign of breathing and there was no pulse. Signs which a first year medical student would have recognised.'

They looked at him with astonishment. The once self-effacing character had become a self-confident individual who spoke with authority.

'Don't get upset, Herr Strahler, nobody's questioning your competence,' said Brenner in a soothing voice. 'What news do you have of Frau Hoenig?'

'Frau Hoenig was the victim of a violent emotional shock, or trauma as we call it,' replied the doctor in a coldly professional voice. 'She was given an analgesic to lessen her pain and her state, on awakening, was judged satisfactory.' He turned to Pierre. 'She would welcome a visit from your wife.'

'Where is Madame Garnier, by the way?' asked Brenner casually.

'She... she's still in bed.'

'Well, well.'

Pierre tried to convince himself there was probably nothing in that last remark and that the superintendent had simply made it in passing. Nevertheless, it struck home.

'By Jove!' exclaimed Harvey suddenly and all eyes turned to him.

'What's come over you, *mon vieux*?' exclaimed Mestre. 'You gave me a fright.'

'I've just remembered something. It's your remark which made me think of it. You suggested just now that the body could have got about by itself....'

'Which is ridiculous!' scoffed Brenner. 'So what?'

'Well, that night, as I already told you, after that fellow forbade me to approach Hoenig's bungalow, I went back and went to bed. I must tell you that, for reasons of hygiene, I always sleep with the windows open. I fell asleep almost immediately and had a terrible nightmare. I dreamt that I was awake and heard steps outside. They were heavy yet

114

soft, as if someone was squelching around in mud. So, still in my dream, I went to the window. The room was in total darkness and I didn't think to turn the light on. And I saw … My God! It was horrible!'

'What did you see?' asked Lippi impatiently.

'Nothing at all at first. It was drizzling and it was too dark. Then, I started to make out a figure under the trees that was moving slowly and making a "plop, plop" noise. It seemed as though it would come up the path and pass in front of my window. And when it came into the light from the streetlamp, I recognised Dr. Hoenig!'

'You watch too many horror films,' mocked Lippi.

'Let Harvey talk,' said Mestre.

'I haven't told you the worst bit. He was moving like a sleepwalker or, rather, like a robot, jerkily with his eyes turned up. I could see him as clearly as I can see you now. His dressing-gown was soaking wet and he had a large knife between his shoulder blades.'

There was a heavy silence in the room and even Brenner himself seemed impressed.

'It wasn't Dr. Hoenig, it was Frankenstein's monster,' sneered Lippi, who appeared nervous nonetheless. He was the only one who made a joke. The others felt a chill down the spine and looked at each other anxiously. Realising that Harvey was visibly terrified, Pierre could not suppress a shiver. Only Brenner remained expressionless.

'You wouldn't have been hitting the whisky bottle a little hard, would you, old boy?' Lippi asked, still facetious.

'Ignore him,' said Mestre. 'Go on.'

'That's all,' said Harvey. 'I don't remember anything else other than I'd had a terrible fright and woke up bathed in perspiration. I still tremble thinking about it.' With those words, he closed his eyes and slumped back on the sofa.

'We're in fairy-tale land,' groused Lippi.

'Harvey's tale was full of information,' stated Prokosch, as if he were turning something over in his mind. 'A fairy tale is like a dream. And there is more truth in dreams than in the real world.'

Brenner looked at him sceptically.

'Like the truth that a dead man can still be alive? Leave such rants to Dr. Freud, Monsieur.'

'Your incredulity is getting us nowhere, Superintendent,' said Mestre, raising his voice.' You should make more effort to understand

115

what Prokosch is trying to say.'

'I do understand one thing, and that's that you're all starting to lose your wits.'

Brenner appeared to make a decision. He opened his cigarette packet and circulated it. Everyone helped himself except Harvey, who sat up and took a pipe out of his pocket.

'If it's all right with you, Gentlemen,' he said calmly, 'we'll dispense with the stories about the living dead. We have more important things to worry about.'

'Such as what?' exclaimed Mestre. 'Everything we have to deal with is an absurdity, a quirk, or a material impossibility, the least of which is the inexplicable disappearance of the corpse. Where do we start?'

'By finding the body, of course,' replied Brenner. 'Without it, we can't do anything. The murderer, realising that the bungalow wasn't under surveillance, took advantage and arranged for it to disappear. Don't ask me how, but I can tell you why. As long as there's no body, we can't prove there's been a crime.'

Harvey let out a cry.

'What is it now,' groaned Lippi.

'I've just thought of something. Since I didn't know before I fell asleep that Hoenig had been stabbed, how is it that in my dream he had a knife in his back?'

***

A sinister atmosphere permeated the small smoke-filled room. The discussion was going round in circles. One hypothesis succeeded another under the weary eye of Brenner whose gloomy expression was piteous to behold. Pierre was seized with an overwhelming desire to leave and breathe some fresh air. Suddenly he was struck by a thought that sent shivers down his spine. Brenner had just shown them Hoenig's notes. What had become of the dossier that had been lying on the table next to him, the dossier that was so damning to Solange? Someone had caused it to disappear, and that could only have been… He felt giddy and clung to the back of one of the chairs.

'I don't feel very well,' he said. 'If you don't need me at the moment, I'll take a short walk.'

'Feel free to leave. But I must see both you and your wife this afternoon, so don't go too far.'

'I... I believe my wife was planning to see Madame Hoenig,' he stammered.

'Quite so. Just make sure she's back before five o'clock. I'll wait for you in the Albergo.'

'Right. I'll tell her.'

'The poor boy doesn't seem his self today,' observed Lippi after Pierre had left.

'None of us does,' said Mestre. 'We're all out of sorts, living on our nerves.'

'How much longer is this comedy going to last?' groused Harvey.

'Well,' said Brenner, 'I'm not going to keep you much longer. I have to go to Monte Verita to see how the searches are going.'

Mestre stubbed his cigarette out in an ashtray that was already overflowing and whispered casually:

'I think I can save you the trouble.'

'What do you mean?'

'Thinking about what Prokosch said just now: that there's more truth in a dream... Suppose we took Harvey's nightmare seriously?'

Brenner looked furious.

'You're not going to start that all over again!'

'For the moment,' continued Mestre, ignoring the outburst, 'it's the only clue we have. Suppose Harvey didn't dream it and he *really* saw Doctor Hoenig that night. And suppose that the Herr Doktor was well and truly alive....'

'That's quite a stretch,' growled Brenner. 'You heard Dr. Strahler – by the way, where's he gone?'

They had to face it: in the heat of the discussion the doctor had slipped out without anyone noticing. Mestre went on:

'You told us, Harvey, that Hoenig was walking along the path that went by your window. Where does that path lead?'

'It leads to the fountain higher up the slope.' He turned to Brenner with a frown. 'But why the devil ask me these questions? I keep telling you it was only a nightmare. I didn't dream that I was dreaming, for heaven's sake!'

'Think about it, Superintendent,' argued Mestre. 'What's the only possible hiding-place in the area? The only place you haven't even thought to search? You'll never guess: it's the grotto. I'm willing to bet that's where you'll find Hoenig, dead or alive,' he concluded calmly.

'In the grotto,' repeated Brenner, with a condescending smile. 'My poor friend, the entrance is sealed by an iron grill embedded in the rock and whose bars are the thickness of a man's arm. You must have a very poor idea of the Swiss police if you think we haven't checked it out.'

'But suppose –.'

'—Suppose what?' exclaimed the superintendent, losing his habitual calm and becoming more and more irritated. 'I'm not crazy enough to *suppose*,' he said, mimicking Mestre, ' that the corpse could have revived itself, got out of the bungalow, locked the door with a non-existent key, gone to terrorise Mr. Harvey in his sleep and, to cap it all, passed through a barrier that ten strong men with a battering-ram couldn't breach to hide in a cavity drilled into a rock.'

'All of which suggests that our philosopher is not completely stupid,' interjected Lippi, serious for once. 'There could be a secret entrance.'

'Oh, no. You're not going to bring up that old chestnut,' barked Brenner, now at the end of his tether. 'Don't drag secret passages into all this on top of everything else. It's beneath you to suggest it.'

'You're right, of course,' agreed the Italian. 'It's such an unworthy trick that no writer worth his salt would even find it necessary to deny its existence to his readers. But, contrary to what you appear to believe, we are not in a detective story. Mediaeval records are replete with underground passages, hidden doors and concealed staircases. Everyone here is aware of the disappearance of the legendary Rosenkreutz. Remember my row with Hoenig: I defied him to shut himself up in the grotto.'

'It's true,' confirmed Mestre. 'We were there.'

'Well, Hoenig accepted the challenge and I believe he was crafty enough to have solved the problem: how to get in and out of that rat-hole without going through the barred entrance. He wasn't a man to believe in miracles, so everything points to him having found a passage.'

'Come to think of it,' observed Harvey, 'I noticed him several times poking around in that area. I thought he was looking for mushrooms,' he added.

Brenner gave a deep sigh.

'So. I don't believe it for one second, but I'm going to have the grotto opened. Even if it's only to prove to you the absurdity of what you're saying. It's highly improbable –.'

'"When you have eliminated the impossible, whatever remains, however improbable, must be the truth",' announced Harvey, pompously. And, when Brenner shot him a hateful look, he added: 'That's not mine, it's from –.'

'— We know!' they chorused.

***

It needed two hours, two robust workers and several metal saws to cut open the grill barring the entrance to the grotto. A policeman squeezed in, armed with an electric flashlight, and emerged a few minutes later covered in cobwebs, coughing and dusting himself with one hand, the other shaking so much that Brenner had to take the torch. 'Well?' he asked contemptuously. The man shook his head silently and, doubled up, made a dash for the bushes.

'Let's go,' said the superintendent. He turned to Mestre and Prokosch. 'You were right, gentlemen. Follow me.'

'Are you coming, Harvey?' asked Mestre.

'Not on your life. The place must be full of rats.'

'I'll stay with Harvey,' said Lippi. 'I'm not afraid of rats, but I'm claustrophobic.'

'Anyway, it's full of rats,' repeated Harvey sharply.

'Undoubtedly, and there must be bats there, too,' chortled Mestre.

'Well, Gentlemen?' urged Brenner.

Inside, the air was heavy and oppressive. The beam of the torch picked out a narrow tunnel in the damp rock, slightly more than head high. After a few metres the tunnel opened out into an oblong cavern, about seven metres long and five wide, which resembled a fantastic junk yard with dust piled high on top of a jumble of old crates, miscellaneous bits of furniture, chairs and moth-eaten sofas. The walls were covered with astrological symbols and impressive effigies of winged demons and other supernatural beings, all eroded by the damp. At the far end of the crypt, a granite plinth decorated with circles, triangles, pentacles and other less familiar symbols supported a rectangular slab on which stood a cobweb-covered cross resembling the primitive Ankh, the *crux ansata:* the key of life of the ancient Egyptians. On either side of the cross were two five-branched copper candelabra coated with verdigris, one upright and one fallen, and in front of it an oriental vase of alabaster held the lone stem of a withered

119

rose. To cap it all, embedded in the rock above the altar, was a black marble stele on which was carved the figure of a woman with a cow's head, between whose horns sat a disc.

Dr. Hoenig was sitting at the foot of the altar, leaning against the plinth as if he were simply asleep: his arms hanging down and his head slumped to his chest. His hair, his face and his dressing-gown were spattered with dust and dirt, and his shoes were hidden under a layer of dried mud. Blood had trickled from his open mouth to his chest. There was blood on the ground also, forming a viscous brown puddle around the body. He appeared to have died slowly and without a struggle, as if his life had leaked out through the tips of his shoes. His right arm was bent, the elbow leaning on his knees and the fingers clutching the handle of a knife whose sharpened blade, about fifteen centimetres long, was covered with brown streaks. It was a simple kitchen knife and its very banality made the scene even more hideous. Some distance from the corpse lay an extinguished flashlight which rolled with a metallic noise when Prokosch accidentally kicked it, causing the others to jump out of their skins.

They were silent for a moment, then Brenner's voice came across loud and clear, reverberating around the grotto.

'Don't get any closer, please. And be careful where you tread.'

In fact, it was almost impossible to avoid the blood. The ground, the rocks and the altar had all been splashed before Hoenig had collapsed, his legs having given way under him like a crude straw man.

'Bravo!' cried the superintendent, with a nonchalance that Mestre felt was forced, 'I have to admit that you were right. Thanks to you, our problem has been solved. All that remains now, because our client, according to all the evidence, was unable to use the front door, is to find the emergency exit.'

'That's not so easy,' sighed Mestre, 'we're still in the realm of the fantastic.'

Brenner turned on him with an infuriated look.

'Here we go again! I know what you're going to tell me. Nobody could have come in through the windows or doors, for the simple reason there aren't any windows or doors. I'm telling you that there's a simple answer. Help me find it instead of arguing about it.'

He ran his hand through his hair. His normally pleasant face seemed suddenly old and weary.

'There must be a passage,' he continued gruffly, 'in the floor or the walls. We're going to have to examine the place inch by inch. Maybe … I don't know. But there must be….'

He moved the flashlight up and down and round in a circle, scanning the rocks that surrounded them. The beam explored the crevices, too narrow and too shallow to serve as passages. It paused for a moment at the niche carved into the rear wall which held, set into the rock, the black marble stele. Then it stopped at the altar and the slab underneath.

'Take the light', he said to Prokosch, handing him the torch. 'Come, Monsieur Mestre, you can take one side and I can take the other.'

'It's damned heavy,' protested Mestre.

'We're going to slide it. You pull, I push.'

With their combined efforts they succeeded in displacing the slab a few centimetres, enough to reveal a crack between the slab and the plinth, at which point they stopped, exhausted. Brenner took back the torch and shone its beam into the fissure.

'Nothing!' he said, straightening up. 'Nothing at all.'

'In any case,' noted Mestre philosophically, 'he would never have been able to lift this mass and place it back where it was.'

'Holy Mother of God!' exclaimed Prokosch. 'How did he get in?'

'No need to call upon the heavens,' said Mestre, wiping his brow. 'The superintendent is right. Hoenig didn't get here through a miracle. He must have found another way in.'

'The walls and the ceiling are all made of granite, and the ground is as hard as rock,' replied Brenner slowly. 'I imagine Mr. Know-It-All will explain how.'

'Alright, let's stop talking about it!' Mestre shot back, with a zest he was far from feeling. 'We found the body, and that's the main thing.'

The superintendent didn't deign to respond and directed the lamp towards the corpse. His hand was trembling a little and, in the dancing light, the dead man's face seemed animated: it was as if the blood was continuing to trickle from his mouth. A phrase came to Mestre's mind and he repeated it out loud: *'"Who would have thought the old man had so much blood in him?"'*

Brenner spun round, surprised by the quotation from Shakespeare,

121

or perhaps by the way it had been said.

'The poor devil must have pulled the knife out and it drained the blood from his body,' murmured Prokosch, who had joined the others.

'Who says it wasn't the killer who pulled the knife out,' mused the policeman, 'and placed it in the victim's hand?'

'To make us think it was suicide, no doubt?' sneered the little Russian.

'It's happened before,' replied Brenner, with an obvious lack of conviction.

He scrutinised the corpse once more, but with such a lack of expression that he appeared not to be seeing it. And then something which had hitherto appeared part of the wool of the dressing-gown came into sharper relief in the light of the lamp. It was on the right shoulder.

Brenner leant over and, watched closely by his companions, carefully placed the object in an envelope.

It was a fine hair, clearly a woman's. And it was a light chestnut colour.

***

Pierre Garnier spent the afternoon in his room. He lay on his bed and tried to sleep. But, even though he was very tired, fear kept him awake. Every ten minutes he looked at the clock, which was relentlessly counting the seconds before the rendezvous arranged by the police. A rendezvous or a summons? Solange would never be there in time and he shouldn't count on it. He reread the note she had left. It said she would be back in the evening. That could mean the late afternoon. He started to listen to the sounds of the passing vehicles, his pulse racing whenever he thought he recognised the purring of the Delahaye. Several times he got up and rushed to the window.

He tried to read, then turned on the radio. The latest news bulletin spoke of a conference about to take place in Munich. For a second he wished there would be war. In the worldwide conflagration, this business would be quickly forgotten. They would be left alone, he and his wife. He almost ordered a whisky from room service, then thought better of it.

Opening the closet where she kept her clothes, he started to inspect them one by one. But they were too numerous. It was impossible to guess what clothes she had taken. And there was no way of telling where she had gone.

On an impulse he picked up the telephone.

'Miss, can you tell me if my wife made a long-distance call from this room yesterday morning?'

'Just a second, sir, if you please. Yesterday morning?... Yes, at eleven fifty-six to Lausanne.'

He thanked her and hung up. Who did she know in Lausanne? He searched his memory. For a moment he was tempted to phone the number, but he feared that Solange would think he was spying on her. What could she possibly be doing in Lausanne? He suddenly realised it was very near to France. Suppose she had crossed the border? No, it wasn't possible, his wife would never do that. But, after all, what did he know? He remembered the bottle of sleeping pills he had found in the drawer. There was no doubt she had given him a dose that night. And in the past, hadn't she committed other acts far more dreadful?

He had to stop. He was becoming delirious, in the grip of the sick thoughts that rattled around in his head. Why was he torturing himself like this? He felt disgusted and ashamed. Instinctively he went to take a cigarette from the jewelled box his wife kept on the bedside table and he noticed the time. It was a quarter to five. Brenner would soon be calling to ask why they were late. He might even come over himself or send a henchman. At any moment there was going to be a knock on the door.

They mustn't find him at the hotel. He needed to gain time while he waited for Solange to appear. Once she was back they could work things out together. He felt a degree of relief as he put on his jacket, knowing that the fresh air of the lakeside would clear his head of dark thoughts. In the lobby he asked the desk clerk if he'd seen the superintendent. The man shook his head and offered him a light. He realised he still had an unlit cigarette in his mouth and threw it in a nearby ashtray.

***

'Just gone half past five,' said Mestre, having just looked at his watch.

'Hell's bells!' exclaimed the superintendent, 'I'd completely forgotten the Garniers.'

There had been a lot of other things to think about. They had rigged up a projection light in the grotto which had allowed them to look into every corner. The medical examiner had concluded his work, his assistants had taken photos and fingerprints and the corpse had been trundled off to the morgue. A couple of policemen were still there, using picks on the floor and tapping the walls with crowbars, in a half-hearted and fruitless attempt to uncover the secret. Brenner, unable to hide his disappointment, continued to exhort them to greater efforts.

Lippi called down from outside:

'You're wasting your time. Let's go and have a drink.'

Receiving no reply, he decided to go and join them, his curiosity getting the better of his phobia. On seeing Lippi, Mestre agreed to his suggestion with relief, and the little Russian signalled his approval as well. The three of them walked towards the grotto's exit and turned to take in the full scene of the crypt. Shorn of its mystery by the relentless light, the esoteric frescos daubed by amateurs, the cabalistic graffiti sketched roughly with charcoal, and the ritual objects taken from junk shops made the place look like a scene from a low budget horror film.

'It all looks so terribly fake,' observed the philosopher in his most scornful tone.

'The Egyptian stele is certainly authentic,' retorted Prokosch, less out of conviction than a desire to show he knew something about antiques.

'Don't believe it!' replied Mestre. 'I'll bet you it's a copy.'

'What Egyptian stele?' asked Lippi.

'The one at the back representing the goddess Isis.'

The Italian went back to study it more attentively.

'That's funny, there's an identical one on the fountain in the park,' he said, stroking it with his hand. 'Come and look, Superintendent.'

'I've already seen it,' replied Brenner. 'It must be worth a lot. It's marble.'

'Marble, my eye,' muttered Lippi through clenched teeth. 'Have you tried to move it?

'And how would we do that? There isn't the slightest crack. It's embedded in the rock and as solid as a – as a prison door,' joked the superintendent. 'I've patted it all over to try and find a hidden spring, as the detectives in your favourite stories do. And anyway, don't you think it's a rather too obvious place for a secret passage?'

'If my friend Garnier were here,' the Italian replied solemnly, 'he would surely recommend you read *The Purloined Letter*. It's one of Edgar Allan Poe's tales,' he explained charitably.

'I don't need to read Edgar Allan Poe to know that it's a sculpture and there's only solid rock behind it.'

'Let's have a look!' growled Lippi. With a forced grin, he picked up an iron bar. It was as if the sight of the goddess offended him and he mistook her for a live human being. Nobody would have been surprised to hear a cry of pain as he planted the iron bar right in her heart.

***

From the cavernous depths a hollow voice could be heard:

'I've reached a sort of tunnel, Superintendent. I'm coming back up.'

A whitish mist floated inside the crypt, composed of particles of plaster and mortar. The stele had been largely broken open and the one intact piece was hanging from a rusted hinge cemented into the rock. Behind lay a black cavity in which could be seen the top steps of staircase that appeared to descend to the bowels of the earth. Suddenly a light pierced the darkness and a hand appeared holding a lamp, followed shortly by a head covered with dirt.

'The passage leads to a series of stone tunnels which seem in fair condition,' panted the policeman, climbing out of the black hole. He waited to catch his breath and continued: 'They're big enough to walk in if you're not too tall and don't mind rats.'

A policeman with grey moustaches stepped forward.

'Begging your permission, sir, I'm from these parts. They must be part of the old aqueduct system which brought the mountain water to the villages.'

'And, on the way, it fed the fountain I told you about,' said Lippi triumphantly. 'When I realised the two steles were identical, I deduced they must mark the access to some sort of underground canal system. In fact, what put me on the trail was that, in ancient initiation rites, Isis was associated with the opening and closing of doors. As someone once said: "It's elementary...." Too bad for the legend of the Sorcerer's Grotto, but at least we now know how Rosenkreutz managed to disappear.'

'"*The solution to a mystery is always inferior to the mystery itself*",' announced Prokosch.

125

'You sound just like Harvey,' said Lippi. 'Is that your own?'

'As far as I know.'

'Bravo! May I quote you?'

'I would like to remind you politely, Professor,' said Mestre, 'that it was I who suggested the existence of a secret passage when I showed that the only place Dr. Hoenig could be was in the grotto. Prokosch can bear witness.'

'If the two of you will allow me,' replied the little Russian, with a malicious gleam in his eye, 'the first to discover it was Dr. Hoenig himself. When Lippi challenged him to shut himself in the grotto, you can be sure he must have studied the problem. I imagine he discovered the old construction plans by looking in the municipal archives and found there was an old aqueduct passing under both the grotto and the fountain.'

'Well reasoned, old boy!' said Lippi approvingly, clapping him on the back. 'That's exactly the conclusion I came to myself.'

'That's enough. Gentlemen, we're closing!' announced Brenner. 'You can continue your nonsense outside.'

'Why do you call it nonsense?' protested Prokosch vigorously as he moved towards the exit.

'Because I was listening to you. You're all assuming that Hoenig got into the grotto under his own steam, which implies he was alive. And we all know he was dead.'

***

A little later, when they all met in the bar at the Albergo, Brenner was forced to admit that the discovery of the corpse raised more questions than it answered:

Firstly, if – as Mestre and the others assumed – Dr. Hoenig didn't die from the knife wound he received, how was it that more than ten other persons (starting with Mestre himself in his initial account) claimed to have witnessed the contrary? And how could Strahler, for his part, been so badly wrong in his diagnosis? Of course, the possibility the young doctor had lied couldn't be ruled out, but what reason would anyone have for doubting his word? Not to mention that still nobody knew how the victim had managed to leave the bungalow, double-locking behind him a door to which he didn't have the key – which led everyone back to where they started.

Secondly, the conjecture, according to which the murderer returned to the bungalow to dispose of the body, using the same method he had used to exit previously, wasn't -- it had to be admitted – any more convincing. How could he have carried the body over such a long distance, from the bungalow to the fountain – particularly if it were a feeble woman – and then dragged it inside the aqueduct, from the fountain to the grotto? It was absolutely impossible.

"Unless she had an accomplice," the policeman said to himself. That would explain a lot of things. He had suspected Solange Garnier from the beginning. In the first place, she was too pretty and Brenner, from experience, was inclined to distrust pretty women. It was true that her description didn't fit that given by agents Mangin and Fantoni. But her only alibi was provided by her husband. There was no obvious motive, that was also true. He only had his intuition to go on. He was following his "copper's hunch" as the hacks who wrote those penny dreadfuls would say. That was why he had waited to question her until he had found a clue to confront her with. And now he had found one.

As for the husband, he had lied about his connections to Dr. Hoenig. Garnier was a brilliant fellow with a penchant for perversity, like so many intellectuals. Only a man gifted with a superior intelligence could have conceived such a diabolical scheme. He had planned the crime and his wife had executed it. It was amazing how everything suddenly became clear.

He tapped the shirt pocket containing the envelope with its precious contents. A short chestnut hair. Collecting some hair samples from the lovely Madame Garnier would be child's play. The lab would do the rest. Hairs are like fingerprints: they're unique to each individual. So. Just a few hours more and the whole business would be wrapped up.

'I'm going to have the Garniers arrested,' he thought out loud.

Mestre choked and knocked over his whisky. Prokosch's eyes sparkled with amusement. Harvey, whom they had found already installed at the bar in front of his third whisky, turned to Lippi and raised his eyebrows.

'What did he say?'

'He said he was going to arrest Pierre Garnier and his wife,' replied the Italian, with seeming indifference.

'You're completely insane,' Mestre finally spluttered, making a sign to the barman to clean up the mess. 'You should warn us before uttering such –.'

'Listen, all of you,' cut in Brenner brutally. 'I've been extremely patient up to now. I've listened to all the nonsense you've spouted and followed your suggestions to the letter and all it's got me is a muddled mess, even though I will acknowledge you've been right on a couple of points. Now it's over. I don't need you any more. If everyone sticks to his trade, the cows will be well guarded.'

'That must be one of those old Swiss proverbs,' muttered Lippi under his breath. 'Better make a note of it.'

'As for you, Professor, you can stop playing the court jester. One more word from you and I'll –.'

'Whoa!' protested Harvey, seeing the superintendent turning a bright scarlet. 'Let's behave like gentlemen, if you please.'

'Yes,' interjected Prokosch, speaking for the first time. 'I'd like to be sure that Superintendent Brenner has fully thought through the consequences. I can see the headlines now: "Two French Citizens Arrested in Switzerland for the Murder of a High-Ranking German Civil Servant." It would cause quite a stir at a time of international tension. I wonder if Berne would appreciate it.'

'Do you mean that?' asked Brenner, suddenly turning pale.

'Certainly. I can't see what you would achieve by doing it, Superintendent. And why, if you're expecting to arrest the Garniers, are you here talking to us instead of questioning them? Why don't you phone Solange Garnier and ask her to come here, with or without her husband?'

'That's the first thing I did when I got here. But she's not in her room and I haven't seen her all day.'

'And yet,' said Mestre, frowning, 'Garnier told us she was in her room.'

'It was a lie,' said Brenner calmly. 'She left the hotel yesterday morning in her car. As for him, he's gone, too. He felt the need to leave this evening around five o'clock and hasn't been seen since.'

'It would seem to me that, if they were accomplices as you claim, they would have left together,' observed the philosopher.

'And they would both be a long way away by now,' added the little Russian.

The superintendent's face reflected a cold determination and he looked at each of them in turn.

'I have no intention of allowing myself to be distracted by your objections every time I make a move,' he said. 'Everything points to him having left to join her. Don't worry, they won't leave the country. Their description has been sent to every border station. So.' He turned to Prokosch. 'Tell your friends in Berne that I'll give them one more chance. But I warn you: if the Garniers aren't here tomorrow morning at nine o'clock, I'll issue a warrant for their arrest.'

***

The door of the baroque church had been wide open and Pierre had taken refuge there. He had strolled for a time by the side of the lake, wandered in the streets of the old town and then stopped in front of the boarding point for the little funicular that carried passengers up the mountainside to the Sanctuary of the Madonna del Sasso. The desire to return to the hotel was balanced by the apprehension of not finding Solange there and the consequent agonising wait. He decided to gain himself some time: "The later I return, the greater the chance she will be there," he argued to himself and, without thinking twice about it, he bought himself a ticket.

The sanctuary and the convent surrounding it were built on an esplanade affording a view across the lake for some ten kilometres, as far as the village of Luino, where it curved towards Italy. The fifteenth century church is a sumptuous religious jewel with low-arching ribbed vaults resting on marble pillars, ceilings decorated with medallions, arabesque sculptures in the round and *bas-reliefs* painted in *trompe-l'œil* . From the moment he entered, Pierre had been dazzled by the profusion of gilding on the walls and the vaults. But his gaze had inevitably been drawn to the Madonna which, at the back of the nave under its marble canopy decorated with arcatures, dominated the chancel and the altar. He had contemplated its surreal beauty, its delicate features imbued with an infinite sweetness, for a long time. And there, as though in ecstasy, Pierre, who had thought he had lost his faith, had found the words of the old supplication on his lips and had prayed for his wife.

He had lost all notion of time and night was falling as he left the sanctuary. At his feet, the lake seemed like a slab of shale set in the drab greyness of the rocks and forests that formed a semicircle around it. The lights of the village came on and, far away at the foot of the mountains, a string of little stars pierced the contours of the dark waters. Almost mechanically he turned his wrist to catch what remained of the light. Was that the time? So late already. He tried to think of Solange but could not bring an image of her to his mind's eye. There was only a sensation of panic and a feeling of dizziness.

"I'm frightened," he told himself. "Not because she's not here. Frightened of seeing her again." And when he found himself the only passenger in the funicular, he felt as if he were a skydiver in free-fall, mouth dry, chest tight – watching the black surface of the sleeping lake rushing toward him.

***

The lobby of the Grand Hotel, by the common consent of its elegant clientele, was a rather depressing place, as is often the case with luxury establishments once they have passed their prime. A few convoluted and fussy contemporary lamps were scattered about the premises, casting their feeble glow on overstuffed furniture, floral columns and the numerous naked goddesses made from alabaster or stucco that stood in contrast to walls made of imitation marble. The only bright light in the vast gloomy space came from above the reception desk, and it made the concierge's bald head glisten and the metallic balls attached to the room keys gleam.

'Please, Dear God, let the room key not be there,' prayed Pierre as he made his way, as if pulled by an invisible force, towards the reception counter where his fate would be decided. He was but a few steps away when he heard his name being called. Instinctively, he turned round.

An old gentleman, half out of his armchair, was beckoning him almost joyfully with a hand waving a newspaper. In the reddish light from under the adjacent lampshade, he stood out against the greenish panels of a screen decorated with nymphs and swans. He was not very tall and appeared to be suffering from a chill even though, despite the warm air, he wore a heavy tweed coat and a Scottish scarf wrapped around his neck. Pierre was sure he'd never met the fellow and yet, as he got closer, he found there was something familiar about the face, even though he couldn't say what.

It would have been hard, nevertheless, to forget the bald, rather large head with its two tousled white tufts on either side; the short moustache, equally white, under a long thin nose; the narrow, stooped shoulders; and, above all, under bushy eyebrows, the eyes, shining with an intelligence both keen and benevolent and hidden behind *pince-nez* from another era.

'Please forgive my presumptuousness,' he said, 'but I saw you come in and took the liberty of calling you. I've come a long way to meet you, sir, and I'd welcome the opportunity to have a few words.'

He spoke text-book French with the fastidiousness of the educated Englishman.

'My name is Carter Gilbert, Arthur Carter Gilbert.'

***

'Here's my card,' he said, handing it solemnly to Pierre, who glanced at it before slumping into a nearby armchair opposite him. 'I'm not surprised you didn't recognise me, because my face no longer resembles the one my publisher insists on putting on the back cover of all my books. That photograph goes back to those far-off days when I wrote my first books and, to be perfectly candid with you, fell in love with a very young person named Solange Duvernois. She was twelve years old and I was fifty-four so, in case you're jealous type, the age difference should reassure you. Then our paths diverged, to coin a dreary phrase. She followed her parents to Germany and I left London for Switzerland, preferring the gulls of Lake Geneva to the vultures of the British Treasury. She had promised to write and she kept her word, or at least whenever she felt the need to confide in her "Uncle Arthur," as she was kind enough to call me affectionately. So I feel I can justly claim to know her as well as you do, or even – no offence intended – better than you do.'

He gave a little chuckle and, fishing a silvered case out of his pocket, offered a disgusting-looking blackish cigarette to his guest.

'I hope I'm not boring you, my dear sir?'

'On the contrary,' replied Pierre accepting the offer in the hope that the tobacco would calm his nerves.

'Good. I must still have feelings for her, given that I agreed to drive who-knows-how-many kilometres at the ripe old age of seventy-two in a convertible with the top down, driven by your wife at breakneck speed – or, as the French say, *tombeau ouvert*: open tomb. I love that expression. I presume you guessed that she'd come to seek my help?'

131

'Where is she right now?'

'In your room, I assume, where she is no doubt taking a bath and making herself beautiful for you. Please remain seated. You have plenty of time to see her. Look here, young man,' said the old man, leaning towards Pierre to give him a light, 'I've invented and solved forty-eight impossible crimes in as many novels. The Swiss authorities, in a number of particularly thorny cases, have seen fit to call on my humble services and – without leaving my office – I've helped to solve quite a few of them. As a result of my success I've been granted access to confidential investigations and to neurologists' reports on the psychology of notable murderers. All false modesty aside, I've come to be regarded as an authority in the matter. I don't say that boastfully: merely to explain why your wife, in her bewilderment, sought me out.'

Pierre drew on his cigarette and was seized by a coughing fit, brought on by the acrid smoke. Carter Gilbert leant back and enjoyed his with an inscrutable air.

'I wonder whether you appreciate her true value,' he said, with an amused indulgence. 'I'm talking about your wife, naturally. She's a woman who, although delicate, secretive and excessively vulnerable by nature, can nonetheless demonstrate great courage and energy when the occasion arises. Why has she never talked to you about her past, particularly her childhood? Most wives, including my own, can talk incessantly about the subject. Because she forbade herself to do so. All the more so because her marriage to you seemed to have freed her from the memories of her past. Her childhood years were a nightmare. Just think, she was only six when her father – .'

'—I know about that,' said Pierre. 'Hoenig told me everything.'

'I was afraid of that,' sighed the writer. 'Do you realise that the very idea that you might learn that she was the daughter of a condemned man – whatever excuses one can make for a crime committed mindlessly for a humanitarian ideal – never ceased to torture her? And I'm sure that pig Hoenig didn't spare you the details of her other youthful indiscretions, either. If you can't appreciate the state of mind she was in when she feared that all the details of her past were about to be revealed, then you're far less intelligent than I'd imagined. And, in fact, she was prepared to go to any lengths to preserve her marriage. To preserve the image she wished you to have of her: accomplished woman of the world, daughter of an eminent diplomat, educated in the best boarding schools, brought up in the world of luxury and good manners. All of which she is, by the way – and to perfection,' he added with a generosity tinged with admiration.

'None of that explains why –,' Pierre started to observe.

'— why she loves you? On the contrary, that explains everything. You have to realise that, like many women who are too beautiful, she's never had any luck with men. One affair after another, which she described to me in her letters in a playful tone which failed to conceal her bitterness and disappointment. Some lasted longer than others, but she always knew they were after the considerable fortune left to her by her adoptive parents. Her first husband, the American engineer –.'

'—her first?' repeated Pierre. 'You mean her third!'

The old man sat bolt upright and the ash from his cigarette fell on his waistcoat.

'The third? What kind of nonsense is this?' he exclaimed, turning crimson.

'But I thought –.'

'Oh! You thought! You thought what? That she'd had three husbands before you? Why not four, or five – or a dozen while you're at it? What on earth put that idea into your head? Are you a madman or an imbecile?'

It was a brutal attack, but Carter Gilbert's paternal tone and the commiseration that could be read on his face stripped it of all offensiveness.

'I – I don't understand anything anymore,' stammered Pierre. 'I –.'

The old man held up his hand for silence.

'I, on the other hand, believe I do understand. It's about time, my boy, that you told me exactly what that swine said to you,' he said with an awkward compassion.

Pierre swallowed hard.

'Everything he told me in that meeting is engraved in my mind. I've thought about it over and over again these last few days.'

'Now's the time to get it off your chest. It will stay between the two of us, I promise.'

He adjusted his *pince-nez* and leant forward as if to concentrate harder. And his piercing eyes stayed fixed on Pierre for the whole time he was talking, displaying frequent glints of anger. The shadows of the two men became lost in the dimness of the vast lobby, its atmosphere oppressive despite the half-open picture windows behind the dusty curtains of red velvet. The hubbub of

133

distant conversations and feminine laughter, accompanied by the noise of silverware, floated in from the terrace where the mildness of the evening had lured out the diners. The two men were unaware they were now alone in their corner of the dark hall – alone because one could not count among the humans the little bellboy standing stiffly in front of a lift that resembled a rosewood coffin, and the receptionist seated behind his counter looking every bit like an evil night-bird of prey, blinking its eyelids in its illuminated cage.

When Pierre had finished talking, Carter Gilbert swore under his breath. He removed his *pince-nez* which had misted up, and, with a fierce concentration, proceeded to wipe them with a large chequered handkerchief.

'Sir,' he began after he had carefully put the glasses back on his nose, 'you have been the victim of a hoax, the most ingenious and the most cruel it has been my misfortune to know. I can assure you of one thing right away: your wife is not a criminal. As far as I know, she has never killed anyone. All the accusations of that charlatan were but a tissue of lies and I will prove it to you point by point.'

He used his fingers to count the arguments.

'In the first place, there never was a criminology conference in London in 1933, and I've never heard of an Inspector Parker of Scotland Yard, except in Dorothy Sayers' novels. Your wife never met, never married and never stabbed a rich old industrialist in a hermetically sealed room – or anywhere else, for that matter – for the simple reason such a man never existed.

'Secondly, in 1931 she was not in Germany but in Argentine with the Duvernois. She could not have been guilty of shooting anyone called Käutner in his locked office in Berlin, because he probably didn't exist either – as opposed to Superintendent Lohmann, who really does exist but only in a detective film released by the German Universal Film Studios.

'Thirdly, there's no reason to think that her so-called "third" husband died of anything other than gastroenteritis, given that individual's notorious abuse – he was a brilliant chemist but a complete failure as a husband – of the martini cocktail. In short, my boy, this whole story about your wife being a calculating murderess is the malevolent concoction of a brilliant but perverse individual who played with your mind with a pleasure I can't begin to imagine.'

Pierre Garnier's resistance to pain was put to the test: he was able to sustain red-hot embers on his skin without flinching. His cigarette burned down to a point between his index and middle fingers without him noticing. Eventually he yelped, looked at it in astonishment, and stubbed it out in the ashtray.

'But why?' he exclaimed. 'Why did the swine tell me all that? Why?'

'Who knows what goes on in the mind of a torturer? For Hoenig was certainly that. Luckily for you, you don't know what experiments he carried out on his mental patients. As refined as they were repellent. But if you're looking for an explanation beyond the purely pathological, my hunch is that, following his public humiliation at the hands of your friend Professor Lippi, he was out for vengeance. And you, my friend, were made to order: bookworm, idealist, overconfident, and above all deeply in love. He hit you where you were most vulnerable, where it would hurt most. And, with his morbid sense of humour, he dropped clues into the narrative that he knew you, in your distressed state, would never think of checking. Inspector Parker, Superintendent Lohmann: yet another way to humiliate you.'

'I behaved like a fool,' sighed Pierre, clenching his fists. 'When I think –.'

Carter Gilbert held up his hand.

'Don't feel guilty, my boy. The tale he spun was, in its way, a small masterpiece of psychology which exploited all the chinks in your armour. Like all the best lies, it was correct in certain minor details, enough to make you swallow the rest. At Solange's request, I can now reveal – if you haven't already guessed – that everything you learned about her birth, her childhood, and the youthful sins she committed later on are all absolutely true. And there's no need to promise me you won't hold a grudge. I'm willing to bet that it will only make you love her more. Now go to her, my boy!'

'Let me shake your hand, sir,' said Pierre, getting up. 'Will you be able to tell us at some point what it all means?'

The old man snorted and tilted his head back in order to look him in the eye.

'But surely you can already see the broad outlines of this affair? The whole story is a pack of lies, but someone has made a truth out of it.'

***

Pierre walked across the lobby, slowly at first, then more quickly, still not fully aware of where he was. It was as if the relief had left his mind drained and his heart beating too fast. He took the steps of the grand staircase two at a time and ran to the room where Solange was waiting for him.

VIII

They were sitting in the dining room in front of a window overlooking the gardens and, further below, beyond the roofs of the town, the lake covered in white mist. They had got up late and were holding hands above the table covered with the remains of breakfast.

'I should have told you all that when you asked me to marry you,' murmured Solange, squeezing her husband's hand even harder. 'But I was ashamed and I was afraid of frightening you away. If you'd ever changed your mind or, even worse, if you'd stopped loving me....'

'Don't think about it, darling. We'll never talk about it ever again.'

'I didn't tell you everything. I did a dreadful thing....'

'Even more dreadful than stealing a diamond bracelet?'

'The diamonds were paste,' she declared.

'I believe you,' he replied with a smile. 'So, tell me. What else did you do?'

She drew her hand away and fiddled with a lock of hair, avoiding his eye.

'Sometimes it seems too awful, but at other times it seems ridiculous. But I can't tell you,' she said, shaking her head so vigorously her hair rose from the nape of her slender neck. 'Uncle Arthur forbade me.'

Pierre frowned.

'You promised there would be no more secrets between us, Solange,' he said gently.

She emitted a quiet scream and clutched her head with both hands.

'It's true,' she murmured.

She raised her head and looked at him with her limpid grey-green eyes.

'You see, darling, it was I who stabbed Dr. Hoenig.'

'Ah! There you are,' said the all-too-familiar voice of Professor Lippi. 'Have you heard the news? Arthur Carter Gilbert is amongst us.'

He rapidly pulled up a chair and sat astride it, obviously excited.

'I've just got back from the Albergo. The old man has taken charge

137

of things. He had a long discussion with the superintendent in private. I don't know what he said to him, but the other came out with a face about six foot long. By the way, do you know that last night that cretin wanted to arrest the two of you? I had my work cut out to convince him it was a stupid idea.'

He looked at each of them in turn, feigning stupefaction.

'Is that all the reaction I get?'

'Where is he now?' asked Pierre in a non-committal voice.

'Who?'

'Sir Arthur.'

'Oh, he went with Brenner to look at the bungalow. But I haven't told you the best bit! When he emerged from his little chat with Brenner, there was a crowd on the terrace, journalists and photographers from Berne, Geneva et cetera, and they bombarded him with questions. He held up his hand for silence and announced cheerfully that there would be a session tomorrow morning, at ten o'clock sharp, in the conference hall of the Albergo and that we were all invited. You'll be coming, of course,' he added with an engaging smile.

'I'm not going,' said Solange in a low voice.

'Is that it?' asked Pierre curtly. Lippi looked at him in surprise.

'One of the journalists asked Brenner – who didn't bother to hide his displeasure – whether he wanted to say anything, but he merely stated that he was expecting the results of the autopsy and the lab report at any moment. And at that point, he said we should all leave and not get in the way of the investigation which, was, needless to say "taking its course."'

There was a silence. Solange was absentmindedly watching a gardener rake dead leaves from the lawn. Pierre picked up the porcelain teapot and scrutinised it intensely, as if it were a rare specimen.

'Well, then…' Lippi began, looking from one to the other with total incomprehension. He stood up and announced he had suddenly remembered some important letters he had to write, and didn't seem particularly surprised when they didn't press him to stay.

***

All in all, the Garniers passed a delightful afternoon, even though the sky was an autumnal grey. Solange used all her seductive wiles to extract from her husband a promise not to pose her any further questions. "Be patient, darling. Uncle Arthur will explain everything at the right time. Believe me, even I am not really sure what happened." They took the *vaporetto* to Magadino where, at a lakeside inn, they lunched very late on fried fillets of local perch. Pierre selected a bottle of wine from Asti: "that cheeky little sparkling wine made famous by Stendhal's *The Charterhouse of Parma*" which she absolutely had to try. Resting her elbow on the table and her head on her hand, Solange raised the glass to eye level for the sheer pleasure of watching the bubbles.

'Admit it, darling: this is one of the happiest moments of our lives. This horrible business has drawn us closer together, finally. But I do wonder,' she added mischievously, 'whether you wouldn't have preferred being the husband of a famous criminal after all. Tell me, wouldn't that have excited you a little bit?'

'I'd like to hear you develop that theory,' he replied, clinking their glasses.

'Not now, darling. This evening, perhaps, in the room, if you're not too tired.'

She sipped the wine but, above the glass, she seemed to look at him anxiously. There was a hint of rings under her grey-green eyes, her hair was slightly ruffled, and a strange smile played on her lips.

He leant across the table and kissed her on the forehead.

'Tell me, just for the record: you wouldn't have put something in my drink last Sunday evening, by any chance? That's what's been bothering me the most. I seem to remember falling onto the bed and sleeping like a log.'

'Last Sunday? It's quite possible. What did we do that evening? Ah, yes, we'd had a very tiring day. Still, you wouldn't want me to wake you up each time I go out to commit a murder, surely?'

She put her head back and he saw her shoulders trembling. But it wasn't from the cold: Solange was laughing.

***

The accumulation of surprising discoveries and incomprehensible events inhibits the emotions and plunges even the most inquisitive spirit into a torpid state.

Such was Superintendent Brenner's experience as he stood with

Arthur Carter Gilbert at the door of the victim's bungalow.

'Is this another joke?' he asked aloud as he realised that, despite all his efforts, the key in his hand obstinately refused to fit the lock.

He noticed that the old man was watching him, a mischievous gleam in his eye, like a street urchin engaged in a prank.

'It's not a joke, Superintendent. You've simply got the wrong key.'

'That's impossible,' muttered Brenner, showing it to him. 'It's the key that Agent Fantoni found on the table next to the victim's body. And it hasn't left my pocket since he gave it to me. Look, Monsieur....' He pointed to the copper plate on the door, inscribed with the number 12. 'I'm not dreaming, it's the same number.'

'Is that so?' said Sir Arthur. He took the key and turned it around in his hand before handing it back to the policeman. Admittedly the numbers are fairly crudely made, but what do you see now.'

'15,' replied Brenner, stupefied.

'Quite so. The 1 is a simple vertical line and the 5 is an upside-down 2. Anyone could have made that mistake. If you're shown into a room by someone opening the door for you, and then you see a key lying on one of the pieces of furniture, you automatically assume it's the room key, particularly if it's showing a number that looks the same. That's what Agent Fantoni thought, that's what you assumed, and that's exactly what someone wanted you to believe. It's such a simple trick that only a truly diabolical mind could have thought of it – a mind cunning enough to know that the most effective schemes are those that deceive by their simplicity.'

'Just a moment,' said Brenner. 'Let me think. There are only two keys for each bungalow, right? One is back in the Albergo. The one we have isn't the right one. So where's the other?'

'Here!' said the old man. And, standing on tiptoe, he reached up and swept his hand along the door lintel, collecting a key that he brandished under the superintendent's nose.

He inserted it in the keyhole, twisted, pushed the door open and entered.

'I'm not a psychic,' he continued. 'I just used logic. When I read the agent's report, I realised straight away that the key found on Hoenig's table couldn't be the right one. Early this morning I came down here to poke about and I found what I was looking for. Then....'

He entered the lounge and went over to the window, opened it wide and pushed open the shutters. The light and the clean air freshened the room, which was giving off an unpleasant smell. Then he turned to the policeman who was blinking and shaking his head in astonishment.

'Afterwards, I put everything back in place and returned to the Albergo where I questioned the receptionist. As I had thought, one of the keys was missing. They hadn't been particularly concerned because it was the key to bungalow 15 which is under repair and whose door is left open because there's nothing inside to take.'

'And the murderer stole it!' exclaimed Brenner, his face lighting up.

Sir Arthur gave a tut-tut of disapproval.

'Don't jump to conclusions, Superintendent.'

'But yes!' exclaimed the other, who seemed to have come alive. 'On the contrary, we have the solution. The woman, after committing the murder, took the good key from the table, put the other in its place, and simply walked out of the door locking it behind her.   And we fell for it. What do you say?'

'I say I've read your report. It's right there in black and white: she wouldn't have had enough time.'

'Let's suppose I was wrong.'

'It wouldn't be the first time. All right, go on....'said Carter Gilbert nonchalantly. Brenner was visibly anxious. He rubbed his chin and his gaze wandered around the room before alighting on the old author's sibylline smile. He took his courage in both hands and declared:

'Well, I'd say that what happened was the murderess returned to the scene of the crime.'

Carter Gilbert uttered a gently mocking laugh.

'Murderers always return to the scene of their crime, that's practically a given.'

Brenner blushed and took a deep breath before going on.

'As I was saying, she returned to the bungalow. She opened the door with the key, pulled the body outside, locked the door and then....'

'And then she dragged a corpse weighing more than two hundred pounds over thirty or forty metres, hoisted it over the rim of the fountain and up to the tunnel entrance, then dragged it again in the dark as far as the grotto. After which, she came back by the same route to place the key on the lintel for the sole purpose, presumably, of giving us the pleasure of discovering it. Doesn't anything about that reasoning

141

strike you as absurd, my friend?' he exclaimed angrily. 'Can you imagine anything more insane in terms of criminal behaviour? You're going to tell me she had an accomplice. A likely story! But even if she had, that wouldn't explain why they went to all those lengths.'

'It's beyond me,' replied Brenner, whose evident despair was painful to see. 'Every time we think we've solved one problem, along comes another. And don't try to tell me you've any clearer idea than I have,' he growled, pointing his finger at the old man, just as the other turned to cross the bedroom, headed for the bathroom.

The sound of heavy steps could be heard in the outer room. The superintendent turned to see a policeman enter the lounge and salute.

'The lab on the phone, Superintendent. They've finished the analyses and want to know where they're to be sent.'

'To the Albergo, of course, idiot!' barked Brenner, sending him away with a flea in his ear.

He went to join Carter Gilbert, whom he found standing on a stool trying to open the skylight.

'We're going to be getting the lab results,' he announced.

'I can tell you what they're going to say,' replied the Englishman in a smooth voice.

'I'd have been amazed if you couldn't,' muttered Brenner. 'But what are you doing on that stool, for heaven's sake? It's already been determined –.'

' – lots of things have been determined.' He stuck his head outside. 'Except that the overhang of the roof juts out below the opening here.'

'So?'

'Nothing.'

He drew his head back inside, took off his *pince-nez* and used them as a magnifying glass to examine the dusty edges of the frame.

'What are you looking for?'

'Anything at all: a piece of material, a hair like the one you found on the body. Unfortunately, your men bungled the job and if there were any clues, they were destroyed a long time ago. Help me down.'

Once his feet were on the ground, he dusted himself off and continued.

'I'll tell you what the lab report contains. In the first place, the hair from the dressing-gown is indeed Solange Garnier's. It's up to you to show how, at the same time, it can belong to the woman in the bungalow despite the testimony of witnesses who swear she had dark hair and was smaller. I can probably help you with that.

'Secondly, as must be expected, only the victim's fingerprints were found on the knife. Thirdly –.'

He stopped and looked around the bathroom.

'Tell me, am I right in thinking Dr. Hoenig had a doctor's bag?'

'Naturally,' confirmed Brenner. 'We left it in the bedroom.'

'May I see it?'

The superintendent shrugged and led him in to the room. A black leather case sat on a low table among a mess of ties, cuff-links and clip-on collars. It had not been properly locked and was untidily open.

'It was like that,' said Brenner. 'We just took a quick look inside.'

'May I?' enquired Sir Arthur.

'I don't want to stop you, but there's nothing interesting there.'

'Really?'

'Yes. The usual shambles: medicines, stethoscope, hypodermic syringe....'

'The syringe has been used recently,' murmured the old man, holding it up to the light. He put it back in its case and pulled out a brownish bottle with a hand-written chemical formula on the label. He uncorked the stopper and sniffed.

'Trichloroethylene,' he mumbled.

'What's that?' asked Brenner.

'A new serum that the Bosch have perfected.'

He re-corked the bottle, put it carefully back in place and turned to face the policeman. The expressive eyes under the bushy brows gleamed behind the *pince-nez*.

'There's no need to wait for the autopsy results, Superintendent. It's exactly as I thought: Dr. Hoenig was under the influence of a powerful barbiturate at the time of his death.'

***

All the foregoing happened on the eve of the masterful discourse given by the phenomenal Arthur Carter Gilbert in which the maestro, like a star shining in the night, dispersed with blinding clarity the shadows engulfing the enigma of Monte Verita. During the fifteen hours preceding that event, he made himself scarce, going first to visit Freyja Hoenig in the clinic to speak at length with her and with Strahler, after which he returned to the hotel. Having tipped the hotel staff lavishly to ensure he would not be disturbed and, as an added precaution, hanging a "Do Not Disturb" sign outside his room, he disappeared from view, thus concealing the spectacle that this writer would have wished to describe to his avid readers as proof of the scrupulous attention, penetrating shrewdness and relentless concentration with which the great man conducted his investigation, surrounded as he was by stacks of reports supplied by Brenner.

Pierre Garnier had promised himself a few quiet moments of escape from the seemingly unending series of tortured moments spent peering into dark mirrors, in the hope of seeing the light. When he returned to the hotel with his wife, he came, wholly unexpectedly, across a new element in the case. It almost handed him the key to the mystery, and launched him on a chase which lasted the whole evening and half the night.

The envelope, on Albergo Monte Verita letterhead, was crumpled and folded in two. Standing there in the lobby and turning it around in his hands, Pierre Garnier felt an uneasy sensation. There was no stamp and no address, only his name printed in large letters. Nothing to indicate the sender. The concierge who had handed it to him had told him it had been found that same afternoon in the pocket of a jacket that had been sent out for dry-cleaning. It transpired that the letter had been delivered by a messenger the previous Sunday at ten past nine. He had noted the day and the hour in pencil on the back of the envelope and it was still readable, although barely. "You and your wife had just left for an excursion on the lake and I must have given it to you Sunday evening on your return," said the man apologetically, "and –.'

'—and you put it in your pocket and forgot about it,' said Solange, who then added:
'Excuse me, it's my fault: I gave your suit to the maid the next day without checking the pockets which, as you well know, my poor darling, is what I make a habit of doing.'

'That, I can't forgive.'

He dropped the frivolous tone:
'Let's not make a fuss about it. The letter is probably of no importance.'

Nevertheless he continued to rack his brains trying to understand what was happening as he fiddled with the letter in his hand. He had an uneasy feeling that it contained something abnormal and menacing. He didn't think he could handle that.

Solange looked at him inquisitively.

'Aren't you going to open it? You seem to be strange, all of a sudden.' She paused and started to laugh. 'Maybe it's a love letter from one of your admirers....'

'Look out, here's Lippi,' said Pierre abruptly.

The Italian came out of the lift and walked past them with his nose in the air, acknowledging them with the merest tilt of the head.

'I'll talk to him,' said Pierre. 'We weren't very polite with him this morning.'

'Whatever you say,' agreed Solange. 'I'm going up to change for dinner. Don't stay too long, darling.'

She left, blowing him a kiss on the way. Pierre joined the professor just as he was about to enter the bar.

'Do you have a letter for me, my dear fellow?' said the Italian affably, and Pierre realised he was still holding the envelope in his hand.

'It's addressed to me,' he replied. 'I was given it at reception. Let me see, what day is it? Wednesday? It arrived last Sunday.'

'There's no post on Sunday,' said Lippi pompously.

'Let's go and have a drink and I'll tell you about it.'

The bar, which had recently been redecorated in the style of an ocean liner, was the most elegant spot in Locarno and boasted a barman who was said to have done his apprenticeship at Fouquet's in Paris. It was the cocktail hour and the pastel outfits of the town's prettiest women formed a charming picture to which Pierre, in other circumstances, would not have been indifferent.

'I'll have a *Turn of the Screw*,' announced Lippi, perching himself on a barstool, 'and I recommend you try one, too. This barman is an artist, a true artist. This cocktail he's created is an absolute marvel and I'm hoping he'll let me have the recipe. After all, it was I that baptised it, in view of its complexity and in homage – as you will already have guessed – to the late lamented Henry James, subtle inventor of so many elegant labyrinths. Here, try it for yourself.'

The barman placed two glasses containing a frosty rose-coloured liquid in front of them.

'It's terrific, as you say,' said Pierre. 'After two or three of these, one's got to be --.'

'One can safely go to four. But start by opening the letter you've been incessantly twiddling in your hands. You said it arrived on

Sunday?'

As Pierre told him about the envelope inadvertently left in the pocket of a jacket sent out for dry-cleaning, the other's growing interest made him uncomfortable.

'Let's see now,' said Lippi. 'It's Sunday, the day of the excursion to the islands. It's the morning. Somebody – let's call him X – sends a letter to you from the Albergo. It must be urgent because he uses a courier. Nevertheless, it doesn't get to the Grand Hotel until ten minutes after you've left. X, who knows about the excursion and is probably in the party, cannot be unaware of this. Given that it must take, at the very least, twenty minutes by bicycle to go from the Albergo to the Grand Hotel, even going at maximum speed, one can infer mathematically that X sent the letter at least ten minutes before going down to Ascona to board the vaporetto. That way, he could be sure that you wouldn't get it until after your return. But your absent-mindedness throws a spanner in the works, and derails his carefully conceived plan. You forget the letter, which you leave in your jacket pocket, and your charming and attentive wife sends it out the next day to the *pressing* – if you'll forgive the use of the Anglicism. And so the letter doesn't reach you until three days after the intended date. *Quod erat demonstrandum*,' he added smugly. 'Now, it only remains to open it.'

'You're a constant source of amazement, Professor,' said Pierre, who was starting to find the whole business rather amusing. He was on his second glass and his anxiety was starting to evaporate. He was motivated by mere curiosity as he opened the envelope, taking care not to tear it, under the watchful eye of Lippi who could barely conceal his impatience.

The thin piece of paper was covered with symbols written in purple ink. There was no signature, nor any other identification of the sender. In the upper left-hand corner was a sketch of something vaguely resembling a skull, but the rest of the page contained nothing but an incoherent string of numbers and signs without spaces, forming a single paragraph. Pierre handed it to Lippi without a word.

The Italian emitted a low whistle and proceeded to examine the contents of the page:
08*=*9=(;+5*)08*5=)+?;45?95;?(38=?780?6!?65006808750>56(8505108 ?(+8)56*;83?+?085;(5>8()805748(=*;5(6.5(05.=(;8+805*:9.488.?6)88578 *;>6*3;.68+)*=8*063*8+5286008+?.5>600=*+?28*3508

'Well,' he said, handing the paper back, 'I assume you've guessed it's a coded message. I think our Mr. X has issued a challenge and wants to play with you.'

'It wouldn't be the first time,' sighed Pierre. 'Now he's even doing it after death.'

'Hoenig?'

'Who else?'

'Why would he have sent you this cryptography sample? It's infantile,' exclaimed Lippi.

'Infantile is the word. Behind that adult façade there was something childish about the man. Childish and monstrous. An impressive intellect captive to the sadistic impulses of a viciously evil child, the kind that pulls wings off flies and puts birds' eyes out. As he grew older, his technique got better. Psychological torture gave him a more refined satisfaction. The exquisite pleasure of playing on the weaknesses and anxieties of others. But it's over; I'm not playing any more. I'm not going to give him posthumous pleasure. I'm going to throw this obscenity of a message into the fire and that'll be the end of it.'

'Hold on,' said Lippi. 'We need to talk about this, but not here. Somewhere quiet.'

He ordered two more cocktails and Pierre followed him to an isolated table near the windows overlooking the terrace. Several couples were dancing outside to the tune of *Such Sweet Thunder*, being played on a gramophone.

If the Italian had been surprised by Pierre's outburst, he tactfully didn't show it. But the despondency that followed the angry declaration hadn't escaped his notice.

'Don't get so upset. Give me the paper and think for a moment: it's not altogether out of the question that he's handed us the solution to the problem.' He held his hand out for the paper, but Pierre threw it on the table.

'Here, take it, if it amuses you to play the detective. You've done nothing else for the last three days. You, Mestre, Prokosch and even Harvey, who fancies himself as Sherlock Holmes. What are you trying to prove? That you're smarter than the police? All you've done is transform a banal and mediocre little murder into an inexplicable and terrifying mystery. As I told you just now, you can count me out. Tomorrow morning, my wife and I are leaving this lunatic asylum. Carter Gilbert may have solved the problem by then, or maybe not. In any case, I don't care any more.'

The waiter arrived with the cocktails.

'Drink!' ordered Lippi.

Pierre drank. The Italian took the paper once more and leaned forward to examine it. After a while, he looked up and stared hard at his friend.

'Listen, Garnier,' he said slowly, 'just one more question. Why would Hoenig draw a skull? He obviously did it for a reason. What does it bring to mind?'

Pierre shrugged.

'The skull, or death's head, is the symbol for a pirate. But I don't see the connection.'

Lippi kept looking at him, a mocking pout on his lips.

'Really?'

'What is it now?' snapped Pierre. 'Why do you all try to find some dark meaning in every little thing? Doesn't it ever occur to you that there are things in life that happen without any explanation?'

'Felix, qui potuit rerum cognoscere causas,' announced Lippi with an almost comical intensity. 'Happy was he who was able to learn the causes of things.'

'Sapiens nihil affirmat quod non probet. A wise man states as true nothing he cannot prove,' retorted Pierre.

'Touche,' replied the Italian.

They smiled at each other.

'So,' said Pierre, who was starting to feel better. 'Hoenig drew a skull. What of it? Suppose he wanted to add a sinister touch to his mysterious text. But I don't see how the death's head gets us any closer to an answer. If the prize for deciphering these hieroglyphics was the equivalent of Captain Kidd's treasure, I still couldn't do it.'

'And supposing it was just that, Captain Kidd's treasure? You disappoint me, my friend. I was expecting more from a noted scholar and devoted reader of Poe.'

Without averting his gaze he took another sip of his cocktail.

It seemed to Pierre as though a veil had been lifted from his eyes.

'Give me that paper,' he almost snarled.

After a few moments he looked up.

'I'll be damned!' he exclaimed. 'It's not a skull it's a scarab.'

'Obviously. Hoenig did it in such a way that this coleoptera looked like a death's head, not just by the shape but by the disposition of the spots on the insect's back. I sensed straight away that it was a clue pointing in some way to the cipher key. I'm not claiming any special merit for that: if you'd kept your head, you'd have arrived at the same conclusion sooner or later. It was actually rather clever on his part. He could create a puzzle that looked insoluble at first glance, but which would be a piece of cake for a connoisseur like you to decipher. There can have been no doubt in his mind that it would be child's play for a Poe expert to compare the present cryptogram with that invented by the author of the most famous of the *Tales of the Grotesque and Arabesque....*'

'The Gold Bug!'

'Precisely. The story of the discovery of a mysterious parchment that put the hero on the trail of Captain Kidd's treasure. Every child has been thrilled by the idea of a key that can unlock a secret code.'

'Wait! Let me think: it was a key based on the frequency of letters in the given language which, since the message was addressed to me, must be my own. All we have to do is to determine the most frequent characters in the text and compare them with those most frequently used in French. Obviously, in the text it's *8*, so therefore –.'

'We can start by assuming it represents the most frequent in French, which is *e.*'

'So the *8* is *e.*'

He took his pen and tore several pages out of his notebook.

'It's preceded by the sign *0*, which is presumably l, assuming the text starts with the definite article *le*. So we have: *8* = *e* and *0* = *l*. Now, what are the next most frequent characters in French....'

They worked enthusiastically for several minutes, taking it in turns to guess and to write down the next discovery. It was Lippi's turn to write and, as he was about to do so, his hand froze in mid-air. A whirlwind of colours and perfume, accompanied by the clicking of high heels, descended the steps to the bar and hastened towards them.

'What does this mean?' asked a familiar soft voice, slightly breathless. 'I've been waiting for you for over an hour, Pierre! And you're not even dressed for dinner!'

Lippi stood up to greet her.

'I'm sorry, dear lady, it was I who detained your husband.'

'Really?' she sighed. 'Then you're no more reasonable than he is.'

She was wearing a short silk dress with a birds-of-paradise motif which showed her legs and the firm roundness of her shoulders to good effect. The indirect lighting of the bar created golden reflections in her hair and her grey-green eyes under dark brows regarded her husband with an air of exasperation that made her even more charming.

'You look even more irresistible tonight in that dress, my little lady,' purred the Italian, offering her a chair, 'Schiaparelli?'

'Oh, it's just a little thing I found in one of those quaint boutiques in Lausanne. But, since I didn't pay very much for it, I was afraid it might be a copy,' she lied, removing her gloves with a studied nonchalance.

Her gaze fell on the papers scattered on the table and she frowned daintily.

'What are you two up to?'

With studied deference, Lippi took great pains to explain exactly what had happened. In spite of himself, Pierre was impressed. He watched his wife's reaction. As usual, her emotions could be read clearly on her face, expressing in the present case a growing enthusiasm.

'It's really exciting!' she exclaimed, blushing with pleasure. 'How clever you are, you men. Can I help?'

'If we don't go in right away, the dining room will be closed,' Pierre pointed out with a feigned earnestness.

She gave him a black look.

'I'm not going in there with you dressed like that,' she said firmly. 'We'll stay here and order some sandwiches. Foie gras and salmon, if possible. And I'll have a cocktail as well. What's that you're drinking? *Turn of the Screw*? What a stupid name! Why not Monkey Wrench or Screwdriver?'

***

Two and a half hours, eight sandwiches and as many Turns of the Screw later, they finally produced a translation of the complete text, which Lippi read out with a rather unsteady delivery:

"The undead in the naos of the thaumaturge where he who united the calvary with Saint Gudule's flower crossed the dried-up Acheron through the door of the exhausted nymph at one hundred and twenty feet in a bee-line from the Bengalese pavilion."

Pierre yawned.

'Well, that didn't get us very far,' he said. 'How can you make any sense of this gibberish? St. Gudule, exhausted nymphs, Bengali pavilions and the like?'

'I confess to being totally in the dark,' replied Lippi. 'I propose we get some sleep and tackle the problem afresh tomorrow morning, with a clear head.'

Solange stamped her foot.

'No! We're not going to give up now, just when we're getting somewhere. Besides, I'm not tired. We have to continue.'

'Don't be childish, Solange.'

'"Don't be childish, Solange",' she simpered, mimicking her husband. 'I'd like to tear your heart out when you talk to me like that.'

'You've had a little too much to drink, darling. You don't know what you're saying.'

'Do you think so? I wouldn't be so sure. You never take me seriously. You think I'm stupid; you constantly treat me like a child, no matter what I say or do. I get so beside myself I really want to kill you!'

'Solange. Listen to me....'

Their voices had gone up a notch in the deserted bar. In the distance, beyond the terrace windows and with a backdrop of grey mist, the necklace of streetlights could be seen as it followed the curve of the quay. The headlights of the occasional car glided silently around the invisible lake.

Lippi gave a discreet cough.

'First of all, my little lady, I don't think –.'

'You're annoying as well! Always calling me *little lady*. I have a name, for heaven's sake.'

'Well then... little Solange... I don't think your husband finds you stupid.'

'No?'

'No. He never misses a chance to tell me how lucky he is to have such an intelligent wife. What's more, we've been three hours working on this document and now we've come to a dead end. If you have any suggestions as to how to proceed, we would be most grateful for them.'

'Really?'

'Really.'

'Well, it just so happens I have one!' Solange announced triumphantly. 'I'll tell you what we're going to do: we're going

151

upstairs to see someone who'll be able to solve it just like that!' she said, snapping her fingers. 'Uncle Arthur!'

'Uncle Arthur?'

'She means Sir Arthur Carter Gilbert,' sighed Pierre. He took her hand, which she pulled away. 'Really, darling, you must be joking: it's after eleven o'clock.'

'You can just be quiet!'

So saying, she gathered her gloves and handbag and stood up.

'Whoever loves me follows me. Let's go!'

***

They walked along a dimly lit corridor, the thick carpet muffling the sound of their steps. Not a sound came from behind the well-polished doors of the bedrooms whose occupants – they go to bed early in Switzerland – were sleeping the sleep of the just. The halls and corridors of the old palace reeked of old-fashioned virtue and respectability. Nothing had changed. On the walls, above the panelling, incredibly melancholic paintings from the Belle Epoque depicted men in morning coats and women in bustle gowns walking along the side of the lake or taking tea in the winter garden. They reminded Pierre of a past that he had never known; a carefree past, full of peace and happiness, that made him only too aware of the dreadful times in which he was living.

Sir Arthur's room was right at the end of the corridor. It overlooked the back of the hotel and, more precisely, the ramp to the funicular. With stubborn insistence he had refused all suggestions to take a suite with a lake view – "the sublime stops me thinking," he had declared bluntly. On the door knob hung a handwritten sign with the badly-printed words "PLEASE DO NOT DISTURB!!!" followed by the solemn warning in huge letters: "I'M BUSY. NO ENTRY."

Solange turned the knob and walked in.

The great man was slumped in a bed covered in sheets of notepaper, his back supported by three pillows and his head leaning on his chest. The light from a tulip lamp reflected from a bald dome fringed by dishevelled tufts. His *pince-nez* were askew on the end of his nose. He was wearing a Chinese dressing-gown embroidered with dragons and everyone could see he was wearing red socks.

'Hello, Uncle Arthur,' the young woman called out as she walked further into the room. I just came to say goodnight.'

'Go away!' he growled, with an angry gesture. 'Clear off! Can't you see I'm working?'

A cheap French romantic novel fell from his knees to the ground.

'It's me, Uncle Arthur,' repeated Solange, taking another step forward. He shaded his eyes and peered into the darkness.

'Ah! It's you, my dear,' he said in a gentler tone. 'How on earth did you get in?'

'You never turn the key in the door, uncle.'

'Because I don't want to be killed in a locked room. Who would solve the problem if I were gone?'

'Please excuse us, sir,' said Pierre. 'We didn't know you were sleeping.'

'Who's there? Well, who is it? Ah! It's you, Garnier. I wasn't sleeping, damn you. I was thinking. If you'd leave me alone, maybe I'd have something to tell you tomorrow morning.'

He peered into the gloom once more.

'Is there someone with you? Haven't you read the sign? I'm busy. Busy. Keep out!'

Lippi emerged into the light.

'Allow me to introduce myself, Maestro. I'm Professor Lippi from Bologna.'

'Professor, indeed. Are you here to teach me how to write detective stories? Something none of your compatriots has been able to do, as far as I know.'

'I am one of your most fervent admirers. You may have read my study of –.'

'I never read, my friend. And above all, books about me. To my mind there are only two authors of any merit: Charles Dickens and Zénaïde Fleuriot. Well, since you're here, you'd better sit down. Sit yourself here, my dear,' he said in a less forbidding tone and patting the bedcover next to him. 'Well, what the devil are you waiting for? I hope for your sakes that you're not here just to bother me. You'd better have a really good reason, or else….'

'The thing is, Sir Arthur,' began Pierre after exchanging looks with Lippi, we're here because of a most serious problem –.'

'Hold on!' ordered the great man, raising a hand for silence. 'Not yet. Just a second… I should have a few cigars left. Oh! There they are, my dear.'

153

It was their ritual. Solange went through the motions of selecting one, rolling it next to her ear, striking a match and lighting it slowly, despite Lippi who was seething with impatience. She held it out to the old man. He took a noisy pull, exhaled a cloud of acrid and nauseating smoke and fell back on his pillows. An air of peace and contentment spread over him. He looked just like an Indian elder smoking a peace pipe, prior to bringing forth a pearl of wisdom.

Pierre coughed. Lippi and he proceeded to recount their story.

'Hell's Bells!' said Carter Gilbert, blinking. 'That's very interesting. It could be highly significant or not. We'll have to see. I don't want to jump to conclusions without having examined it thoroughly, but it could be the missing piece of the puzzle. I can't say just yet.'

Pierre took the papers out of his pocket and handed them over. Carter Gilbert took a quick look at the original message, then handed it back, keeping only the translation. He studied it for a minute of two, then let it fall on to his knees. He picked up his *pince-nez*, placed them on the piece of paper, crossed his hands over his stomach and closed his eyes.

'Are you sleeping, sir?' asked Pierre, hesitantly.

The old man blinked and peered about myopically.

'Ah! It's you, Garnier,' he replied. 'I wasn't sleeping, I was cogitating, sir. If you did the same instead of bothering me, you'd no doubt find the answer to this infantile puzzle.'

He went back to his cogitation and reached out for his cigar, which had gone out. Automatically, Lippi struck a match and leant over to offer him a light, but he waved the professor away.

'But before I provide it, it's best to clarify the story a little. We mustn't forget that we're dealing with a man who, throughout his entire life, had engaged in manipulation and who, according to all the evidence, had prepared this senseless joke in the pursuit of rational goals. I'm summarising what you've told me and I'll tell you what I think about it: on Sunday morning, before boarding the boat, Hoenig sends a letter by courier to the Grand Hotel. That way, he can be absolutely certain that our friend Garnier will find it on his return. He knows he's dealing with a Poe expert who is certain to decipher it. But not straight away, obviously. At the time, the recipient will believe it to be a joke or a hoax and not rack his brains to find the answer to the riddle. It won't be until the next day, when he will learn the double

154

news of the murder and of the disappearance of the body, that he'll make the connection between those mysterious events and the secret message. So, what will he do? He'll get to work and translate the message immediately. After which, he'll communicate the results to the police, which will lead them to find what they're supposed to find at the precise time and place the plan calls for. That's how it was supposed to happen. But things didn't quite work out that way.'

He sighed, eyes half-closed in contemplation of the cigar that he hadn't got the courage to light again, and allowed himself to fall back against the pillows with his arms crossed.

'Are you trying to say, Maestro, that Hoenig hid his killer's name in the message?' said Lippi in a voice so soft it was almost a whisper.

'What on earth are you thinking, Professor? That the victim knew ahead of time that he was going to be stabbed and by whom? Well, I'm going to surprise you: in point of fact, you're not very far from the truth. Indeed, one might say you were burning. But to go from there to believing that Hoenig would write down the name of his murderer and arrange for it to be known only after his death... Rubbish! You're breaking all the rules of detective fiction by pulling a hitherto unknown clue out of a hat, and one which just happens to contain the key to the whole business. No, I won't have it. Whoever perpetrated this crime constructed it like a *good* detective novel. But something didn't work as planned. It's as simple as that. Does anyone have a match? ... Thank you.'

Above the flame reflected in the mirrors of the room, the old man's eyes looked at each one of them in turn. He seemed amused, although his face expressed a determined concentration.

'I hope you realise, Uncle Arthur, that they don't understand a word of what you've been saying,' observed Solange gently.

'I can't tell them any more, my pretty, not yet. It'll have to wait until tomorrow morning. I have a vague picture of the whole business in my head, but I won't be able to explain anything until I've checked out all the pieces to see precisely how they fit.' He took the piece of paper from his knees and waved it in their direction. 'What you did was very good. It answered the only question left open.'

'Thank you,' replied Lippi, who was beginning to get back his confidence. 'Perhaps you might care to explain what it means.'

'Well, that's what I'll do,' declared the old man, in the tone of someone who has decided to share a confidence. 'That way, you won't have disturbed me for nothing. Although, with a little thought, you could have saved yourself the trouble.'

He took off his *pince-nez*, rubbed the bridge of his nose, and put them back.

'Let's see,' he began. 'In your view, what's the meaning of *undead*?'

'I've never heard that expression,' replied Pierre. Most people say "phantom" or "spectre" or even "vampire" but nobody says "undead."'

'Well then, you haven't read my novel *The Case of the Undead Corpse* which, for once the French publisher has translated intelligently as *L'Affaire du cadavre vivant*. In the present case, the good doctor – for it refers to Hoenig himself – simply wanted to inform you that he was still alive. It's so obvious that there was no chance you would get it. Next: what is a *naos*? The professor will tell us.'

'I seem to remember it's the hidden part of the temple, the part closest to God, to which only the high priest has access.'

'Perfect. I won't insult you by asking what is a *thaumaturge*.'

'A man who performs miracles,' said Pierre.

'A magician, a sort of sorcerer,' added Lippi. 'It can only mean….'

Pierre clapped his hand to his head:

'The Sorcerer's Grotto! Of course!'

'I didn't need to tell you. The rest is exceedingly simple. The word *calvary* is evidently used in the sense of….'

'I think I'm beginning to get the hang of it. It's a synecdoche!' exclaimed the Italian.

'It's more of a metonymy,' Pierre offered timidly.

Solange rolled her eyes.

'How stupid you both are! It's simply a cross.'

'Bravo, my dear. As for *Saint Gudule's flower*, even though I know nothing about the good lady, I presume it means the rose and he who united it with the cross was none other than the famous Rosenkreutz, i.e. rose plus cross.

'After that discovery, the rest is plain sailing. Acheron is the river of the Underworld, so *crossed the dried-up Acheron* must refer to the Sorcerer's escape from the grotto using the underground aqueduct, and I'm guessing that the *door of the exhausted nymph* is the dried-up fountain he used to get out.'

Pierre nodded.

'That's correct. Also, in Latin – you can check this with Lippi –

nymph can also mean fountain.'

'I thought as much. So, to summarise: the message is simple, ingenious, and at the same time, explicit. And the gist of it is: Hoenig is alive and well and can be found in the Sorcerer's Grotto, from which Rosenkreutz escaped by using the dried-up aqueduct that leads to the fountain located one hundred and twenty feet in a beeline – a straight line – from the Bengali pavilion, in other words the bungalow.

'And now that you've got what you came for, go, all of you. Get out and leave me alone.'

Far away, somewhere in the town, a clock struck midnight.

'That's all well and good, Maestro,' said Lippi firmly, 'but it doesn't get us anywhere. A host of problems still remain, for example –.'

Solange made a sign for him to be quiet. The old man had closed his eyes. He remained perfectly still, but for the regular rise and fall of his chest.

'OK, you two, out you go,' she hissed forcefully.

She held the door open and was the last to leave. Pierre could have sworn that, at the last moment, just as she was closing the door, the old man winked at her.

157

IX

There was another storm that night. Even though they had gone to bed at one o'clock, Pierre couldn't sleep. For almost the whole night the thunder had rumbled, the rain had beaten down on the windows and the wind had made a loud racket all around the hotel. For her part, Solange had had a troubled sleep. At two thirty in the morning, as she was mumbling words in an incessant stream, he thought for a moment about waking her. He himself dropped off around three o'clock and only woke when the maid brought in the breakfast.

He couldn't take any more. He would have liked to be able to forget all the unknown quantities of this affair, even the ridiculous story of the coded letter. A puzzle in the style of Poe, what nonsense! Even from the hereafter, Hoenig continued to mock him. But he couldn't get the riddles out of his mind. Every time a new fact was uncovered, the mystery deepened. Instead of bringing enlightenment, everything kept getting more and more complex in this frightening brain-teaser.

Sitting up in bed, as the clarity of the electric light met the greyness of the early day, he read the morning newspaper and tried to convince himself that the events were real. It all appeared so incredible now, sitting this mundane environment where one could see the teapot, the toast, the butter and the little pots of jam placed carefully on the tray, or hear the water running in the bathtub, sounds of doors and footsteps, happy conversations and all the peaceful and confused background noises of a hotel waking up.

Under the headline: GREAT HOPE FOR PEACE, the news of the start of the Munich conference covered the front page, together with photographs of the four attendees. The photos seemed to have been selected from the archives of some morgue. Pierre recognised one of the four faces as Hitler, whose deceitful and murderous appearance belied the optimism of the title. Chamberlain looked inane and Daladier's smile was more like a grimace. Mussolini appeared in full regalia, his chin imprudently in the air as he descended a monumental staircase.

Arthur Carter Gilbert's discourse was, more modestly, announced in the local news pages. Would the great writer be able to shed light on the mystery of Monte Verita? asked the journalist. His coverage of the affair was reasonably accurate, even though it put rather too much emphasis on the supernatural aspects and failed to mention any suspicions attaching to the attendees at the symposium that had just ended.

Pierre had finished his breakfast, and was anxiously imagining what Carter Gilbert was going to say, when his wife came out of the bathroom. She was wrapped in a flannel bathrobe and her hair was swept up under a knotted towel. Her face was smooth and her skin was fresh but her eyes appeared swollen. The scent of *eau-de-toilette* permeated the room.

'You're not up yet?' she said sitting down in front of the dressing-table. 'Hurry up, or you're going to be late.'

'So you're not coming with me?' he asked, knowing the response. 'What are you going to do?'

'I'm going to the clinic. Freyja Hoenig gets out today. She's going to be all alone. I imagine Strahler will be at the lecture.'

'And afterwards?'

He looked at her reflection in the mirror. Her eyes seemed unusually wide as she applied mascara to the lashes, an operation that seemed to require all her attention.

'Afterwards, I'm coming back to pack our bags. You can take the car. Come straight back here after the lecture and we'll leave at once. We'll stop for lunch on the way.' She turned round. 'You can't imagine how happy I am that this nightmare is over. What about you?'

'I'll tell you at the end.'

'Come here,' she said. She put her cheek against his hip as she looked up at him in the mirror.

'Don't worry, darling. Uncle Arthur will fix everything. He'll explain the role I had to play. I don't know why I couldn't bring myself to tell you,' she murmured, pressing herself more firmly against her husband. 'Sometimes it seems too ridiculous; at other times it's too frightening. Anyway, I don't know what's behind it all. Someone killed this odious man and I know it wasn't me.'

He leant down and kissed her on the forehead.

'Don't think about it any more, darling, there's no point in even

160

talking about it.'

'But I do want to talk about it, because I'm the cause of all this evil. You see....'

She stopped herself and changed the subject, while mechanically applying her lipstick.

'You know, Pierre, the happiness I feel right now will be nothing compared to how I shall feel once there's an explanation of this whole dreadful business.'

***

A light drizzle fell upon the Albergo in the wan light of a grey sky. It was a chilly morning, so much so that many were wearing coats and scarves and those waiting outside the room were walking up and down as they talked, to warm themselves up. The rain from the previous night had washed the terrace clean. Water dripped from cherry-laurels and spindle trees and slid with each gust of wind off the hanging leaves of the palm trees. The damp smell of autumn rose from the clumps of trees in the park. Down below, mist hung over the lake. People were leaving the building already. Suitcases were stacked up in the hallways. There was a general atmosphere of melancholy and departure.

Pierre tried to calm himself by thinking about the weather. It would be better in Italy, he told himself, once they'd crossed the border. He moved towards a group dominated by Lippi's tall silhouette. The only ones with him were Prokosch, Mestre and a handful of disinterested onlookers. Mestre told him Harvey had left on the first train out that morning without taking the time to say goodbye.

Pierre felt like running away. He didn't care about the dénouement of this senseless business and he wasn't even surprised at his own lack of curiosity. He prepared some brief words of departure: "I shan't stay for the lecture. I just came to say farewell. We have to leave right away in order to be in Venice by nightfall." But his scrupulous nature rebelled subconsciously against the feeling of cowardice he would experience afterwards. What would he say to Solange? What would she think of him?

Talking about anything at all; fretting about the delayed start of the lecture: it was still putting off the moment of truth. And so he stayed.

'Terrible weather.'

'Terrible weather.'

'Musn't complain. It's been a pretty good week.'

'When are you leaving?'

'Today.'

'I leave tomorrow,' said Mestre. 'We'll keep in touch, OK?'

The siren of a police car coming up the ramp became louder. Brenner appeared at the door of the bar. He looked upset. Despite the cold, he wore his rumpled summer suit and a rather loud tie. It was obvious from his face that he hadn't slept for twenty-four hours. He squinted in the direction of the parking space where a fat policeman was emerging from behind a clump of laurels kepi in hand.

'Where is Sir Arthur?' barked Brenner. 'What's happening, for goodness' sake?'

His manner changed dramatically when he addressed subordinates.

'He's coming, Superintendent. He was sleeping like a log and we had the devil of a job waking him up. He's furious, sir,' he added, wiping his brow.

The old man emerged, accompanied by two more policemen. Their very size made him look even smaller. An overcoat several sizes too large from him, and obviously borrowed, flapped about his fragile frame. His *pince-nez* were askew and the tufts of hair stood up on either side of his great bald head. He was fuming. He walked straight up to Brenner with a menacing look on his face, spluttering about attacks on individual liberty and Gestapo-like methods.

The Superintendent ignored the remarks and saluted him courteously. The he turned to the first policeman.

'What about Strahler? Have you found him? We can't start without him.'

Strahler had not been in the hotel the previous night and Brenner, convinced he would be found at the clinic, had dispatched the man there.

The policeman stood to attention.

'Impossible, sir.'

There was something in his voice which caused everyone to look up.

'What's impossible?' Brenner asked acidly.

The officer leant forward and his voice took on a despondent tone.

'To find Stahler, sir. He's left, Superintendent. He's gone away with the Hoenig woman. They've packed their bags. They've gone.'

162

***

Sir Arthur Carter Gilbert's discourse and the debates that followed it were reported in the official minutes of the symposium. But the academic style employed could not capture the truly remarkable spectacle the great man offered his audience, nor the indelible impression of a formidable intellect at work behind the vast bald forehead and the expressive little eyes twinkling behind the *pince-nez* perched on the end of the long nose. The man who had invented and solved nearly fifty criminal puzzles, who had shaken up the world of mystery fiction with his theory of impossible crimes, was there seated on the stage, as calm and immutable as the lord of heaven and earth on judgment day; or, rather, like an antique soothsayer about to pronounce upon the flight patterns of birds or the entrails of a slaughtered sheep.

The old man was there, gracefully holding his *pince-nez* in one hand while gesticulating with the other to lend force to his demonstration. Due to his elevated position, it was possible to see, under the table, that his trousers were too short and his red socks were twisted, a fact which would not have drawn so much attention if they had been worn by other ankles but which – illustrated by magazines and the jeers of the street urchins – filled the spectators with an almost religious respect. Before him sat every detective in the canton, the entire local press, a considerable number of dignitaries and noted academics, and those few foreigners that had decided to stay following the interruption of the symposium – the rest, having opted to go home instead, cursed themselves for it for the rest of their existence.

'In the course of my numerous – too numerous – conferences,' Sir Arthur began nonchalantly, 'I have noticed that the public prefers the particular to the general and the concrete to the abstract. I was proposing, therefore – initially at least – to keep to the material aspects of the affair all you reasonable people have come here about, and to limit myself to the discussion and resolution of a crime which, for once, did not spring from the busy typewriters of Dorothy Sayers or Agatha Christie.'

He looked around the audience with his little twinkling eyes, eliciting the occasional smile or growl of approval and then, to the surprise of all, banged his fist on the table.

'I WAS WRONG!' he exclaimed, in a voice which set off echoes all round the hall. 'I was wrong because you see, good people, the big problem with this story of locked doors and walking corpses is that

163

there is no material evidence to base it on. As I believe has been said between these very walls, nobody planning a criminal enterprise would, under normal circumstances, dream of employing such ridiculously complicated methods. Unfortunately, in the present case, it turns out that's exactly what he did. We're dealing with someone who, by all the evidence, created an irrational situation in the pursuit of rational ends. Once seen from that point of view, everything becomes logical. BUT BEWARE! The logic in question does not follow the rules of real life. That's why it seemed to me from the moment I became involved in this affair – and I already made this clear to several among you – that someone must have prepared a plan that caused events to occur according to the rules of detective fiction. That is to say the routine steps of police investigations – material clues, fingerprints, infinitesimal particles of ash collected by the likes of the maniacal Sherlock Holmes which could only have come from a particular cigar shop in Valparaiso that only has a single client – seem to be solecisms, completely out of place here. We must thus limit ourselves to the discussion and abstract resolution of an intellectual problem, a million miles from the sordid reality of everyday life.

'This matter, you see, doesn't fall in the category of realist but of intellectual, implying intelligence and not just imagination: what we call the detective story. I'm not talking about those slices of life, seasoned with violence and other obscene spices, that American readers habitually consume these days. Nor the French version, which suffers from anarchy and vulgarity, as practised by Gaboriau, Leblanc and Leroux and the Belgians Steeman and Simenon, men of letters who can be readily forgotten.' There were several disapproving coughs from the audience and even one voice crying "No!" Carter Gilbert raised a conciliatory hand. 'I exclude, however, the delectable *Mystery of the Yellow Room*, whose excellent argument has survived even its frightful editing,' he added, to considerable applause.

'No, I'm talking about those gentle novels where the action takes place between civilized people and which have perfected the suppression of human life in a peaceful English village, on a Cunard ocean liner, or in the most respectable boarding houses in Brighton. Crime there is civilized and avoids bloodshed. There, all is logic and reason, good manners and cups of tea. Let us be thankful for that kind of detective story: like a modern-day version of the epics of chivalry, it has managed, in these troubled times, to uphold the classic virtues. It is

164

maintaining order in a time of universal disorder.'

There were several bursts of applause and even some shouts of agreement. Carter Gilbert silenced them by modestly raising both hands. Then he continued:

'I shall now speak on the subject of –.'

'Could the speaker please get to the point,' asked a voice, with exaggerated politeness.

'I shall now speak,' continued Carter Gilbert smoothly, 'on the subject of a fundamental problem in this kind of fiction, that of a body in a locked room which nobody has left – .'

One of the symposium organisers, seated on the front row, raised his hand.

'Forgive the interruption, Sir Arthur, 'but that point was the subject of an earlier paper by Professor Lippi.'

'I know, my friend: I've studied the transcript. I merely wanted to add a modest codicil to that scintillating lecture, that I borrow in all humility from the impeccable De Quincey: understand that to have discovered a problem is not less admirable – and, I might add, is more ingenious – than to have found a solution. As everyone here knows, Edgar Allan Poe invented the detective story. In The Murders in the Rue Morgue he posed a formidable problem, but the solution he proposed – and here I beg young Garnier's pardon ....'

Adjusting his *pince-nez*, he found Pierre sitting between Mestre and Lippi, and made a gruesome grimace in his direction which was obviously intended as a welcoming smile.

'As I was saying, the solution he proposed is far from the best possible. It requires obtuse investigators, a window with a broken nail and an anthropomorphic ape. I myself have written innumerable locked room stories. I've used asphyxiating gas introduced through a keyhole, a dagger shot from a rifle, an Indonesian arrow dipped in molasses and cyanide, a pistol attached to a piece of elastic that fires bullets made from rock salt, an electrified chessboard and so on. I even read one the other day that should make you laugh. The murderer, finding himself in a house surrounded by six inches of snow, escaped by clinging on to the string of a kite. I ask you, the string of a kite?'

'Where's he headed with all this?' whispered Lippi in Pierre's ear.

'All that is by way of explaining,' continued Carter Gilbert, as if he'd heard Lippi's question, 'that the most satisfying solutions are also the most simple. So simple, in fact, that they appear evident. And so evident that nobody dares think of them! So Professor Lippi, pre-occupied in his lecture with listing the most weird and complicated methods, overlooked the clearest and simplest. I assume it was negligence, for I cannot imagine anyone deliberately ignoring a model of the genre, an elemental solution of exquisite simplicity, invented in 1892 by my compatriot Israel Zangwill in his novella *The Big Bow Mystery*. It is simple, it is convenient, it is easy to put into practice and it should have pointed you in the right direction....'

'I confess my ignorance,' said Mestre in a low voice. 'What solution is he talking about?'

'Shhh!' said Pierre. 'I'm trying to remember.'

Lippi, who had been drumming his fingers on his trouser leg for several moments, stood up.

'Good grief, Maestro, you've just said the contrary. Let me see, how did you put it exactly? Yes: you said that in this business the murderer had used ridiculously complicated methods.'

'You haven't been paying attention,' replied Carter Gilbert irritably. He detested being interrupted. 'It's true I did speak about insanely complicated arrangements. But I never said it was the murderer who had done the arranging. I stressed the fact, as I recall, that *someone* had prepared a plan according to the rules of detective fiction. Someone very clever, I must admit. The staging of a murder in a lighted room, with two witnesses who were *expected* to be there, already reeked of trickery. But when the woman with the knife vanishes, and the corpse disappears from a double-locked room, and on top of all that there's a cock-and-bull story about the living dead and a bewitched grotto that's only been put in for show... all that is too studied, too staged, too mysterious. The spectacle had been slowly and carefully prepared in order to make you all lose your wits, up until the precise moment, chosen by the author, when the skein would have been untangled and all the threads laid out bare in the blink of an eye for all to see.'

His bulging, myopic eyes scanned the auditorium. With the thick lenses, he looked like an owl.

'And as for you, devotees of unsolvable riddles and inextricable mazes, and you, professionals trained in scientific investigation and tough interrogation....'

His gaze lingered on the police officers grouped together at the rear of the hall as he continued:

166

'You allowed yourselves to be mystified and you fell for it hook, line and sinker. Yes, gentlemen of the police, trained as you are to answer an unglamorous calling in the parishes of sordid crime and mundane news items, it pains me to say that, under the disastrous influence of the lovers of puzzles, riddles and brain-teasers, you allowed yourselves to be hoodwinked as well. You accepted without question the myth of the impossible crime, the only miracle that a prosaic mind gifted with sound common sense will accept as a challenge.'

He raised his hooded eyelids as if expecting a protest. But, seeing Brenner imposing silence on his men with the wave of a hand, he continued:

'You see, the real problem was to find out who had committed the crime and why, not to try and guess how it was done. Your efforts to explain the puzzle only impeded its solution. As for the rest of you, the disciples of Edgar Allan Poe,' he went on, turning to Pierre and his colleagues, 'you should have remembered the detective story is a mystery novel, strange in appearance but simple in concept. Because the most important element in a mystery is that the secret be simple. The ingenuity of the construction has as its sole objective the concealment of the truth. So, good folk, do you know what my reaction was when I plunged into the witness' depositions? I said to myself: "Don't bother with the set-up, old chap. Focus on the crux of the matter and forget about all the wild goose chases." And I say the same thing to you: "Get to the heart of the problem and forget all the tall stories."'

'No!' declared Lippi categorically. 'It's just a bit too easy... We were all prepared to hear you out to the end. But you're restricting yourself to theoretical considerations that we all know by heart. I've elected myself spokesman of those whom you have chosen to denigrate: we're getting a stronger and stronger impression that this whole business is actually beyond you, that it's outside your area of competence and that it was stupid on our part to think you'd be able to crack it.'

The old gentleman locked eyes with him and literally began to swell with anger.

'He's joking, Sir Arthur,' Pierre called out, without waiting for the first rumblings of the storm. 'You stressed the fact that someone prepared a plan along the lines of a detective story....'

The response was a growl.

167

'I did indeed.'

'But maybe you don't know who prepared the plan?'

'What!' roared Carter Gilbert, eyes flashing. 'Would you care to make a bet?'

At last Sir Arthur was penned in. All that remained was to give him his head. His anger subsided like an overcooked soufflé and he stretched out in his chair, hands across his waistcoat and thumbs twiddling. His little eyes surveyed the audience once more. He seemed amused, even though there was a wrathful expression on his face. Suddenly his eyes half closed.

'Well, then, I'll tell you,' he said, as if he'd decided to impart a confidence. 'I haven't said anything so far because I naively assumed you'd all guessed. It was Dr. Karl Hoenig.'

Lippi fell back on his chair, mouth open. A hubbub arose in the auditorium, punctuated by exclamations of astonishment. The Swiss, usually slow to show emotion, were visibly agitated. Only Brenner managed to keep calm. He adopted an expression of ironic amusement and forced himself to adopt the tone of one intent on being reasonable:

'If I understand correctly, Sir Arthur, you're saying that Hoenig was responsible for organising a stage production down to the last detail, in such a way that he could be peacefully murdered?'

'That's perfectly correct, Superintendent,' replied Carter Gilbert in the same reasonable manner. 'Except for the small detail that the good doctor did not intend to be murdered. The killer simple took advantage of a situation handed to him on a plate.'

'And do you also claim that, once murdered, he locked himself in the bungalow?'

'Precisely. If he hadn't been double-locked inside, how could he have proved to the world that someone else had succeeded in doing...what he was planning to do himself?'

'And what exactly was he planning to do?' asked the Superintendent, whose calm façade was starting to crack, in an unnaturally calm voice.

Laboriously, Carter Gilbert pushed his chair back and put his feet up on the table. He looked defiantly at the "No Smoking" sign on the wall and extracted a cigar from his pocket which he proceeded to light with a match he struck against his heel. The cigar went out almost at once, but he continued to draw on it as if he hadn't noticed. Outside the hall, the rain had started to come down again. It lashed the windows of the auditorium.

The dark and sparse foliage of the trees moved with an eerie slowness against the background of grey fog. Someone went to turn on a switch and Sir Arthur waited until the light came on before he continued.

'I think it's high time to clear up this mystery. It started right here, in this very hall: this peaceful place where, exactly one week ago, the learned Professor Lippi of Bologna – a fine dialectician – gave a lecture. I have the minutes in front of me, and for those of you who were not present I shall briefly give the gist of it. The professor held forth on the subject of inoffensive crimes imagined by an elite and conceived with sophistication, by which we – busy bees and delicate tasters – all make our honey. My own master, the noble Gilbert Keith Chesterton, to whom I humbly tip my hat, caused his Father Brown – a man of God able to reconcile miracles with logic, and the most brilliant detective in the history of detective fiction – to say: "A crime is a work of art," and "The criminal is an artist; the detective is only a critic." You're free to smile, take offence, or simply marvel at the paradox. Professor Lippi took it as his own and embellished it with all the facets of his scholastic talent.

'Here, in a few words, is Professor Lippi's thesis: he puts forward the notion that the detective story, considered as a work of art, is not an imitative art. He rejects the burden of reality and only ever expresses his own point of view. In this bizarre world where crime disguises itself as fiction, real objects lose their natural function so as to play the role of accessories in the service of the illusionist, the manufacturer of false miracles that is the creator of the detective fiction in question. In the ingenuity of the concept as much as in the strangeness of the form, plausibility is deliberately sacrificed to aesthetics. The probable is no longer what it has every right to be considered as: the surest guarantor of fiction. Instead, the reader, manipulated and mystified, is led to reject it out of love of the improbable. He only has eyes for lies, optical effects and illusions.'

Sir Arthur struck another match. But the phosphor broke off and fell out of reach. He gave up lighting his cigar and let his eye wander around the hall. His gaze fell on Lippi who was looking at him thunderstruck, for he could not remember having said all that, and so well. Sir Arthur frowned and asked him in a loud and treacherous voice:

'I hope I construed your ideas correctly, Professor?'

In response to a jab in the ribs from from Pierre, the Italian leapt to his feet and responded with a mumbled sound that Sir Arthur chose to take as approval. He took from his pocket a large handkerchief covered in red squares the colour of his socks, and proceeded to blow his nose forcefully. He continued:

'And then you changed your tone. You couldn't help amusing yourself at the expense of detective fiction. You caricatured the clichés and the norms. Sacrilege! You dissected impossible situations under the rubric of "hermetically sealed rooms" and you mocked the hocus-pocus, the bizarre techniques and the far-fetched solutions that authors such as I have produced in abundance in our works. You asserted vigorously that "This kind of thing can't happen in real life."

'All that for what? So as to affirm that those who try to extend the field of detective fiction into the everyday world are victims of a complete and total aberration?'

'Exactly,' exclaimed Lippi, folding his arms. 'That's precisely what I think.'

'And I'm not too far away from your way of thinking,' said Carter Gilbert approvingly, an expression of benevolent understanding on his face. 'We have never pretended, I and my colleagues, that our little inventions, our clever tricks, our shady schemes, would find a place in real life crime. Nevertheless, something's bothering me.'

He lowered his large head on to his chest, tapped his forehead with the tips of his fingers, and looked up abruptly.

'Tell me, my boy,' he asked as if making a Herculean effort to remember, 'aren't you the same Umberto Lippi from Bologna who has put forward in numerous intellectual publications the idea – borrowed, between ourselves, from that rascal Oscar Wilde – that literature serves as a model for life and makes it in its image?' He pointed an accusing finger. 'Haven't you written that life imitates fiction far more than fiction imitates it: that the copy is the reflection? And that one can interpret it in light of the rules and conventions that govern narrative speech?'

Lippi tried to stand up, but he was not given the chance.

'Stay where you are, sir. I have the floor. I'm not going to be dragged into a byzantine argument. Paradoxes are extremely dangerous things. They are reversible by their very nature and one can prove anything from them.' His expression softened and a conciliatory smile appeared on his face. 'Don't get me wrong, my friend. I'm not trying to beat you into submission. I'm simply trying to show that those who listen to you can only be befuddled by the apparent discrepancies in your discursive thought; and that the good Dr. Hoenig, who was lying in wait during your lecture for the slightest error in reasoning, jumped in with both feet.'

He leant forward and wagged a finger at the audience at large:

'Don't think that Dr. Hoenig could have believed for a second that there was a single case in the annals of crime that could be tied to a locked room problem. Because, for heaven's sake, such a thing doesn't exist. And he made the claim for the sole purpose of contradicting you, confident that the strength of his reputation would suffice to hide the lie. It's the kind of shameless bluff practised by his master, Adolf Hitler. But it failed in this instance because his adversary wouldn't back down. The professor challenged him to provide proof of his claim. The good doctor collapsed like a pricked balloon and our friend rubbed it in by ridiculing him and denying him any means of escape. Which, let me tell you, isn't a wise thing to do when faced with someone so unquestionably evil.

'It was intolerable for that runt claiming to be a member of the master race to be publicly humiliated in that way. He marched off, his face red as a beetroot from anger and shame, only too aware that he had provided a free spectacle for the crowd of intellectuals and academic pedants he despised so much. He was going to show them how a genius of crime could introduce the famous problem of the locked room into a real-life situation, setting all those great minds to work in search of the solution. If everything had turned out as planned, he would have extracted a spectacular revenge, which was his intention.

'Now, for it to work he needed an accomplice. I should say two, for it was the second one who betrayed him. But more of that later. Once you grasp the essential thread of this affair – in this case the fact that Karl Hoenig needed someone to play the lead role in the play he was planning to stage – everything else follows. You see, good people, I saw straight away that the whole story was a fabrication. I could make out the main thread of Hoenig's plan: a feigned attack on him by his accomplice. But who would be mad enough to accept a role in this farce unless they were obliged to? He needed someone he could hold in his power, an innocent puppet dancing at the end of a string without asking too many questions about what was going on around him.

'Luckily for him, but unfortunately for us, the good doctor stumbled upon the ideal accomplice, someone who would fulfil all the necessary conditions better than anyone else: a woman whose name I shall withhold for now. Some of you know her and some of you have spoken to her, and she has been unjustly suspected. If truth be told, she is the real victim of this sinister plot. And, listen to me the rest of you....' Here he pointed his finger at the group of police officers. 'I strongly advise you to leave her alone. Otherwise I shan't hesitate to broadcast to the four corners how you jumped with both feet into a trap that anyone with half a brain could have seen right away was a set-up. For you see, fellows, just because you've seen someone commit a murder doesn't make them guilty!'

He nodded his head slowly and chuckled. Then, with a superhuman effort, he managed to re-light his cigar. He took a long puff and continued:

'Let's talk a bit about this woman: she's very pretty, elegant and possessed of a charming naivety. Thirty years old, or thereabouts: the ideal age of femininity. She has enormous admiration and respect for her husband. She likes to swim, to dive, to laugh, to play tennis and to drive fast cars. She's perfectly sane and healthy. Her only problem is to have committed a number of youthful indiscretions that attracted the attention of the police and caused a slight scandal in polite society. In addition – and I'm not going into detail – she is an adopted child and is ashamed of her origins. And, to cap it all, she has never discussed her past with her husband, whom I believe to be a decent man and who would, had she told him everything, immediately have given her a kiss of absolution. Are you beginning to get the picture?

'Let us now go back in time a few days, to the evening Hoenig set eyes on her. This monster has an elephantine memory – without wishing to cast aspersions on those amiable and gracious pachyderms. She hasn't changed much in twelve years. He recognises her, or rather identifies her, immediately. Without losing a moment – he's a policeman at heart – he telegraphs his office to send him her file. It might come in useful. And come in useful it certainly does, beyond his wildest expectations. He's found the centrepiece of his little machination. He threatens to expose her to her husband, and frightens her out of her wits. He gets the young woman exactly where he wants her. She agrees, under considerable duress, to play the part of the murderess in his macabre little play.

'For it really is a play he's putting on: a horrifying spectacle worthy of the Grand Guignol. Imagine a locked room murder taking place under footlights, on a brilliantly illuminated set, under the eyes of two spectators with front row seats, who won't miss a second of the show. I'm speaking, of course, about the two agents posted in the bungalow opposite, whom Hoenig has known about for some time, and whose presence is vital to the success of the spectacle. What gets me really upset,' he growled, blowing a large puff of smoke towards Brenner, 'what gets me really angry, is that you could have unravelled this whole business straight way if you'd paid attention to the revealing comment they made right there in their report: "We had the impression of being at the theatre," they said. And they were bloody well right!

'Getting back to the role of the woman. Obviously it was important she not be recognised. Her sex appeal had to be hidden during the entire performance. Her figure would be concealed under a raincoat too large for her, she would wear a brunette wig under her scarf to hide her real hair and she would have no make-up. Funny how a couple of locks of hair and an absence of make-up can transform a face. She would appear smaller as well because she customarily wore high heels. Do you gentlemen remember how small your wives appeared the first time you saw them without high heels? So, what do you think? Not a bad job of work, was it?'

He took off his *pince-nez* and polished the glasses. For a few seconds he appeared perilously close to falling backwards.

'Now you've got some idea of the overall scheme,' he continued, recovering his balance and placing the *pince-nez* on the end of his nose once more, 'let's get into more of the detail. Our charlatan needs an assistant. He takes Strahler into his confidence – poor Strahler, the lost soul, the slave he leads about by the nose. He asks him to go to Milan and bring back one of those trick knives whose blade collapses into the handle and squirts out fake blood. I know for a fact you can find cheap ones in those little shops around La Scala. So. Now you have a grasp of some of the details. But, believe me, you're a long way from understanding the whole thing.

'Having got the woman's role sorted out, Hoenig will now go after the husband. Why? He had nothing to do with the humiliation Hoenig had suffered. But he took the professor's side and is supposed to be his friend. And anyway, he's a decent young man, intelligent and sensitive, with perhaps a little too much imagination. The ideal prey for this manipulative creature, capable of torturing an innocent and peaceful individual for the sole pleasure of having fun with him. He tells Pierre about his wife's past and the minor misdemeanours she has wrongly concealed from him. But that's not enough for his creative spirit. He weaves into his account an outrageous and wholly fabricated story of mysterious unsolved crimes of which the unfortunate woman is supposed to be guilty. And our gullible friend, his nose buried in the detective stories which fill his imagination, swallows it all hook, line and sinker. When he learns on Monday morning of the events of the night before, how could he not suspect the woman in the bungalow of being his wife? Didn't she have an excellent motive? Hoenig was going to unmask her and had to be killed. Don't laugh, my friends! We would have fallen for it the same way, you and I, existing as we do on a diet of fantasy. Dr. Hoenig, you see, understood our psychology perfectly. He knew how to hit the right nerve and he derived pleasure from hearing us squeal. It was the most terrifying, the most diabolical trait of his character.'

Very gingerly, Carter Gilbert placed his feet back on the platform. In the silence that followed, several in the hall thought they heard the creaking of old joints. The atmosphere in the hall was stifling. The windows were steamed up. A cloud of black smoke hung over Sir Arthur's head. He crushed his cigar under his heel and continued in a flat voice.

'I shan't spend much more time on the least important and most obvious part of the business: the grotesque drama played out in the lounge of the bungalow, behind the well-lit glass, just like the mannequins in a shop window. The night, the drizzle, the fine rain that left imperceptible droplets on the glass: all contributed to making the scene credible. Add to that the evil atmosphere that emanated from Dr. Hoenig and you have a fair idea of the impact of the scene on the two witnesses. Having said that, let's examine what happened after the "murderess" finished her act. One might have thought that, to the extent that she manifests any emotion at all, she would leave the scene at once – she is, after all, supposed to have killed a man – but no. She calmly opens the windows, leans out to grab hold of the shutters, then shuts them very carefully. The gestures, in fact, of an actress who has just finished a performance and is now pulling the curtains closed so as to prevent the spectators seeing how the tricks were executed.

'Working out what happened after the curtains were drawn is now child's play. (Incidentally, it's the infantile aspect of this burlesque machination that gives it its sinister aspect. It makes one think of the sick games of a retarded child.) Anyway, it's obvious that the "corpse" gets up, accompanies the "murderess" to the bathroom, and helps her climb up to the skylight. That's where she loses the famous hair that's later discovered on the dressing-gown. She slides through the opening – after all, she's young and fit – grabs the overhang of the roof, launches herself outwards and lands on the ground outside the grass strip surrounding the bungalow, where she would have left footprints. You can see what happens next: Hoenig closes and locks the skylight and it's done. It's only taken a few seconds. As for the front door, I think Hoenig probably locked it just after the visitor came in. By the time the two agents arrived at the bungalow, nobody could get in or out. The "murderess" is already a long way away. She gets back to her car, puts it in neutral so as not to make a noise, gets rid of the wig in a dustbin and returns calmly to the hotel.

'Hoenig only has to wait for the people from the Albergo to arrive. He lies down on the carpet, at the spot where he fell down earlier, makes sure that the handle of the fake knife is still attached to his back, and plays dead. And everyone falls for it.'

A voice spoke from the audience.

'Not so fast!'

Mestre had stood up on his chair. He was trying to control himself but he appeared very agitated.

'There are several of us here who were in the bungalow. We know what we saw. The corpse lay there in front of us for at least ten minutes, motionless as a log. Not the slightest flutter of an eyelash. No sign of breathing. I'm asking all those who were there: can any one of you honestly say you thought for even a second that the doctor was still alive? Come off it! Not even the greatest actor who ever lived could have played dead with such perfection.'

'If you would be good enough not to interrupt me before I've finished, that would save quite a bit of time,' replied Sir Arthur stiffly. He continued:

'I admit that objection had me floored for a minute. But I found the answer in Hoenig's bag: a flask of trichloroethylene.'

He repeated the word "trichloroethylene" as if savouring a sweet.

'If there are any doctors among you, they will know it is a powerful anaesthetic perfected two or three years ago by a German laboratory. It's taken intravenously. Do I need to list the symptoms it induces in the patient? Eyes rolled upwards, breathing slowed almost to

175

a stop, pulse almost imperceptible. That is the state in which the good doctor was found: *perinde ac cadaver...* in the manner of a corpse. That explains, with the fake bloodstain on the dressing-gown and the glasses broken when he fell on the floor – an unpremeditated accident which happened when he mimicked his own fall – the perfection and the realism of the set-up... Are you convinced yet, young man?'

'Excuse me, *Maître*, I won't interrupt any more,' murmured Mestre, sitting down.

'If not,' continued Sir Arthur, 'I can show you the autopsy report that confirms the presence of the product in the victim's bloodstream. In view of the delay for it to take effect, I believe Hoenig must have given himself the injection shortly before he welcomed his visitor. The poor fool! He must have known that the product could also cause heart arrest. And, in fact, someone else made sure it was arrested by a different method....'

'Oh! My God!' cried Pierre spontaneously, like Archimedes proclaiming "Eureka."

'Well,' said Carter Gilbert gently, 'is it possible that the solution has occurred to Monsieur Garnier? What finally put you on the right path, my boy?'

'Your allusion just now to Israel Zangwill's novella, *Maître*. I've just remembered the method.'

'And what was it?'

'As you said, *Maître*, it's extremely simple. Two people appear simultaneously at the door of the crime scene; one breaks the door down and goes in first; he announces in horrified tones that someone has slit the victim's throat; taking advantage of his companion's bewilderment – the two or three seconds where he is struck dumb and blind in amazement – he does the deed unnoticed.'

Pierre ran his hand nervously through his hair, then whispered in a low voice:

'Does this mean that we know the murderer, Sir Arthur?'

'We'll talk about the murderer in a few moments. The problem which should occupy us, the problem that we should solve before even asking how the murderer did it, is still the motive. In other words, who had an interest in seeing Dr. Hoenig dead?'

Sir Arthur leant forward. For the first time, he spoke with a smile on his calm face.

'Look here, good people,' he said, looking yet again around the auditorium, 'you've only considered events from their phantasmagorical aspect and you've forgotten the great old adage: *is fecit cui prodest* – the guilty party is the one that benefits. When I read the statements made to the police, it seemed to me that I should limit my suspicions to two people: young Strahler and Freyja Hoenig. Only those two really had a motive. You've all remarked, while apologising for spreading gossip, about the way those two behaved like turtledoves. However, they had a cast-iron alibi: at the time of the crime they were sitting at the back of the bar, hand in hand in the half-light. And also, I have to confess that as a creator of criminal fictions, I was very disappointed by the banality of that solution. The secretary who kills his employer is, after nearly fifty years, the most frequent murderer in detective literature, followed by the impeccable butler and the fake invalid in the wheelchair. And, of course, in a good detective story, when A is killed it is out of the question that B, to whom all evidence points, is guilty; it must be the innocent-seeming C.

'Now we get to the accidental part of the affair, the bit that wasn't premeditated. A few moments ago I spoke about a situation being handed to the criminal on a plate. At the start, Hoenig asks Stahler to get him a trick knife; what's the next thing he asks him to do? It's not difficult to guess, in the light of what we now know. He tells him: "I need you to do something else. You're going to be the one who examines the body in front of several witnesses, and you're going to pronounce me dead." There's an obvious question that arises here: why is Hoenig so sure that Strahler will play his part in this sinister drama? We know the young man is poor. He can't afford to upset his master. One word from Hoenig and he can say farewell to any chance of a career. But I don't think that's the real explanation. I'm going to tell you the reason he has a hold over Stahler, and it will surprise you. You see, the husband was perfectly aware of the idyll between his wife and his secretary. Don't think he was jealous. Jealousy is a human sentiment. For this perverse and theatrical creature, the romance is a golden opportunity to manipulate the two lovers like marionettes.'

'Just a second!' came Brenner's voice from the back of the hall. 'If I understand correctly, you're suggesting this was a *crime passionel:* the lover kills the husband for his mistress' sake. But why go so far as to commit murder? What stopped the two of them disappearing one fine morning to go and do their cooing somewhere else?'

'For one very good reason,' sighed Sir Arthur. 'Her maiden name.

Frau Hoenig is Sarah Goldberg. She's Jewish.'

He himself appeared startled by the theatrical tone of this last revelation, and he proceeded more calmly, although not without a degree of vehemence:

'Nobody suspected. Being tall and blonde, she could easily pass for an Aryan. And with the German goddess's name her husband had saddled her with – Freyja, the wife of Odin – it's easy to see the hold he had over her. He could force her to do his will. All her family is in Germany so you can imagine the reprisals if she had fled with her lover. She also had a personal fortune from which her husband profited brazenly, another reason why he would never have let her go.

'We'll never know how long Strahler had waited to kill him. But he'd never had the means to do it. And now the opportunity to commit the perfect murder falls into his lap, provided by the very person he wants to eliminate. Who wouldn't see that as the hand of fate? The lovers talk and decide to act. Strahler buys a second knife similar to the first, but a real one that will serve its proper purpose. At the time the doctor has arranged for his "murder," they arrange to be seen together by a dozen or so witnesses. No, they aren't demon lovers. What they're doing is extremely simple. They're just profiting from the Machiavellian trap created by that devil Hoenig and hoisting him on his own petard.

'Allow me to address those of you who were there at the crime scene and yet didn't see what was happening under their own eyes. Remember: Strahler rushes forward to examine the victim, just as any doctor would have done. He kneels – turning his back towards you – and performs the habitual tasks. Then he announces the death. At that point Madame Hoenig throws a fit. All that is so normal, so *expected*, that Sherlock Holmes himself wouldn't have found anything suspicious. Everyone crowds around the poor woman. Straher has at least a minute when nobody's paying him any attention. He removes the fake knife, brings the real one out from under his jacket, and plunges the blade up to the hilt in exactly the same spot. Did the corpse shudder? I don't know. Whether or not, you can be sure the victim, already unconscious, didn't feel a thing,'

During the awful silence that followed, Pierre glanced at his neighbours. Mestre rolled himself a cigarette. His hands trembled a little and he spilt some of the tobacco. "*Plaudite cives*: applaud, citizens," murmured Lippi through clenched teeth. But nobody felt like applauding. Sir Arthur's brilliant little eyes behind the thick lenses; the rabbit smile under the drooping moustache; in fact the whole silhouette with him sitting, fingertips touching like one of the judges of Hell weighing the souls of the dead, inspired in everyone a mixture of respect and fear. He lit up another cigar and the flame was reflected for an instant in his lenses. Not a single muscle in his face moved.

'Now, let's look at what happens next,' he continued in a voice dripping with a nonchalant irony. It's particularly unpleasant, although it does offer some limited interest from the point of view of deduction. I shan't retrace the plan conceived by Dr. Hoenig. Whatever its ingenuity, it didn't entirely satisfy him. He wanted, not only to show that a locked room problem could occur in life just as in a novel, but also to meet the challenge laid down by Professor Lippi.

'Remember: "Shut yourself in the grotto and... disappear." A mediocre enough puzzle, truth be told, not at all worthy of appearing in a self-respecting novel because it relies on the old trick of the underground passage. By consulting a few old maps, the doctor has little trouble in discovering the secret and decides to crown his dramatic opus by an effect which, though simple enough, is sufficiently spectacular to appeal to the charlatan in him. I shall only mention as a matter of form the banal exchange of keys that will enable him to get out of the locked bungalow – an elementary piece of hocus-pocus that, mystified as you already were, good people, you fell for like a ton of bricks. In short, he's ready to play at zombies and to enter the grotto by what one might regard as the emergency exit, a grotto in which he fully expects to be discovered the next day. As he needs to be sure about that, and as he is – to put it bluntly – not altogether impressed with your perspicacity, he reveals his hiding place to young Garnier by means of a secret message of a disconcerting simplicity whose key is borrowed from a children's story by Edgar Allan Poe!

'Imagine his triumph if and when he appears on this very platform where, today, I have the humble privilege of addressing you. Think of it! An auditorium chock full of erudite academics, eminent specialists, authors of learned tracts and scholarly theses will have allowed themselves to be duped by a practical joke that would put a first year student to shame! See him licking his chops at the prospect of your complete humiliation!

'But throughout this affair the farcical gets mixed up with the tragically horrible. Strahler has botched the job. The blade – as the autopsy shows – has only just touched the cardiac muscle. A mortal wound, but not immediately fatal. It causes internal bleeding, but the handle of the knife blocks the wound and prevents the blood from oozing out externally. Hoenig is now alone in the bungalow. The effects of the anaesthetic are starting to wear off. He's gradually regaining consciousness. He feels no pain. He has no idea he's dying and his brain orders him to finish the job at hand.

'He leaves the bungalow, locks it behind him with the good key he hid under the awning and puts it back in place. He walks straight ahead, the knife firmly planted between his shoulder blades, with the steady and regular step of a robot or a sleepwalker. His eyes are drenched by the rain. Without his glasses, he can't distinguish anything more than two metres away. He bumps into trees and rocks. Blood leaks from his wound. But the draining of his force does not drain his willpower. The only idea that penetrates the fog in his brain is that he must follow his original plan. He reaches the fountain. He manages to displace the slab which pivots shut behind him. If only he can get down the small flight of steps leading to the aqueduct....

'He can. He finds the flashlight which he'd carefully placed there. Almost as a reflex, he switches it on. Now, bent double, breathless, unsteady on his feet, scraping his head on the roof, he moves forward agonisingly slowly in the tunnel....

'It's hard to imagine the effort his body had to make. A normal man, mortally wounded like that would have succumbed almost immediately. But Hoenig is a man built to last, and a fighter. God knows how, he drags himself as far as the grotto. There, he starts to recover his senses. The anaesthetic has worn off completely. Pain grips him, dull and diffuse at first, then sharper by the second until it's tearing him apart. He tries to seize the handle of the knife and, with a superhuman effort, succeeds in pulling it out. At that instant, he understood. When the blood burst from the wound as if from a severed hosepipe; when it flowed from his mouth; when his legs gave way under him and the world started to darken before his eyes. He tried to call out, in vain, because his throat was choked with blood. At that moment, Karl Hoenig realised something he had not thought possible: that all the hatred, all the planning, all the stage management had turned against him. He knew he was about to die.'

A long silence fell upon the audience. Pierre looked at his watch. He felt drained. His only thought was for his wife who was waiting for him in the hotel.

Sir Arthur removed his *pince-nez* and rubbed his eyes for a long time.

'I'm exhausted. I need at least a week of solid sleep. I believe that's the end of the story.'

'Yes,' said Brenner glumly. 'Yes, it all fits together. I'll send out an arrest warrant for Strahler and his accomplice. There's one small detail, however. I know you went to see them. Why did you let them get away?'

Sir Arthur put his glasses back on and looked at him with astonishment.

'Did I let them get away? Not exactly. I told them I was abreast of events and I told them the whole story. You probably won't believe me, but they were smiling and holding hands. I added: "My friends, I'm going to leave the room now. You know where your duty lies, don't you? I advise you to make a voluntary statement to the police." He, still smiling, replied "Yes." And I added: "Well, I'm going now. If I thought that your confessions would be taken seriously, I'd never have given you that advice. Personally, I could never tell a tribunal what I've just told you. I'd look as though I'd concocted a novel as unlikely as any the old man has written over the course of his career." I think they understood.'

He stood up shakily, wobbled and clutched the table.

'My friends, I've just committed a new crime,' he said. 'I've just given a lecture.'

***

Another conference ended the following evening, a date that History recorded as Friday, September 30th. It gave rise to the famous statement: "You were given the choice between war and dishonour . . . you chose dishonour and you will have war." Pierre and Solange Garnier paid no attention. They found themselves in Venice and had better things to do than read the newspapers. Albert Mestre was mobilised the following year and fell in June 1940 defending a bridge on the Somme. His unfinished treatise on *Non-Being and the Absolute*, published by La Liberation, is regarded today as one of the fundamental works of post-war philosophy. As for Professor Umberto Lippi, an untimely quotation from Cicero ("How long, Catalina, will you abuse our patience?") made in the presence

181

of *Il Duce* at the opening of the congress of writers in Rome– although made in Latin – earned him an immediate dispatch to an island in the Tyrrhenian Sea. He spent his time applying his theories of narrative to the composition of a vast and labyrinthine mediaeval detective story which turned out to be unreadable and achieved no critical or commercial success. Superintendent Brenner swore he would not be taken in again and devoted his career from then on to cushy investigations of minor housebreaking and domestic crimes.

On the day after the armistice, the Garniers left France for the United States where Pierre obtained a chair at Harvard University. They lived happily and had no children. Sir Arthur Carter Gilbert passed away in 1960 at the age of ninety-two. His body was found in his bedroom. It was hermetically sealed and no key was ever found.

Epilogue

The *poulet Gabrielle Dorziat* was bubbling slowly in the casserole. Solange dipped a morsel of bread in the sauce, brought it to her lips and took the time to taste it. "Maybe I used too much rosemary," she murmured to herself. She judged that the sauce had sufficiently reduced and added mushrooms, tomatoes, olives and a handful of grapes. She stirred them with a wooden spoon and added a pinch of coriander and paprika. She tasted it again. "There, it's perfect," she announced appreciatively. She liked things to be perfect. She glanced at the clock. It showed half past seven. Pierre had promised to be there by eight. He had a meeting at the university – God knows the poor darling hated meetings! – and by the time they sat down to eat the sauce would be so velvety and its taste so subtle that only a true gourmet would be able to analyse it.

In the impeccably organised kitchen – the smallest utensil had its proper place – the battery of copper shone brilliantly. Through the open door she could see the crystal and the silverware laid out precisely on the dining-room table, the bottle of Chateau Lafite reclining in its basket and the twisted red candles in the chandelier. The tiny gift packet was hidden under a napkin – it contained a platinum signet ring engraved with their entwined initials. Solange allowed herself a moment of relaxation, serving herself a small glass of port with a sigh of satisfaction. It was the twenty-seventh of October, the date of their wedding anniversary. She had prepared everything herself, having given their maid the evening off. She lit a Muratti and pulled towards her the folded newspaper from where it lay on the side-board, the headlines and short article clearly visible:

DEMON COUPLE FOUND IN ARGENTINA

From our correspondent in Buenos Aires. The International Criminal Police Commission has located the secret hide-out of Hans Strahler, the diabolical murderer of Dr. Karl Hoenig in 1938, and his accomplice Freyja Hoenig. The couple were living under an assumed

183

name in a hotel in Mar de Plata. Under questioning by the police, the couple denied any involvement in the murder of the eminent scientist. Nevertheless the Swiss authorities have initiated extradition proceedings. If they are successful it is possible that light will eventually be shed on one of the most mysterious crimes of this century.

She crumpled the newspaper into a ball and went to toss it in the rubbish bin, then crossed over to the window overlooking the garden behind the house. Her face was reflected in the dark glass. It was a soft and pretty face with calm grey-green eyes under half-closed lids. A slight smile danced on her lips. She thought:

"There won't be any extradition. In a few months it will be war. It was dear Dr. Hoenig who told me so and he was certainly in a position to know. It's a pity that little Strahler wasn't arrested after all. He was a feeble coward. He had a thousand reasons to kill Hoenig but couldn't summon the courage. And it's a shame that Freyja wasn't really guilty at all. She deserved to die, if only for being unfaithful to her husband. I've been married several times and I would have died rather than do such a thing."

She looked at her reflection with satisfaction and put a lock of her chestnut hair back in place. Outside, above the darkened garden, the pale lights of the nearby town seemed to absorb half the sky.

She turned to look at the clock again. Pierre would be here soon, but the last few minutes were always the longest. She carefully rinsed the glass she had been using, placed it on the draining board, cast a last look at the immaculate kitchen and went into the lounge where the only light was the glow from the flames dancing in the chimney. The room was at the front of the house and the bow window looked out over the path leading up to the door. From there, she could see the headlights of the car as soon as it reached the gates. She stood in front of the glass reflecting the firelight. In the night outside, the blood-red light seemed to float in the foliage of a chestnut tree. Someone standing on the lawn could have made out the slender silhouette of the young woman and the pale white of her bare shoulders, but certainly not her face nor the smile on her lips.

"It was pure madness to commit a murder in the window of such a well-lit room, right under the watching eyes of those men. I knew they were there, of course, and they were part of the scheme of things. The original plan was plain and simple, without any embellishments. When

Dr. Hoenig threatened to tell my husband everything, I was forced to accept the role he wanted me to play. I confess I played it rather too realistically, but he didn't have time to bear any grudges.

"Afterwards, things got so complicated that I realised only Uncle Arthur would be able to sort them out, so I had to go and ask him for help. It's true that, once again, the police weren't much of a risk because nobody could explain how I'd got out of the bungalow. But I didn't want my husband to harbour any suspicions about me. I love him and I'm determined to spend the rest of my life with him.

"Uncle Arthur was really clever to have found an explanation taking into account all the facts such as I presented them. It was amazing to watch him do it, because I haven't his intelligence, and it would never have occurred to me to pin the murder on poor little Strahler. He had the motive and the desire but he had no willpower and proved it by running away.

"I wonder what I would do if I ever saw Uncle Arthur again. I'm sure I'd be sorely tempted to tell him what really happened, but I wouldn't want to vex him because he's so proud of his explanation. The fact is, all those great brains were embarrassed by the whole affair, because quite frankly they were completely thrown off the trail – and I found that terribly amusing. Perhaps it was the simplicity of it all that fooled them. Perhaps the solution was just too obvious. This time I took the idea from the story of the purloined letter that Pierre spoke about in his lecture. I told myself that if someone were to commit a crime in plain view and right under the noses of witnesses, our great amateur detectives would never solve it because there would be just too much evidence. When they look for the author of a crime, they can only think about the complicated methods they would have used to commit it. But I'm not very intelligent and I didn't have time to work out a brilliant plan. I had to silence Hoenig quickly before he revealed all my little secrets in his lecture the following day. I gave Pierre a sleeping draught, I got rid of that joke accessory Hoenig gave me and I took a real knife from the hotel kitchens which are empty at that time of night. Then I took the route to Monte Verita. Everything happened exactly as the witnesses described. And then I came back to bed with my husband.

"That's what I would tell Uncle Arthur if I saw him again and I know it would disappoint him because he went to such lengths to invent that amazing story. Although I wonder if he didn't guess the truth, all the same. He's certainly clever enough for that, and there are so many other secrets between us. I know he loves his little 'Alice' – as he calls me – very much (Alice in Wonderland, of course). That's why I won't tell him anything.

"I won't tell him how I got out of the bungalow after stabbing Hoenig, either, or how I hermetically sealed all the apertures on the inside. No. I didn't get out through the skylight, dear Uncle Arthur. That would have been incredibly inconvenient and undignified to boot. There again, I had to make it simple by necessity, as well from choice. When I was growing up I must have read a thousand locked room mysteries, by Uncle Arthur and many others. and I was always disappointed whenever the author concocted a solution that was extravagant, unlikely, or ridiculous. I have a taste for the simple and I've perfected two or three methods, but none that could have applied in this case. They found the door locked from the inside, and yet nobody could have done it from the outside because it had been under observation all the time. The bungalow was effectively sealed and simple common sense would tell you that nobody could have escaped.

"Therefore, while the two agents were checking round the bungalow, unable to open the door, the shutters or even the famous skylight there shouldn't be any doubt that I was locked inside. And while one of them stood guard while the other ran for help, it should be equally obvious that I was still inside. But if we accept that evidence we come hard up against a material impossibility, as Uncle Arthur would say: once the door had been opened and the lounge, the bedroom, the bathroom and all the nooks and crannies had been searched, it had to be admitted that – apart from the unfortunate Hoenig himself – there was nobody on the premises. I had to have got out by means of some hocus-pocus, therefore. That's what prompted Uncle Arthur to invent that incredible explanation, which everyone believed simply because it was complicated."

She cocked an ear to the sound of a distant vehicle travelling on the main road, but it wasn't the familiar purr of the Delahaye and she experienced a fleeting disappointment. She took up her train of thought again and a kind of rapture could have been read on her face. She continued:

"I don't much like citing famous quotations at the end of almost every observation, as Pierre's friends do. But it does seem to make sense that, once you've eliminated the impossible, what's left, however improbable, must be the answer. I was still inside the bungalow when all those people arrived, and if nobody saw me it's simply because I made myself invisible. I can see Uncle Arthur's face from here if I told him that, and his disapproving air. 'Non, no, Uncle Arthur,' I'd say. 'There's no diabolical trick, I didn't violate the laws of nature and I didn't resort to witchcraft.' I'd let him mull it over for a while and then I'd explain everything.

"'Let's look,' I'd say, 'at what happened when they arrived in front of the bungalow. There were, first of all, the people who were at the bar – including Strahler and Freyja, of course – plus the hotel manager and the agent who'd gone to find him. Say about a dozen. They didn't take the time to count because it was raining cats and dogs and they only had a flashlight to see by. And don't forget the other agent who'd stayed behind to stand guard. The manager unlocked the door with his key and when it was flung open in the small entrance hall the manager, the agent and all those craning their necks to see only had eyes for the body of Hoenig which was clearly visible in the brightly-lit lounge, beyond the interior door that I had taken care to leave wide open. The agent went in first and rushed straight to the lounge which he inspected rapidly before moving on to the bedroom and the bathroom. The manager, on his orders, had stayed by the door to the lounge so as to bar access, except for little Strahler whom he allowed in to examine the victim. Meanwhile, all the others were milling around in the dark, either in the doorway or in the entrance hall itself, jostling one another and each trying to get a better look over the manager's shoulder. As for me....

"'Yes, Uncle Arthur, you guessed. I was standing in a corner of the hall, where I had taken the precaution of removing the bulb (which turned out to be unnecessary, as not one of them thought to turn on the light switch.) Once they were all packed together inside, I naturally melded into the crowd and of course nobody noticed. Because, you see, Uncle Arthur, I was *mentally* invisible.

"'When all those honest folk swear there was nobody but them in the bungalow, they mean nobody resembling the woman in the raincoat who was seen stabbing the victim. And when the agent posted at the outside door testifies that nobody left other than those he had seen going in, he doesn't mean nobody at all left. He means he didn't see anyone he could suspect of being the murderess. In fact there really was someone in the middle of all those people in the hall; someone who did walk out under the nose of the watchman; but it was, as I say, a mentally invisible human being.

"'I can't take this much longer,' Uncle Arthur will roar (he's quick to lose his temper). 'Who is it? What does he look like? What kind of clothes was he wearing, because I assume he wasn't naked?' 'Of course not, Uncle Arthur,' I'll reply, blushing. 'He was wearing quite a nice red and gold uniform with a short brass-buttoned jacket and a pillbox cap, which enabled him to pass unnoticed. You see,' I shall continue modestly, 'there are people in every grand hotel that nobody ever notices because they are part of the furniture like the potted palms, the revolving door and the lift cage. One remembers the head doorman with his majestic air, the friendly concierge, the sympathetic face of the barman, even the chambermaid if she's pretty enough, but everybody ignores the little bellboys, yet they have emotions just like everyone else.

"'Do you want to know how I did it? It was very easy. While my dear husband was asleep, I put on a raincoat that came down to my ankles under which, I'm ashamed to say, I was only wearing my undergarments. The service personnel's cloakroom is on the corridor leading to the kitchens. I had all the time in the world to find a uniform of my size, and even slightly larger – I'd noticed beforehand that the bellboys at the Grand Hotel wore the same uniform as at the Albergo, of course. I put the raincoat back on; I drove to Monte Verita; I parked under the trees where nobody could see; and I knocked on the door of the bungalow where the good doctor was waiting for me to start his little show.'

"'You know the rest. After I closed the shutters I took off the headscarf and the brunette wig – which hadn't really served much purpose – and collected the compromising document from the table and stuffed it down the front of my pants. Then I made the mistake of leaning over the body to make sure it wasn't still alive – he seemed well and truly dead but Hoenig hadn't told me he'd be taking an anaesthetic. That's when I must have lost the hair that almost got me arrested. I stuffed the wig and scarf in the pants of the bellboy's uniform, after first donning the pillbox cap and tucking my hair in underneath. All I had to do then was take off the raincoat and wait in the darkened corner of the entrance hall.

"'When the others arrived, everything happened just as I expected. Everything, that is, except Freyja Hoenig's collapse, which actually helped quite a lot, I must say. The manager noticed me, asked me what the devil I was doing there – he seemed to think he'd seen me before –

and sent me to the Albergo to get some brandy. I didn't need to be asked twice and left in a hurry. I ran past the agent who didn't even look at me. I got back in the car, slipped the raincoat back on, and drove back to Locarno. Needless to say I got back into the Grand Hotel through the servant's entrance, the same way I had left earlier. I tore the dossier into a thousand pieces and put it in a dustbin along with the wig and the scarf. I put the bellboy's uniform back into place and went up to the room to nestle against my dear husband where I slept like a log the rest of the night.'

"It's really a great shame I can't confess the truth to Uncle Arthur – it almost makes me cry. I can imagine him drawing thoughtfully on one of his awful cigars and casually letting drop the question he would be sure to ask: 'There's just one small detail I don't quite understand, my dear. What did you do with the raincoat after you took it off in the bungalow?' 'You'll never guess, Uncle Arthur: Archibald, my American husband, worked for Dupont de Nemours. The laboratories there created a new synthetic fibre, water resistant and very light. They named it Nylon and it will soon be on the market. Meanwhile, my late husband had a raincoat made for me that would fit in a handbag or, in this case, under a bellboy's jacket. Which is exactly what I did and it was practically invisible. I was sorry to have to get rid of it, because it was useful on so many occasions!'"

She uttered a strange laugh as a beam of light shone on her face, which a cruel expression had made to seem suddenly older. The blinding headlights swept the lawn and the trees, creating a host of moving shadows. The sinister expression vanished, to be replaced by a joyful smile as she tore off her pinafore and threw it on the sofa.

Her face became the face of a pretty wife, and she ran out to meet her husband.

APPENDIX: NOTES

Monte Verita in History

Monte Verita does exist and is a popular tourist destination and conference centre. Henri Oedenkoven did establish Monte Verita as an "Individualistic Vegetarian Cooperative", which became an *avantgarde* cult that attracted such internationally known figures as Isadora Duncan, Hermann Hesse, Carl Jung, Jean Arp and Paul Klee. Josef Stalin was rumoured to have contemplated a visit. It was eventually shut down by the local authorities. There is, alas, no record of Oedenkoven vanishing from a locked grotto.

A Real-Life Locked-Room Mystery

When Professor Lippi challenged Dr. Hoenig (Chapter II) to produce one single real-life locked room mystery, the good doctor could well have cited an event that had taken place forty years earlier and not so very far from where the symposium was taking place.

On 10 September 1898, Empress Elisabeth of Bavaria was stabbed in the heart with a sharpened file by a young anarchist named Luigi Lucheni as she was walking along the promenade of Lake Geneva with her lady-of-courtesy, Countess Sztaray, about to board a steamship for Montreux. Due to the narrowness of the wound and the strong pressure from her corset holding the bleeding down, she did not die immediately but, feeling weak, went to her cabin to lie down. Once the corset was removed, several hours later, death was almost instantaneous.

Although not technically a locked room crime, it could easily have become one had there been no witnesses to the attack and had the empress locked her cabin from the inside. In fact, it is thought by at least one locked room expert (Roland Lacourbe, John Dickson Carr's French biographer) that the delayed assassination was the inspiration for Gaston Leroux's *The Mystery of the Yellow Room,* published in France in 1907, which Carr himself declared to be the finest locked room mystery ever written.

Echoes of John Dickson Carr and others
(WARNING: this section contains SPOILERS)

Anthony Carter Gilbert is obviously based on John Dickson Carr himself.

Although the explanations of the locked room murder are themselves original, there are inevitably echoes of Carr's and other authors' works:

---the murderer as the person who initially examines the body first appeared in Israel Zangwill's *The Big Bow Mystery* (*1892)*

---the victim aiding the "murderer" to escape and locking the door after him first appeared in Anthony Wynne's *The Case of the Red-Haired Girl (1935)*

---the murderer remaining in the room hidden, then mingling with the incoming crowd, was used by John Dickson Carr in one of his earliest short stories *The Shadow of the Goat (1928),* although it was not the first such appearance in the literature.

---it was Carr also, writing as Carter Dickson, who wrote of a slender murderess disguising herself as a boy (although not a bellboy) in *The Plague Court Murders (1934)*

---the idea of a murderer being psychologically invisible originated in G.K. Chesterton's *The Invisible Man (1911)*

Like Carter Dickson's detective Sir Henry Merrivale in *She Died a Lady (1943),* the elderly protagonist of *The Riddle of Monte Verita* deflects suspicion from the true murderer, who is allowed to escape.

The ill-fated Solange Garnier is in good company among Carr's persecuted leading ladies: Marie Stevens in *The Burning Court*, Fay Seton in *He Who Whispers (1946)* and, above all, Lesley Grant in *Till Death Do Us Part (1944).*

Indeed, the evil Hoenig behaves very much like the victim Gilman in that last Carr novel: he fabricates the story of a diabolical murderess perpetrating impossible crimes, and he puts the same choice to the hero of confronting the alleged villainess or not.

The Author's Note

In his Author's Note, M.Török declares his intention to write an impossible crime novel that obeys the rules of what is often called Golden Age fiction; to write it in a manner faithful to the French language usage of the time; and to end the story with the last sentence of *La Chambre ardente*, the French translation of Carr's *The Burning Court (1937)*, the words of which had made an everlasting impression on him. Thus the last line of *The Riddle of Monte Verita* reads: "Her face became the face of a pretty wife, and she ran out to meet her husband."

Alas, M.Török was not to know that the French translator of *The Burning Court* (Maurice-André Endrèbe, himself a writer of locked room fiction) had taken liberties with the narrative flow of Carr's epilogue, with the result that several of the paragraphs at the end of the French version had had their order changed from the English original.

Essentially, there are two threads running through the epilogue: (i) rational explanations of the murders as reported in newspaper articles (ii) musings by Marie Stephens, one of the principal murder suspects, to the effect that she perpetrated the crimes by using her black magic skills.

In the original English version, Marie's musings and her rush to greet her husband precede the quotes from the newspaper, so the epilogue closes on a prosaic and decidedly unromantic note.

In the French version, the newspaper stories come first and the last thing we read is Marie's thoughts as she prepares to run out to meet her husband, with the result that the French version leans more towards the supernatural.

When Carr learned of Endrèbe's changes, he liked them so much he contemplated modifying his own work to incorporate them.

For the record, the last sentence of *The Burning Court* is: "At this point there was some commotion, and Judge David R. Anderson said that, if any more laughter were heard in a court of justice, he would order the court to be cleared."

Readers can decide for themselves which is the more memorable ending.

None of the foregoing notes and observations should be taken as a criticism of M.Török's elegant, intelligent and ingenious work. Indeed, in the translator's humble opinion, he has succeeded admirably in his stated goal.

John Pugmire
March 2012

47353237R00107

Made in the USA
Lexington, KY
07 August 2019